SPECIAL MESSAGE TO READERS

THE ULVERSCROFT FOUNDATION
(registered UK charity number 264873)
was established in 1972 to provide funds for
research, diagnosis and treatment of eye diseases.
Examples of major projects funded by
the Ulverscroft Foundation are:-

- The Children's Eye Unit at Moorfields Eye Hospital, London
- The Ulverscroft Children's Eye Unit at Great Ormond Street Hospital for Sick Children
- Funding research into eye diseases and treatment at the Department of Ophthalmology, University of Leicester
- The Ulverscroft Vision Research Group, Institute of Child Health
- Twin operating theatres at the Western Ophthalmic Hospital, London
- The Chair of Ophthalmology at the Royal Australian College of Ophthalmologists

You can help further the work of the Foundation
by making a donation or leaving a legacy.
Every contribution is gratefully received. If you
would like to help support the Foundation or
require further information, please contact:

THE ULVERSCROFT FOUNDATION
The Green, Bradgate Road, Anstey
Leicester LE7 7FU, England
Tel: (0116) 236 4325

website: www.foundation.ulverscroft.com

Wiley Cash is a native of western North Carolina, a region that features prominently in his writing. This is his first novel, and was inspired by a true story. He and his wife live in West Virginia, where he teaches fiction writing and American literature.

A LAND MORE KIND THAN HOME

One Sunday, nine-year-old Jess Hall watches in horror as his autistic brother is smothered during a healing service in the mountains of North Carolina. The unimaginable violence that follows must be untangled by a local sheriff with his own tragic past.

WILEY CASH

A LAND MORE KIND THAN HOME

Complete and Unabridged

CHARNWOOD
Leicester

First published in Great Britain in 2012 by
Doubleday
an imprint of Transworld Publishers
London

First Charnwood Edition
published 2013
by arrangement with
Transworld Publishers
A Random House Group Company
London

British Library CIP Data

Cash, Wiley.
    A land more kind than home.
    1. North Carolina- -Fiction.
    2. Large type books.
    I. Title
    813.6–dc23

    ISBN 978–1–4448–1441–5

Published by
F. A. Thorpe (Publishing)
Anstey, Leicestershire

Set by Words & Graphics Ltd.
Anstey, Leicestershire
Printed and bound in Great Britain by
T. J. International Ltd., Padstow, Cornwall

This book is printed on acid-free paper

M.B.C.
FOR YOU, BECAUSE OF YOU

Something has spoken to me in the night
. . . and told me I shall die, I know not
where. Saying:
  '[Death is] to lose the earth you know,
for greater knowing; to lose the life you
have, for greater life; to leave the friends
you loved, for greater loving; to find a land
more kind than home, more large than
earth.'

— THOMAS WOLFE,
YOU CAN'T GO HOME AGAIN

Adelaide Lyle

1

I sat there in the car with the gravel dust blowing across the parking lot and saw the place for what it was, not what it was right at that moment in the hot sunlight, but for what it had been maybe twelve or fifteen years before: a real general store with folks gathered around the lunch counter, a line of people at the soda fountain, little children ordering ice cream of just about every flavor you could think of, hard candy by the quarter pound, moon pies and crackerjack and other things I hadn't thought about tasting in years. And if I'd closed my eyes I could've seen what the building had been forty or fifty years before that, back when I was a young woman: a screen door slamming shut, oil lamps lit and sputtering black smoke, dusty horses hitched to the posts out front where the iceman unloaded every Wednesday afternoon, the last stop on his route before he headed up out of the holler, the bed of his truck an inch deep with cold water. Back before Carson Chambliss came and took down the advertisements and yanked out the old hitching posts and put up that now-yellow newspaper in the front windows to keep folks from looking in. All the way back before him and the deacons had

1

wheeled out the broken coolers on a dolly, filled the linoleum with rows of folding chairs and electric floor fans that blew the heat up in your face. If I'd kept my eyes closed I could've seen all this lit by the dim light of a memory like a match struck in a cave where the sun can't reach, but because I stared out through my windshield and heard the cars and trucks whipping by on the road behind me, I could see now that it wasn't nothing but a simple concrete block building, and, except for the sign out by the road, you couldn't even tell it was a church. And that was exactly how Carson Chambliss wanted it.

As soon as Pastor Matthews caught cancer and died in 1975, Chambliss moved the church from up the river in Marshall, which ain't nothing but a little speck of town about an hour or so north of Asheville. That's when Chambliss put the sign out on the edge of the parking lot. He said it was a good thing to move like we did because the church in Marshall was just too big to feel the spirit in, and I reckon some folks believed him; I know some of us wanted to. But the truth was that half the people in the congregation left when Pastor Matthews died and there wasn't enough money coming in to keep us in that old building. The bank took it and sold it to a group of Presbyterians, just about all of them from outside Madison County, some of them not even from North Carolina. They've been in that building for ten years, and I reckon they're proud of it. They should be. It was a beautiful building when it was our church,

2

and even though I ain't stepped foot in there since we moved out, I figure it probably still is.

The name of our congregation got changed too, from French Broad Church of Christ to River Road Church of Christ in Signs Following. Under that new sign, right out there by the road, Chambliss lettered the words 'Mark 16:17–18' in black paint, and that was just about all he felt led to preach on too, and that's why I had to do what I done. I'd seen enough, too much, and it was my time to go.

I'd seen people I'd known just about my whole life pick up snakes and drink poison, hold fire up to their faces just to see if it would burn them. Holy people too. God-fearing folks that hadn't ever acted like that a day in their lives. But Chambliss convinced them it was safe to challenge the will of God. He made them think it was all right to take that dare if they believed. And just about the whole lot of them said, 'Here I am, Lord. Come and take me if you get a mind to it. I'm ready if you are.'

And I reckon they were ready, at least I hope so, because I saw a right good many of them get burned up and poisoned, and there wasn't a single one of them that would go see a doctor if they got sick or hurt. That's why the snake bites bothered me the most. Those copperheads and rattlers could only stand so much, especially with the music pounding like it did and all them folks dancing and hollering and falling out on the floor, kicking over chairs and laying their hands on each other. In all that time, right up until what happened with Christopher, the church hadn't ever had but one of them die from that carrying on either, at least only one I know about: Miss Molly Jameson, almost eleven years ago. She was seventy-nine when it happened, two years younger than I am now. I think it might've been a copperhead that got her. She was standing down front on that little stage when Chambliss lifted it out of the crate, closed his eyes, and prayed over it. He wasn't more than forty-five years old then, his black hair cut close and sharp like he'd spent time in the army, and he might have for all I knew about him. I don't think a single one of us knew for sure where he came from, and I figure anyone who said they did had probably been lied to. Once he finished praying over that snake, he handed it to Molly. She took it from him just as gentle as if someone was passing her a newborn baby, this woman who'd never had a child of her own, a widow whose husband had been dead for more than twenty years, his chest crushed up when his tractor rolled over and pinned him upside a tree.

But like I said, she held that copperhead like a baby, and she took her glasses off and looked at it up close like it was a baby too, tears running down her face and her lips moving like she was praying or talking to it in such a soft way that only it could hear her. Everybody around her was too wrapped up in themselves to pay any attention, dancing and carrying on and hollering out words couldn't nobody understand but themselves. But Chambliss stood there and watched Molly. He held that microphone over his heart with that terrible-looking hand he'd set

4

on fire years before in the basement of Ponder's feed store. I'd heard that him and some men from the church were meeting for worship down in that basement, drinking lamp oil and handling fire too, and I don't know just how it happened, but somehow or another Chambliss got his sleeve set on fire and it tore right through his shirt and burned his arm up something awful. They said later that his fingers were even melted together, and he had to pull them apart and set them in splints to keep them separated while they were healing. I didn't ever see his whole arm because that man didn't ever roll that right sleeve up, maybe the left one, but not that one. I reckon I can't blame him. That right hand was just an awful sight, even after it got healed.

Like I said, Chambliss stood back while Molly handled that snake and he watched her catch hold of the Holy Ghost, and when he felt like she was good and filled up with it he went to her and put his good hand on her head. Then he took up that microphone and prayed into it. I remember just exactly what he said because it was the last time I ever heard that man preach. It was the last time I ever stepped foot inside that church until now.

He said, 'O dear, sweet Jesus, take this woman and fill her up with your spirit from head to foot. Fill us all, sweet Jesus, with your good Holy Ghost. Lift us up in your name, dear Lord.' And when he said that, he put his good hand under her elbow and helped her lift that snake up over her head. He moved away real slow, and she just held it there above her like she was making sure

5

God could see it, her eyes closed tight, her feet running in place, her mouth alive and moving in a prayer she probably hadn't ever prayed in her life.

When she lowered that copperhead is when it happened. The first time it struck it caught her just under her left eye, right along her cheekbone. And when she went to pull it off her face it got her on her right hand, right in between her thumb and her finger, and it wouldn't let go. She hollered out and cracked that snake like a bullwhip, but it was too strong. Chambliss dropped his microphone, and him and two of the deacons laid her down right there in front of the church. They held her still and finally got that snake's fangs to turn her hand loose. You could tell by the way they handled it that they didn't want to hurt it, and they didn't want themselves to get bit either. Chambliss picked it up just as gentle as he could and then opened the top of that crate with the toe of his boot and let that thing slide right back inside. Everybody stopped their dancing when they heard Molly hollering, and soon the music stopped too. That church was quieter than it had ever been until Chambliss got down on his knee beside Molly and put that microphone up to her lips like he expected her to say something. 'Go ahead,' he said to her, but all you could hear was the sound of her panting like she couldn't catch her breath. Somebody brought her a glass of water, and those two deacons helped her raise herself up and take a drink. When they sat her up, you could see that her cheek had started to turn blue, and they had to tip the water glass into her mouth because her lips were almost swollen shut.

'Sister Jameson,' Chambliss said, 'you've stepped out in faith, and we're all witness to that belief you have in the love of Jesus Christ to protect you and keep you safe, whether it's here with us on this sinful earth or at home with him in glory.' Whispered 'amens' rose up out of the congregation, and people waved their arms over their heads in hallelujah. 'I'm going to ask the rest of the deacons to come up here with me and lay their hands on you, Sister, and maybe the good Lord will let us pray you through this.' The sound of folding chairs being pushed across the linoleum rang out, and groups of men went up on the stage and kneeled around Molly and laid their hands on her and prayed different prayers, some of them in tongues, some of them calling on God and asking him to save her. Chambliss stayed knelt down beside her and kept his eyes closed, his good hand on her head, the burned one still holding on to the microphone.

'God's sent his angels,' he whispered. 'I can hear their footfalls up on the roof above us; I can hear their wings just a-fluttering, Molly. God's sent his angels to be with you this very morning, and we don't know if they're here to watch over you and keep you with us, or if he's sent them to carry you home to glory, but we feel them here with us, don't we, and we feel Jesus's love washing over us this very minute.' He looked up at the congregation. 'And all God's people said, 'Amen.''

'Amen!' the people hollered back. Chambliss stood up and looked out at us, and then he looked back down at Molly where she was laid out and surrounded by all those men who were still busy praying over her.

'But the world ain't made up of God's people,' he said. 'The world ain't given to know what we know. The world ain't going to understand this woman's faith; it ain't going to understand her wanting to take up that serpent to conquer the Devil. And I can tell you that the world ain't ever going to understand the will of God in allowing her to come home to him.'

'That's right!' someone hollered out. 'Hallelujah!'

'But we know,' Chambliss said. 'We know what's at work here. We know God has a plan for his people. We know God lets only the righteous into Heaven. We know God brings only the worthy home.'

'Amen!' another voice said.

'And I tell you,' Chambliss said, 'it's a good day when one of us goes home. It's a beautiful Sunday morning when one of us is called back to Jesus. Hallelujah!' He dropped his hands to his sides and shuffled across the front of the church like he was dancing. 'It gives me joy to see it! No tears. No sadness. Hallelujah! Just joy. Joy that this woman's going home. We got that good Holy Ghost power up in our church today, praise God!' He looked over to where Mrs. Crowder sat behind the piano, and he nodded toward her and she took up playing and pounding away at the keys. The drums and the guitar picked up after

8

that, and before I knew it the congregation had started in on 'Holy Ghost Power' and everyone had took to dancing and singing like nothing had ever happened, like they'd all done forgot that Miss Molly Jameson was dying from a snakebite right there in front of us, the music so loud and pulsing you could feel it in your chest. A couple of deacons picked Molly up and carried her out of the church, right down the middle aisle, right past everyone there, but not a single one of them people even seemed to notice.

A few days later I was down at the post office in Marshall when I heard a woman at the counter telling the postman about how Molly's sister-in-law came over to the house and found Molly dead in the garden on Wednesday evening. Said she was out there laying facedown in a row of tomatoes, a spade still in her hand.

'What took her?' the postman asked. He wet his finger with his tongue and counted out dollar bills for the woman's change, and he laid them out on the counter like a fan.

'They don't know exactly what got her,' the woman said. She tore a stamp from the sheet the postman had just given her, and she licked it and smoothed it out on her letter before handing it over to him. 'But they reckon a snake must've been hiding in them tomato plants. By the time they found her on Wednesday her right hand had turned black, and she had a black lump under her eye too. It was just as round and hard as it could be,' she said. 'Shiny too, like a ripe apple but for the blackness.'

They buried Molly that Friday, and Chambliss

9

preached her funeral.

After that I understood that my church wasn't no place to worship the Lord in, and I realized I couldn't stay. I'd been a member of that church in one way or another since I was a young woman, but things had been took too far, and I couldn't pretend to look past them no more. If having Molly Jameson die right in front of that church didn't convince Carson Chambliss to stop his carrying on, who's to say that somebody setting themselves on fire and burning down the church would change his mind? There wasn't no amount of strychnine that could've got him to stop; wasn't no kind of snake that man wouldn't pick up and pass around.

Even though that newspaper in the windows kept folks from seeing inside that church, I figure everybody in town knew what was going on, and it wouldn't be long before they had the law down there trying to break it up. I didn't like none of it one bit at all, and I knew if it wasn't a safe place for an old woman, then there wasn't no way it was a safe place for children, and so I prayed on it and I prayed on it, and that's when God laid it on my heart. *Addie*, he said, just as clear as day, *you need to get out of that church, but you know you can't leave them children behind.* And I knew then that I'd have to stand up to Carson Chambliss, that I'd have to tell him that what he was doing was wrong.

I got down to the church early that next Sunday morning, the week after Molly Jameson was killed, and I pulled up just as Chambliss and Deacon Ponder unloaded the last of the crates out of the back of Ponder's pickup truck. I got out of my car and stood there watching them. Chambliss must've had some kind of premonition about my business because when he saw me he stopped what he was doing and looked at me, and then he handed his crate over to Ponder.

'Would you carry this inside for me, Phil?' he asked. 'I'm going to stay out here and visit with Sister Adelaide for a bit.' He slammed the gate on the truck bed, and Ponder nodded his head and smiled at me and walked on inside the church. Chambliss dusted off his hands and walked over to where I was standing by my car. 'You're here awfully early,' he said. His eyes narrowed to keep out the sun, and then he lifted his good hand to shield them from the light. His face was ruddy and weathered like most men's faces up here who've spent too much time working in the sun or smoking too many cigarettes, or maybe both.

'I wanted to get here early because I need to talk to you about some things,' I said.

'What things?'

'About what all has happened,' I said. My voice was shaking, but I tried my best to hide it because I didn't want him knowing I was scared of crossing him. 'I want to talk to you about what happened to Molly last Sunday.'

'What do you need to talk about?' he asked me. 'You were there. You saw it. She stepped out in faith, and the Lord took her home.'

'But it ain't right,' I said. 'It ain't right what y'all did to her.'

'What do you mean, 'It ain't right'?'

'It ain't right what you done with her after church,' I said. 'Taking her home and laying her out there in the yard and just leaving her, hoping somebody would find her before the animals started eating at her. People got a right to know about these things.'

'What people?' he said. 'Everybody who really loved her, everybody she loved, they all know what happened.' He pointed at the church. 'They were all right inside this church when it happened. Nobody else deserves to know anything more than that. Besides us, nobody in this world needs to know anything at all. It ain't going to do her a lick of good, and trouble is all it's going to bring us.' He dropped his hand from his eyes and squinted against the sun.

'Folks talk,' I said. 'Especially in a town like Marshall, especially about a church like this. Putting up newspaper so they can't see inside ain't going to keep them from talking.'

'Well,' he said, 'I trust the folks of my congregation to know who needs talking to and who don't. But if you got any ideas about taking our business outside this church, then I think you'd better tell me now. I need to know that I can trust members of my congregation with the Lord's work.'

'That's fine,' I said, 'because I can't be a part of this no more.'

'What do you plan on doing?' he asked.

'I can't be a part of this no more,' I said again. 'I'm leaving the church, and I want to take the children with me.'

He smiled and just stood there looking at me

like he was going to laugh in my face.

'Is that right,' he said. 'You're just going to take the children out of my church and teach them in your own way, teach them your own beliefs. What do you think gives you the right to do that?'

'Before the hospital got built I delivered just about every child that ever stepped foot inside this church,' I said. 'And I delivered just about all their mamas and daddies, too. I ain't claiming to be in charge of their spirits, but I have a job to see them safely through this world after bringing them into it. And I can tell you this ain't no place for children to be,' I said. 'It just ain't safe.'

'Sister Adelaide,' he said, 'I've been pastoring this church long enough for you to know that we protect our children, and I can tell you that I wouldn't never let a youngster take up no snake or drink no poison or nothing like that. But you've been here long enough to know that what we do here is the Truth and our children need to see it. Our children need to be raised up in it.'

'And you should know that children can't keep no secrets about what they see either,' I said.

He folded his arms across his chest and kind of rocked back on the heels of his boots. He turned his head and looked out over the river toward downtown Marshall like he was thinking about what I'd said. Then he turned his head and looked back at me.

'Can you, Sister Adelaide? Can you keep a secret?'

'I can,' I said. 'But I'd rather not know any secrets that need keeping, and I won't know

13

them if I stay out of your church. A church ain't no place to hide the truth, and a church that does ain't no place for me. Ain't no place for children neither.'

★   ★   ★

Chambliss never forgave me for taking the children out of that church. He warned me then that in leaving the church I was leaving my life as I'd known it, and that those folks wouldn't ever accept me the way they once had and that I'd always be an outsider. I told him I wasn't leaving the church, I was just leaving him, but I knew he was right. I lost friendships I'd had just about my whole life, and it hurt me. It still does. But for ten years I kept those children out, kept them safe. Once the service started, I'd take them across the road and down to the river when it was nice and warm, or folks would just drop them off at my house in the wintertime or if it was raining. We'd have us a little Sunday school lesson, then they'd play outside. Sometimes we'd make things, color pictures, and sing songs. But I didn't step another foot inside that church for ten years, and I hardly said more than a 'hello' to Carson Chambliss in all that time. And for a while there it was real nice, that little truce. I had my little congregation and he had his, and we didn't have hardly anything to do with each other. I felt like I was doing what the Lord wanted me to do with those children.

But I should've known it couldn't have gone on like that, and I should've known that something terrible was going to happen again. But there was just no way I could have guessed it would happen to one of mine. I tried to keep them children out of that church, and for ten years I did, but that ten years didn't do nothing for Carson Chambliss but make him ten years older and braver and ten years more reckless too. And here I was on a Thursday afternoon, sitting outside a church I thought I'd never see the insides of again, waiting to talk to a man I was afraid of being alone with. It was the only time in my life I'd ever gone to church out of fear.

I sat out there in my car with the windows rolled down and my keys still swinging from the ignition, and I stared at the church through all that bright heat and thought about him sitting in there in all that dark and waiting. The sound of that gravel dust getting blown through the parking lot could've been bare feet shuffling across the hallway the night before, when Julie was standing in the doorway watching me hunched over the bed in my funeral clothes. I finished folding the covers down, then I turned around and settled myself by the quilt that was slung over the footboard, and I smoothed out my dress and looked up at her. She didn't have a black dress to wear because she'd had to leave so many things behind right after it happened, and I ended up giving her one of mine. It hadn't been worn for years, and I reckon it had fell out of fashion well before I'd come to own it, but she seemed glad to have it and it looked just fine on her. She almost looked like a young girl, even though she was a woman a couple

15

years past thirty who'd just buried her son. When we'd come in from the funeral, she'd gone into the bedroom across the hall and closed the door. I heard the old springs on the bed give a creak when she laid down on it. I imagined her in there on that bed with her eyes wide open staring at the ceiling until the room got too dark to see it. Then she'd opened the door and come across the hall with her hair let down just as long and pretty as it could be. About the color of sweet corn. I could see she'd done a little more crying.

'You fixing to turn in?' she asked me. I nodded my head and tried to smile at her.

'I was thinking about it,' I said. 'You need anything before I do?'

'No, ma'am,' she said. 'I think I'll be all right. I just want to tell you again how much I appreciate you letting me stay here. Shouldn't be but just a while. Just till I decide what I'm going to do.'

'Lord, girl,' I told her, 'you can stay here just as long as you're needing to. You don't need to make no kinds of decisions, especially not tonight, especially after what all has happened.' She looked down at that pretty yellow hair where it draped over her shoulder and fell down to her chest, and she picked up the ends of it and swished it over her fingers like she was dusting something off her hands.

'Pastor told me he wants to see you,' she said. 'Tomorrow afternoon, down at the church. He said about three o'clock.' She dropped her hair and used both her hands to move it back behind

16

her shoulders, and then she raised her face and looked at me.

'I wish he could've told me himself,' I said. 'And I wish he'd been out there today at Christopher's funeral. Don't seem right that he wasn't.'

'He thought it'd be better if he didn't come,' she said. 'After all that's happened, I mean.'

'Is that right?' I said. 'A little boy dies during his church service, and he thinks that's a reason to stay away. It don't seem right to me.' I stood up from the bed and turned on the lamp on the bedside table and went to the closet where my nightgown hung on the back of the door. 'I don't reckon you want to go down there with me?'

'He said he wanted you to come alone,' she said.

'I can't say I'm too surprised by that,' I said.

* * *

There wasn't a single car out there in the parking lot besides mine and Chambliss's old Buick. I opened the door and put my feet out on the blacktop and looked across the road where the land sloped down toward the riverbank. Downtown Marshall sat about a mile or so up the river, too far away to hear the sounds of cars or people's voices or other things you might hear on a Thursday afternoon in a little town. It looked to be real still, like there wasn't even anybody on the streets at all. I looked back toward the church and saw the green field spread out behind it, the trees rising up from the woods

17

farther out at the field's edge. There weren't any sounds except for that little bit of breeze and the sound of the river running softly across the street. I climbed out of the car and closed the door and just stood there for what seemed like forever, trying to wrap my head around what might've happened up here on Sunday night, trying to imagine what was going to happen to me.

I can tell you that opening the door and stepping inside that church was like walking right into the dark of night. The newspaper over those windows blocked out the sun, and with that dark wood paneling on the walls it took a good while for my eyes to get used to all that blackness; I couldn't hardly see a thing until they did. Once my eyes got fixed right, I could see where the broken linoleum tiles exposed the bare cement floors after those coolers had been yanked out. It hadn't hardly changed a bit in ten years. I followed the floor tiles down the center of the room where the folding chairs parted to lead you down to the front of the church. I could just barely make out Chambliss sitting in a chair right up there on the first row. His back was to me, and he didn't even turn around when the door closed behind me. He didn't turn around when he spoke to me either; he just sat there looking straight ahead.

'Sister Adelaide,' he said. 'I was hoping you'd decide to come in.'

'Julie said you wanted to see me,' I said. 'And here I am.'

'And here you are,' he said. 'I'm glad you

18

came. It's good to have you inside our church again.' He put his arm across the chair beside him and finally turned his head and looked at me. 'Come on up here and have a seat by me.' I could see his face good now, and except for that silver hair around his temples, he hadn't changed. His eyes looked just as cool and distant as they always had.

I walked down the center aisle past them rows of folding chairs. It was dead silent in there because he didn't have that window air conditioner on or none of them floor fans running, and that hot, stifling air almost took my breath away. When I got down to the chairs in the front, I saw that he had one of them wooden crates sitting on the floor right by his feet. It had a little hinged trap on the top of it, and I could see that the clasp on the trap was undone. I stood there looking down at it, and then I looked over at Chambliss. He was staring up at me and smiling like he'd just thought of something funny to tell me. His left arm was still across the back of the chair beside him. He took it off the chair and patted the seat.

'Sit down,' he said. I didn't want to sit that close to him, so I walked in front of him and took a seat a few chairs over to his right. When I did, he moved his arm and covered his right hand with his left, like he didn't want me staring at just how awful that burned-up right hand looked. We both sat there real quiet for a bit. I crossed my ankles and leaned forward just a little until my back wasn't touching the chair, and he just sat there with his feet flat on the floor, his hands in his lap, the left one covering up the right so I couldn't hardly see it.

Somebody'd hung all kinds of pictures and calendars on the front wall behind the stage, and just about every one of them had a picture of Jesus Christ on it: Jesus praying in Gethsemane; Jesus at the Pentecost; Jesus holding out his hands to Doubting Thomas to show him the places where those nails had gone right through. From where I was sitting I could see there was an old calendar from Samuels' Funeral Home and some other ones from a couple of stores in Marshall and Hot Springs and one from the old bank. Some of them calendars were so old you could only look at the pictures because you couldn't hardly read the lettering on them. In between all those calendars and all those pictures, right there in the middle of the wall, was a big framed painting of Moses taking up a serpent in front of the burning bush. I sat there and looked at that picture of Moses and thought about how he watched that staff come alive right there in the dirt, and I wondered how he must've felt when the voice of the Lord commanded him to pick it up by its tail. I looked from that painting to the crate where it sat on the floor in front of Chambliss.

'I know the sheriff's been out to see you,' he said.

'Yes,' I said. 'He has. A couple days ago.'

'And I reckon he had him a few questions about what happened up here on Sunday.'

'He had some questions,' I said. 'But I didn't have any answers for him. I told him I couldn't speak for what y'all do up here in this church. This ain't my place anymore, even though I've been a member of this church for fifty-something years, it ain't been my place for a very long time. That's what I told him.'

'What is your place, Sister Adelaide?' he asked me. He turned his head and looked at me with just about the most blank expression I've ever seen on a man's face. I stared right back at him too, and then something caught my eye, and when I looked down I seen that that awful hand had made a fist and he was using his left hand to try and cover it up, but it was almost like he couldn't do it, so instead he took to rubbing his fingers back and forth across the back of that hand, and I just sat there and stared at them fingers and I couldn't take my eyes off them.

'What is your place?' he asked me again. His fingers stopped moving, and he opened his fist and laid both his hands flat on his thighs. I looked up at him.

'My place is with the children of this congregation,' I said.

'Is it?' he asked.

'That's where I say it is.'

'You know your Bible, don't you, Sister Adelaide?'

'I do,' I said. 'I know it very well.'

'Then you should know Matthew 9:33,' he said. 'If you know your Bible, then you should know it says that 'when the demon was driven out, the man who had been mute spoke.' And I reckon you should probably know Matthew 17 too, about the man who brought his son to Jesus because he was sick with a disease brought on by a demon and the disciples didn't have the faith enough to heal him.'

'I know both of them stories,' I said. 'I've read them both many, many times.'

'They ain't no stories,' he said. 'You can believe me when I tell you that.' He looked away from me toward the front wall where all those pictures of Jesus were hanging up. 'Jesus took that boy from the book of Matthew,' he said, 'and he healed him. He told the disciples they didn't have the faith enough, and he promised them that if their faith was even as small as a mustard seed, then they could move mountains.' He looked away from the pictures and turned his head back toward me. 'That's all it would've taken, Sister Adelaide, just that little bit of faith, but they didn't have it. They didn't have faith enough to cast that demon out. Jesus had to do it himself.'

'You ain't no Jesus,' I said. 'And Christopher didn't have no demon in him. He was born that way; I was there when he came into this world, and I can tell you God makes us how he needs us to be. I'd think about that the next time you go off on some idea about trying to change things you ain't got any business changing. I might be afraid of tempting that kind of power.'

He smiled at me like he thought what I'd said was funny, but I wanted to tell him that I didn't mean for it to be no joke. He turned his head back to the front wall and took to rubbing his fingers back and forth across the back of that hand again. Well, I'd had all I could stand of his talk and his little Bible lesson, and I just wasn't going to sit there and stare at that hand no longer than I had to. I uncrossed my ankles and smoothed out my skirt and got ready to stand up to leave, and when I did that's when I felt it right there on the back of my neck.

What he did next I can't even picture quite good enough to tell just how it happened, but when I felt it on my skin I knew right then what it was; it felt just like the hand of a dead man, just as cold and clammy as it could be. He grabbed me by the neck just above my shirt collar and forced me to my knees right there in the front of the church, and when he did I heard the toe of his boot kick open the little trap on that crate. He let go of my neck and got ahold of my arm, and before I even knew he was going to do it he'd already stuck my arm down inside that crate, and he used that hand he'd once set on fire to hold it there. I tried to jerk it out, but he was just too strong, and when I tried to stand up he leaned one of his knees down on the back of my shoulders. My feet scraped at the floor, and I kicked at one of the metal folding chairs behind me in the front row. It fell over and the crash echoed along the floor. Chambliss acted like he hadn't heard it. I kept kicking my feet, looking for something that would help me stand, but there wasn't nothing there.

Chambliss stood above me and held on to me tight like I was some kind of hog he was fixing to butcher and he was afraid of me getting away before he'd done it. I tried again to jerk my hand free, but he held it there tight, and I could feel the cold, smooth skin of his fingers where they wrapped around my arm.

'Shhhh,' he whispered. 'Don't fight it now. Don't fight it.'

I gave up then and quit struggling with him, and I can tell you that's when I took to praying. I closed my eyes and turned my head away from that crate, and that's when I heard it inside there; it was real quiet at first, like a light wind rustling dry cornstalks, but then that rattle got louder and louder until I just couldn't make myself pretend it was nothing else. I squeezed my eyes shut just as tight as I could, and I imagined feeling the prick of its fangs, something like a bad bee sting, and I imagined that venom coursing itself through my veins on the way to my heart. I pictured myself pulling my arm out of that crate after it struck me, the skin on my hand already turning black around the two puncture holes and the blue veins rising up all cloudy with poison. I pictured Miss Molly Jameson, how her face had swelled up, how she'd struggled to breathe, how they'd found her laying out there in her yard without the least idea of how she'd got there. I tell you that I thought I was going to die, and I did my best to get ready for whatever it was that was going to happen after I did.

'You ain't afraid, are you?' Chambliss whispered. I tried to say something to him, but it was like the words got caught in my throat and I couldn't cough them up good enough to speak. He gave my neck a hard squeeze and shook me good, and when he did I felt that rattler buck

24

against the roof of its crate and I thought I'd been bit for sure. 'Are you afraid!' he hollered at me then.

'No,' I finally said so quiet I almost couldn't hear myself. 'I ain't afraid.'

'You ain't got to be afraid if you believe,' he whispered. 'If you got your faith, there's nothing in this world that can hurt you. Not the law, not no man neither. Ain't nothing you need to fear but the Lord himself.'

Once he said that, I felt that hand let go of my arm, and I pulled it out of the trap on that crate just as fast as I could and tucked it under me with my other hand. I heard him close that trap with his boot, and then I heard him behind me setting that folding chair back upright. I still had my eyes closed because I was too afraid to even open them, and I stayed there on my knees on the floor with my arms pulled up under my chin like I was praying. I heard his footsteps come around in front of me, and he bent over and closed the latch on that crate and picked it up by its handle. I could tell he was standing right there over me because I heard him breathing heavy, but other than that it was quiet again, so quiet it was almost like nothing had happened.

'Hope to see you on Sunday,' he finally said. 'If you get a mind to it, come on inside and join us for worship.'

I stayed hunkered down there in the front row of the church and listened to his footsteps as he walked down the center aisle toward the door. I heard him open it up and step outside, and when he did my eyes sensed the explosion of light the

25

door let in even though I had them closed just as tight as I could. He was outside, but I stayed froze just like that until I heard the sound of his car engine revving; I still didn't move when I heard him pull out onto the road and head out toward the highway. Once I was sure he was gone, I opened my eyes and tried to look around to get my bearings, but the light from the door was gone, and I knew my eyes would have to fix themselves against the blackness that had once again taken over the church.

Jess Hall

2

I followed Joe Bill farther down the riverbank
than we'd ever gone before. We stopped at the
bridge and came up a new path from the river
through the bright morning sunlight and crossed
the road toward the woods on the other side. We
walked along the railroad tracks where you could
smell the dusty ties getting baked dry in the heat,
and then we went into the trees and crawled
through briars and over rotten limbs and didn't
say a word to each other until we stood in the
shade on the edge of the woods and stared across
the field at the back of the church.

It was so hot that my hair and my shirt were
soaked through with sweat, and I figured that if I
told somebody I'd just been baptized in the river
with all my clothes on, they would've believed it.
I could feel that sweat running down my legs
beneath my blue jeans, and I knew it would start
itching me when it dried. I untucked my shirt
and wiped my face, and then I tucked it back
inside my jeans because Mama had told us over
and over that we'd better keep our shirts tucked
in while we were at church, especially on Sunday
mornings. She always said Joe Bill's mama didn't
care one bit about what he looked like at church,

and I reckon she was right, because he'd untucked his shirt and unbuttoned some of its buttons too. He reached up and grabbed a tree limb and pulled it down and held on to it. I looked around for a limb that I could pull down and hold on to too, but there wasn't any that I could reach. Joe Bill was eleven and I was nine, and that meant he wasn't just two years older than me, he was two years taller too.

I watched a hot breeze come across the field and move through the high grass on its way to us. I looked over at Joe Bill as the breeze pushed his cowlick off his forehead. His hair was blond, but in the shade it looked almost as brown as mine because it was wet from him sweating so much. He looked over at me, and then he looked back toward the field.

'It's right there,' he said, nodding toward the back of the church.

I looked across the field, but I didn't know what I was supposed to be looking at because I hadn't ever been behind the church before. Up front it had big windows that somebody had covered over from the inside with newspapers so long ago that they'd been turned yellow from the sun. There was only one window around the back of the church, and it had a rusted old air conditioner sitting up inside it.

'Right there,' Joe Bill said. He raised his hand and pointed his finger out across the field to where that air conditioner hung out of the window. There were some rotten-looking boards blocking in the sides of it, but it almost looked like it might be too heavy for them boards to hold it up in there. 'You see it?' Joe Bill asked.

'I see it,' I told him. He looked over at me again, and then he took a step closer like somebody might've been watching us and he was afraid they'd hear what he was about to tell me next.

'There's gaps in between them boards and the window frame,' he said. 'If you get up close enough, you can see right in there.'

I looked at that air conditioner, and even though I couldn't hear it from where we were standing, I could see it blowing hot air down into the grass right under the window. The church was painted white, but around the bottom it had turned orange from where dirt and mud had splashed up from the grass during rainstorms.

'I bet he's still in there,' Joe Bill said.

'You think?'

'I bet he is,' he said. 'It ain't been long since Mr. Thompson came down and got him.' Joe Bill let go of the limb he'd been holding, and it whipped right past my ear and snapped back up into the tree.

'Hey!' I hollered out. 'You just about took my dang ear off!'

'Shhhh!' he whispered. 'Be quiet.' He closed his eyes and dropped his head and for a minute it looked like he was fixing to pray, but then he opened his eyes real slow like he'd just woke up from a nap. 'Listen,' he said.

'To what?'

'You can't hear that?'

'Hear what?'

'Listen,' he said again.

I dropped my head and closed my eyes just like I'd seen Joe Bill do, and for a minute I couldn't hear nothing at all except for a few birds fussing in the trees above us and the sound of the breeze coming through the dry grass, and after a minute I couldn't even hear that. But then, real slow, the singing of the crickets raised up out of the woods behind me and their chirping sounded like somebody was scratching a spoon across a clean dinner plate, and past that, across the railroad tracks on the other side of the woods, I could hear the river running slow toward Marshall, and it was so soft that I wondered if I was making it up or remembering the sound of it just because it was supposed to be there. Then I couldn't hear nothing until I turned my ears to listen for what was in front of me out there in the field where the grasshoppers and the katydids hummed in the high grass. That was a noise I'd always heard without even knowing I could hear it, and when I heard it, I could finally hear what Joe Bill was talking about. At first I heard it like a heartbeat, and I felt it in my chest like a heartbeat too, like it was inside my body thumping up against my ribs because it wanted to get out. It made me think about the Madison High marching band at the football games and the marchers with the drums strapped to their chests and the feeling you get inside you when they march out onto the field at halftime with the batons and the horns and the drums and all that noise they make. And now I could hear other noises floating just above the sound of that heartbeat: the electric guitar came

30

out over the field like a crackly old radio that wasn't tuned in good, and the sound of somebody banging away on the piano followed behind it. All of a sudden I knew that what I was hearing was music, and when I opened my eyes I knew it was coming from inside the church. I looked over at Joe Bill.

'It's music,' I said.

'I know,' Joe Bill said. 'They must be singing in there.'

We stood in the shade and listened to what we could hear of the music coming across the field. Every now and then I could hear people's voices, and it sounded like they were shouting.

'Are you going to take a look?' Joe Bill asked me.

'I ain't decided yet,' I said, but deep down I wished I could tell him *no* because I was scared to death of going all the way across that field to spy on folks inside the church. Mama had told me and Stump it wasn't right to spy on grown-ups, and one time she caught us hiding up in the barn listening to Daddy and Mr. Gant hang the burley. When she found us, she took us inside the house and whipped us good across the backs of our legs with one of Daddy's old belts.

'I told y'all not to go spying on grown-ups,' she said. 'Especially your daddy. You don't need to know the kinds of things a man like him talks about.' But I already knew what kinds of things men like my daddy talked about. They talked about burley tobacco and farming and other men they knew who got new cars or new girlfriends or whose wives had got sick and died without nobody expecting it. I couldn't figure out what was so special about that kind of talk that made it something me and Stump couldn't hear. I wanted to tell her that all Daddy talked about was the kind of stuff folks talk about while they're working or while they're sitting around and visiting. Only thing she ever talked about was God and Jesus and Pastor Chambliss and what all they had going on down at the church. Sometimes I wanted to say, 'If it's so great down there, then why can't you get Daddy to go with you?' and 'If it's so wonderful, then why can't me and Stump go inside too?' I wanted to tell her that I got tired of hearing about that kind of stuff, but I didn't say nothing about what I thought because I didn't want her getting out that belt and whipping me again.

Joe Bill reached out and punched me in the shoulder. 'Come on,' he said. 'You ain't being a sissy, are you?'

'You go on up there,' I told him. 'You're the one that wanted to come up here so bad, and I ain't letting you get me in trouble. They're going to be getting out here pretty soon, and my mom will have a fit if she catches me spying.'

'It ain't even close to noon yet,' Joe Bill said. 'On Sundays they don't even let out until one. It's going to be a while. Besides, it ain't *really* spying anyway. I bet she would've let you go inside with Stump if you'd have asked. It ain't wrong to look in there just because you didn't ask.'

'They didn't ask *me* either,' I said. 'Mr. Thompson came down and got Stump, not me.'

But even as I said that, I was glad Mr. Thompson hadn't come down to the river looking for me. I didn't want him holding my hand and leading me across the road to the church like he did with Stump. He was old and bald except where he had pale yellow hair sticking out from behind his ears. It was the color of dead grass, and his face and his arms and hands were covered in dark brown spots that looked like big freckles. His old yellow eyeballs were always wet, and they looked too big for his head, like they might just pop out on you any second. That morning, when Mr. Thompson reached for him, Stump put his hand behind his back and got up close to me. Even Miss Lyle made a face like she didn't want Mr. Thompson touching Stump.

'Come on, Christopher,' Mr. Thompson said. 'Don't be afraid. I've come down here to tell you that today's your special day. We want you to worship with us this morning.' His breath smelled like Stump's and my clothes after we played outside during the wintertime.

'Why is it his special day?' Joe Bill asked.

'Because,' Mr. Thompson said, 'the Lord's called him.' He went to take Stump's hand, but Stump wouldn't let him touch it. He'd closed his fingers around something and made a fist and he wouldn't open them. 'What's he got?' Mr. Thompson asked. I looked at Stump.

'Let me see your hand,' I said. Stump put his hand behind his back again and stood there looking toward the river like he couldn't hear me. 'Stump,' I said, 'let me see what you've got.' He finally opened his hand, and when he did I saw that he'd picked up a little piece of quartz that he must've found while we were down at the river skipping rocks with Joe Bill. He was always doing that, picking up shiny rocks and keeping them in his pockets until we got home. We had a whole shelf in our room where we kept the rocks we collected. We even had us a big purple quartz rock about the size of a baseball that Daddy had found when he was turning his tobacco rows. I held out my hand to Stump. 'I'll keep that for you,' I said. 'I won't let nothing happen to it. I promise.' He dropped the quartz into my hand, and I slid it into the back pocket of my blue jeans. Then me and Joe Bill just stood there and watched Stump and Mr. Thompson walk across the road toward the church.

I didn't want Stump to go inside there without me, even though Mama'd told me over and over that I wasn't old enough to go to church with her just yet. But she'd also told me over and over that I should always look out for Stump and make sure that nothing happened to him, that I was like the big brother and he was like the little one. But I figured that what she'd said didn't matter now, and I felt awfully little just standing there watching Mr. Thompson take Stump's hand and lead him across the road.

There was a black drop of blood starting to scab on my arm where something must've scratched me on the way through the woods, and I took my finger and picked the scab off and rubbed the blood back and forth across my skin. It left a rusty trail through the hairs on my arm. Me and Joe Bill had been standing in the shade so long that the sweat on my legs was getting dry and it was starting to itch. I wiped my finger on the back pocket of my blue jeans to get the blood off, and then I scratched my legs with my fingernails until they stopped itching. I could feel that music beating inside my chest from clear across the field.

Joe Bill squatted down in the grass and put his elbows on his knees. Then he picked up a stick and started snapping it into little pieces and tossing them out in front of him. He didn't look at where they landed because he was too busy staring at the back of the church where that air conditioner sat up in that window and shook like it might break those boards and fall out on the ground any second.

'What do you think Stump's doing in there?' I asked. Joe Bill didn't say nothing for a long time, and then he laughed and broke off the last little bit of that stick and tossed it into the grass. He looked up at me and smiled.

'He ain't singing,' he said. 'That's for sure.'

'Well, he's in there for some reason,' I said. 'Mr. Thompson said it's his special day. Maybe my mom wanted him to be with her.'

'But why?' Joe Bill said. 'He can't even talk or sing or nothing.'

'That don't matter,' I said. 'Maybe he's old enough to go to church with them. He's thirteen. He's older than you.'

'So what,' Joe Bill said. 'I'm smarter than him. At least I can talk.'

'Just because he can't talk don't mean he ain't smart.'

'My brother says if you can't talk, then it means you're dumb,' Joe Bill said.

'Well, your brother's an asshole,' I said, and as soon as I said it I knew I shouldn't have. Joe Bill turned real slow and looked up at me like he couldn't believe I'd said it either. We stared at each other for a minute, and then I squatted down beside him and picked up a stick and started snapping it into pieces so I wouldn't have to look at him while he was staring at me.

'Don't talk about my brother,' he finally said.

'Don't talk about mine either.'

'I'm just telling you what Scooter told me,' Joe Bill said.

'I don't care what he told you,' I said. 'Why do you stick up for him all the time? All he ever does is beat the crap out of you.' Joe Bill stood up straight and looked at the church, and then he looked down at me.

'You going up there or not?' he asked. 'Because if you ain't I'm going back down to the river before Miss Lyle starts looking for us.' I didn't say nothing; I just sat there snapping that stick into little pieces until it got shorter and shorter and I stared out across the high grass toward the church and thought about what I should do. Joe Bill sighed real loud and turned around and started walking into the woods. 'I should've known you'd chicken out,' he said. 'You always do.'

I tried to picture what Stump was doing inside the church with that loud music pumping and all those folks singing and hollering, and then I thought about how he wouldn't be able to tell me one word about what he'd seen. I figured that if I was ever going to find out what they did in there then that morning might just be my only chance. 'All right,' I hollered. 'I'll go.' Joe Bill stopped walking and turned around and looked at me. 'I'll go if you come with me,' I said. 'If I get caught, then you're getting caught too.'

'Finally,' he said. He walked out of the woods toward me. I watched him for a second, and then, without even hardly thinking about it, I crept out of the woods real slow to the edge of the field where the grass was tall and bright yellow in the sunlight and I hunkered down and set out across the field like I was afraid I'd bump my head on something if I stood up too tall. The field seemed like it went on forever once I was out of the woods, and I figured that if I stood up straight I'd be able to see the road in front of the church and I could probably even see part of the river where it ran toward Marshall. I knew that meant that anybody driving by might be able to see me too, and I was afraid of Miss Lyle coming up the riverbank across the road and spotting me any second. I got down just as low as I could and I bent my knees almost to the ground and kept walking.

When I got about halfway across the field, I stopped and looked back and saw that Joe Bill hadn't even moved yet. I waved my hand for him to follow me, but he smiled and shook his head and I knew that he'd been lying about coming with me. I thought about going back, but I didn't want Joe Bill calling me a chicken again, even if he was one himself. And then I thought about

Stump being in there with Mama and I looked out over the grass at the back of the church and I saw that air conditioner vibrating in the window, and I figured I'd already come too far to think about turning around.

I looked back at Joe Bill again and he whispered something, but he was too far away for me to hear what he said. He put his hands around his eyes and looked at me like he was trying to block out the sunlight. I turned around and walked toward the church, and soon I was close enough to make out the song they were playing, and I knew it was 'Have Thine Own Way, Lord.' Sometimes Mama sang that song to me and Stump before we went to bed at night, and the words popped into my head like I was lying in bed and singing right along with her, but instead I was out there in that field behind the church, hunkered down and walking low to the ground with that song singing itself in my head.

★   ★   ★

A little bit of roof hung off the back of the church, but it didn't offer hardly any shade at all, and by the time I made it to the church I could feel the sun burning through my shirt. I looked at my shadow where the sun threw it up on the concrete wall in front of me, and I thought about how easy it would be for Mama or Mr. Gene Thompson or Miss Lyle or somebody else to come around the corner of the church any second and catch me spying. I imagined seeing their silhouettes move against the wall while they

38

crept up beside me. I could almost feel somebody tapping me on the shoulder, and I tried to think about what I'd say to somebody if they found me back there.

The air conditioner hung in the window just about eye level with me, and when I stood by it I heard that it was rumbling so loud that I wouldn't be able to hear somebody sneaking up on me. It was so loud that I couldn't hardly hear the music coming from inside the church. When I got closer I felt the heat coming out of it, and that hot air poured down into my shirt collar and blew back my hair like I was riding in my daddy's truck with the windows rolled down.

I stood there in the sun with the hot air blowing on me, and I looked up and down the right side of the air conditioner until I saw a tiny crack up toward the top of the window between the concrete and the plywood where a little bit of light was coming through from inside the church. I looked around for another crack that might be lower, but I couldn't find one, so I stood on my tiptoes and reached up and grabbed ahold of the old, rotten window ledge and pulled myself up just a little so I could see in. The music inside the church came through the wall and pounded against my knees.

I raised myself up just as high as I could, but before I could even look inside I saw something out of the corner of my eye. I let go of the ledge and dropped down to the ground and stepped back, and as soon as I did I saw another silhouette thrown up against the wall right beside mine. I turned around and started to run toward the woods, but before I could even get going my nose smashed right into Joe Bill's chest and he grabbed my shoulders to keep me from knocking him down. His eyes were wide open, and he was looking right at me. He put one hand over my mouth like he was afraid I might holler out, and then he put his finger to his lips.

'Shhhh,' he said. We stood there looking at each other for a minute, and then he moved his hand off my mouth so I could talk. 'Did I scare you?' he whispered. He smiled like he thought it was funny.

'Dang it, Joe Bill,' I said. I pushed him as hard as I could to get him out of my face.

'You better hush,' he said, just loud enough so that I could hear him over the air conditioner and the music pounding on the other side of the wall. 'Did you get to see anything yet?'

'I ain't had the chance to look,' I whispered. I pointed up to where light from inside the church was showing through the crack between the board and the wall, and then I watched Joe Bill cup his hands around his eyes and peer through it for a minute. He looked back at me.

'They're just singing,' he whispered.

'Let me see,' I said.

'Go over to the other side and look for another crack,' he said. 'This one's too high for you.' I tugged on his shirt and tried to pull him away, but he wouldn't move, so I ducked under the air conditioner and found another crack to look through. It wasn't quite as high as the one I'd been looking through before, but I still had to get up on my tiptoes and prop my arms up on

40

the window ledge so I could see in. I got both my elbows up on the ledge and braced my knees against the wall, and then I cupped my hands around my eyes just like I'd seen Joe Bill do.

I could see right into the church; it almost felt like I was inside there, standing right down front on the little stage and looking into the people's faces out in the audience. They were all singing just like Joe Bill said they were, but the guitar and the drums had stopped going and the only sound was the singing voices and somebody I couldn't see banging away on the piano. It was a whole lot darker in there than I'd thought it'd be, especially with the sun so bright behind me, and I couldn't see too far past the first couple of rows. I looked around and tried to catch a sight of Mama and Stump, but it was just a small crack that I was looking through and I couldn't quite see everything inside there.

Everybody inside was standing up from their folding chairs and clapping their hands to the music. Some of them swayed back and forth and sang with their eyes closed. That air conditioner rattled and rumbled right up against my head so loud that I couldn't hardly hear nothing else for it, and that hot air poured onto my face and blew into my hair, and it seemed like I could feel that hot air getting pumped out of the church and right onto me and Joe Bill.

It didn't take long for my shoulders and my elbows to get good and sore from holding up my weight, and I dropped down to the ground to give them a rest. I ran my fingertips over my elbows and used my fingernails to pick off the flecks of dried paint and pieces of old wood that had gotten stuck on my skin. Joe Bill ducked under the air conditioner and came over to my side.

'This is boring,' he whispered. 'All they're doing is singing. I think we should leave.'

'Then go on back to the river,' I said, but I hoped he wouldn't because I didn't want him leaving me up there all alone. He watched me pick at the dried paint on my elbows, and then he looked back across the field toward the trees.

'I just think we should get going,' he said. 'They'll be letting out here soon.'

'But I haven't even seen Stump yet,' I told him. 'That's the whole reason we came up here.'

'I'm just thinking that we shouldn't be doing this,' he said.

'Now who's acting like a chicken?' I asked. Joe Bill stood there for a second, and then he ducked under to the other side of the air conditioner. I turned back to the window and got up on my tiptoes again and raised myself up with my elbows and cupped my hands around my eyes to peer in through that crack.

Not a single one of the people inside had sat down yet, and somebody was still banging away on that piano even though it looked like they'd all stopped singing. Just about every one of them had their eyes closed, and some of them had their hands up over their heads like they were waving big at somebody who might be too far away to see them.

All of a sudden, Pastor Chambliss flew right past my eyes and then disappeared, and the way he was moving looked like he might've been dancing or skipping or hopping down in front of the church. A second later he flew by again, and then he came back and stood right in front of me. I could see him good. He stayed there with his back to me and Joe Bill, and he just stared at all those people where they swayed back and forth with their eyes closed and their hands waving way up over their heads, their fists opening and closing like they were trying to reach up and grab something out of the sky.

Pastor Chambliss had his hair buzzed so short that you couldn't hardly notice the little bald spot right there in the back, and I probably wouldn't have noticed it myself if he hadn't been sweating and the light hadn't caught it. He looked like somebody who'd been in the army to me, even though he was probably too old to be a soldier now. The back of his blue dress shirt was dark with sweat, and the shirtsleeve on his left arm was rolled up past his elbow, but he had that right one buttoned tight at his wrist, and I knew why — his right hand was scary to look at: bright pink and wrinkled up. He kept that right sleeve rolled down tight, but he couldn't keep his hand hidden; everybody in the church had seen it, and most of them had probably got so used to it that they never even thought about it anymore. But I'd thought about that hand all weekend long because I'd seen it out in the bright sunlight two days before, and I saw the whole arm it was attached to too, and I'd seen where that pink skin ran up to his shoulder and covered his chest like chewing gum does when you blow a bubble and it pops and spreads itself out across your cheeks.

★ ★ ★

On the Friday before, after the school bus had dropped me off at the top of the road, I'd found Mama and Stump sitting on the porch steps like they were waiting on me. They were both holding small wooden boxes that looked like cages with handles on them, and when I got close enough to hear what she was telling Stump I heard the handle squeaking where Mama swung her box back and forth in front of her. She looked up and smiled when she saw me.

'There you are,' she said. 'How was school?'

'What are y'all doing out here?' I asked.

'Waiting on you,' she said.

'What for?'

'Because I figured you might want to go out and catch a few salamanders for y'all's room.' I dropped my book bag by her feet on the bottom step, and I looked at the wooden box where she held it in front of her. She held it out to me, and I took it by the handle.

'You serious?' I asked.

'Well,' she said, 'y'all been wanting some, and I figured you might as well have them if you can take care of them. We'll have to find something to put them in, but this'll do for now. I'll take your book bag inside, and you can go on down to the creek if you promise to keep that shirt and those pants clean.'

'I will,' I said. I looked at the box in my hand.

44

'Where did you get these?'

'From a friend,' she said. 'He's letting me borrow them just so y'all can use them. But we can't keep them, okay?'

'Okay,' I said.

She picked up my book bag and stood up from the steps and turned to go into the house, but she stopped and looked back at me and Stump. 'See if you can catch five salamanders,' she said. 'I think that would be plenty for us to have. So see if you can catch five.' I looked at Stump like I couldn't believe what she'd just said, and I swung my cage by its handle and bumped it against his like I was making a toast.

'You ready?' I asked. He jumped up from the porch, and we started across the yard toward the creek at the bottom of the hill.

But we didn't catch any salamanders. We couldn't even find a single one. It was probably the only time I'd ever gone off looking for salamanders that I couldn't find them, and when we walked back up the hill toward the house all we had in those little boxes was a few sticks and some blades of grass that reminded me of the terrarium we had in my classroom at school.

My pants were soaked up past my knees and I carried my shoes with my socks stuffed down inside. I was afraid that Mama was going to be mad at me for getting so dirty, especially after I'd told her I wouldn't. Stump had left his shoes on while he was walking through the creek, and I could hear water sloshing around in them and they squeaked when he walked. I knew Mama wasn't going to like that either.

We came up alongside the house, and I stopped beside the rain barrel. It sat up off the ground on some concrete blocks, and the gutter ran down into it from the roof. I squatted down and turned the spigot. I heard bubbles come up inside the barrel when the spigot opened and the water started pouring out.

'Wash off your hands,' I said to Stump. 'We'd better wash our shoes too. Mama's going to be mad if we bring all this mud in the house.'

He sat his box down in the grass by the rain barrel, and he held his hands under the water and rubbed them together to get the dirt off.

'Stick your shoes under there too,' I said. He picked up one of his shoes and held it under the water, and I found a stick and used it to scratch the mud off the sides of his shoe. Then he held the other one under there and I did the same thing. Stump turned off the spigot, and when he did we heard them inside the house. I looked up at the window where Mama and Daddy's bedroom was, and me and Stump stayed kneeled down there in the grass and listened to them. They were making the same noises that we heard them make in the morning sometimes when they didn't know we were awake yet.

Stump stood up straight and looked up at the window, and he turned his head like he was trying to hear them better. He tossed his shoes onto the ground behind him and walked up closer to the house.

'One of them's going to look out that window and see you,' I whispered. 'If they do, they'll come outside here and wear us out for spying on them.'

I turned the spigot back on and put my shoe under the water and scratched some more of the mud off the bottom with that stick. Stump walked right up against the house and reached up his hands to the window ledge like he was thinking about pulling himself up to look in.

'You'd better stop it,' I whispered louder, and I reached out that stick and poked him on the back of his leg. He looked back toward me and stepped away from the window, and then he put his hands flat on top of the rain barrel and grabbed on to the gutter and pulled himself up. I turned the spigot off, and I heard that big bubble inside there float up to the top again.

'Stump,' I said, 'you'd better get down. That ain't going to hold you,' but he acted like he couldn't even hear me. 'You'd better get down,' I said again.

When I stood up, I could feel the mud and wet grass squishing between my toes, and I could hear Mama and Daddy's bed squeaking inside their room. Stump put his hands on the window ledge and stood on his tiptoes on top of the rain barrel and tried to look in there. I saw the concrete blocks under the rain barrel move just a little, and then it leaned a little to the side like it might tip over. I put my hands on the sides of it to try and keep it from falling, and I felt the water in there roll around from side to side.

'Stump,' I whispered. I reached out and tugged at his leg, but he just stayed up on his tiptoes and tried to see in the window like he didn't feel me pulling on him. 'It ain't going to hold you,' I said. I tugged at his leg again, and when I did all that muddy water on his feet made him lose his balance. His feet went out from under him, and he fell on his butt on top of the rain barrel. It ripped loose from the gutter and tipped toward the yard, and Stump slipped and fell up against the house and landed on top of those concrete blocks. The rain barrel turned over in the grass with its top busted off. Water poured out onto the ground and ran down through the yard, and Stump just laid there on his back on top of those concrete blocks.

I heard Mama's voice through the open bedroom window. 'What was that?' she said.

'I don't know,' a man said. I didn't recognize the voice, but I knew it wasn't Daddy's. 'I'm going to go see,' the voice said. 'You stay right here.' I heard the bed squeak like somebody was standing up. 'You stay right here,' the voice said again. I knew whoever's voice I heard was coming out to find us. I looked down at Stump.

'Get up,' I said to Stump, but he wouldn't move. I kneeled down and tried to stand the rain barrel upright, but my feet kept slipping in the wet grass and it was too heavy to move. Stump just laid there with his eyes closed like the wind had got knocked out of him, and then he reached around behind him like he'd hurt his back. I heard the bedroom door open.

'Get up, Stump,' I said, but he just laid there and looked over my shoulder at the window above me like he couldn't move. 'They're coming out here,' I whispered. I reached down

48

and tried to pull him up by his hand. 'Get up,' I said again.

I heard the screen door slam shut around front, and I turned and hightailed it toward the woods beside the house. I ran until I didn't think anyone could see me, and then I stopped and laid down flat on my stomach behind some tree roots and looked back toward the yard. I could see the rain barrel where I'd pushed it back up, and I could see where the gutter had gotten bent and broken, but I couldn't see Stump at all because he hadn't stood up yet.

I laid on my stomach in the woods and waited on whoever I'd heard to come around the corner of the house and find Stump, and then I remembered that my shoes were still up there and I knew they were going to find them and tell Mama and she'd wear me out because I should've never let Stump climb up there because we shouldn't have been spying. But I forgot about all that when I saw Pastor Chambliss. I only saw his face at first because he peeked around the corner like he'd been hiding from somebody and was checking the side of the house to make sure it was safe to come out. He stood there peeking around the corner at the rain barrel, and then he walked into the side yard and I could see him good. All he had on was a dirty old pair of blue jeans that he had to hold at the waist because he wasn't wearing a belt. He'd pulled his boots on over his blue jeans, and he stopped walking and bent over and pushed his jeans down over the tops of his boots. When he bent down, I saw the inside of his right arm and how bright pink and shiny it was. When he stood up straight, I saw that the pink, wrinkled skin covered his chest and ran up his neck too. He looked out toward the woods beside the house, and I got as flat as I could on the ground behind those roots so he wouldn't see me. He walked over to the rain barrel and stopped, and then he just stood there looking down at Stump like he was surprised to see him laying there. Pastor Chambliss bent down and sat the rain barrel up straight. Then he fixed the top where it had come loose. He pounded on it with his fist and shut it tight. I heard the screen door slam, and then I heard Mama's voice come around the house from the front porch.

'What was it?' she hollered. Pastor Chambliss whipped his head around and looked toward the front yard.

'Nothing,' he hollered. 'Go back inside.' He turned and looked down at Stump again.

'You sure?' she said.

'Yes,' he hollered. 'It ain't nothing. The rain barrel tipped over, that's all. Go on back inside.' He squatted down like he was getting a good look at Stump, and then he reached behind the rain barrel with that wrinkly arm like he was offering Stump his hand so he could help him up. 'What did you see, boy?' he said. He waited like he expected Stump to say something, and then he laughed. He turned and walked back to the front. I got a good look at that bad arm, and I saw that it didn't even have any hair on it. I laid there in the woods behind those roots and stared at his arm until he'd gone around the corner of the house toward the porch steps and I couldn't see him anymore.

That night, while me and Stump were getting ready for bed, I asked Mama what had happened to Pastor Chambliss's hand that made it look like that. Stump and I were already in the bed, and she was folding some of our clothes and putting them in the dresser and she was hanging our dress shirts in the closet. With the closet door open I could see Stump's quiet box sitting up on the top shelf. Mama'd made it for him when he was little because she said when the world got too loud Stump needed a quiet place where he could go off and be alone. She took one of Daddy's shoe boxes and wrote, 'Quiet box — do not open' on the side of it. I could read her handwriting from where I laid in the bed. She'd never let me see what was inside the quiet box, and I'd always been afraid to even ask Stump because I was afraid she'd find out that I'd been messing with it.

Mama had just picked up the shirt I'd worn to school that day when I asked her about Pastor Chambliss's hand, and, instead of hanging it up, she just held it out in front of her and stared at it like she was looking to see how clean she'd been able to get it.

'What do you mean, 'What happened to his hand?'' she asked. She finally put my shirt on a clothes hanger and hung it in the closet. Then she reached down into the laundry basket again.

'How'd it get that way?' I said. 'Why's it all pink?' She turned around and looked at me. I saw that she was holding the blue jeans that I'd gotten wet and muddy down at the creek.

'What's got you thinking about that?' she asked.

'I don't know,' I said. 'I was just wondering.' She turned back toward the dresser and folded my jeans and opened a drawer and put them inside. She sighed.

'Would you believe that once upon a time, back before the Holy Ghost got ahold of him, Pastor Chambliss was on fire for the world and the things of this world burned him up?'

'What does that mean?' I asked.

'It means that he wasn't living for the Lord,' she said. 'He was on fire for the world. But now he's on fire for the Lord Jesus, and nothing in this world can ever burn him again.' She kept on folding clothes without looking back at us. Down the hall in the living room I heard the sound of Daddy reclining in his chair. Then I heard the television set turn on.

'What's the rest of him look like?' I asked. 'Is it all burned up too?' Mama grabbed the rest of the clothes out of the laundry basket and stuffed them into one drawer without even folding them. She picked up the basket and turned around and stood by the door and looked at me and Stump where we were laying in the bed.

'Why would you ask me that?' she finally said.

'I don't know,' I said. 'I just wondered.'

'I've never thought about what the rest of him looks like,' she said. 'And you shouldn't be thinking about things like that either. Go to sleep.' She turned off our bedroom light and closed the door. I heard her walk down the hall to her and Daddy's bedroom, and I heard the door close and the sound of her kicking her shoes off onto the floor. The bed springs creaked when she laid down.

I laid there in the dark with my eyes open and stared up at the ceiling. Then I rolled over on my side and looked across the bed at Stump.

'Stump,' I whispered. He opened his eyes slowly and looked at me. 'What did you see when you were up on the rain barrel?' We stared at each other for a minute, and then he closed his eyes and turned over on his other side. I laid there and looked at the back of Stump's head, and I pictured Pastor Chambliss coming around the corner of the house and asking him the same thing: 'What did you see?'

I rolled onto my back and stared up at the ceiling again, and then I closed my eyes as tight as I could and tried to say my prayers, but no matter how hard I tried I couldn't help wondering if that pink, burned-up hand had touched my mama.

★ ★ ★

But now Pastor Chambliss held his Bible in that burned-up hand inside the church, and I remembered what Mama'd said about him being on fire for the Holy Spirit, and I thought about him bursting into flames and giving off all kinds of heat, and how that air conditioner might just be pulling it out of the church and blowing it right onto me and Joe Bill.

The air conditioner and that piano were going

too loud for me to hear what Pastor Chambliss was saying, but it looked like he must've been preaching into the microphone because he had his Bible in his hand and he raised it and pointed it at everybody. He walked back and forth, and for a few seconds I couldn't see him, but then he came back to where I could watch him and when he did he had a woman on the stage with him; I knew it was Mama before I even saw her face. I raised myself up a little higher to get a better look, and when I did I saw Stump standing right there beside her. I felt something tugging on the back of my shirt, and I realized it was Joe Bill. He'd come around under the air conditioner and was standing beside me.

'I just saw Stump,' he said. He tugged on my shirt again, and I balanced myself on one of my tiptoes and kicked at his hand to get him to stop. 'Hey,' he whispered up at me.

'I see him too,' I said.

'Why is he down front?'

'I don't know,' I said. He let go of my blue jeans and ducked under to the other side of the air conditioner again.

I couldn't see anything except the back of Stump's head, but I could tell he was looking all around the church at all those people and I saw that now most of them had their eyes open and they were looking right back at him. Pastor Chambliss held his Bible with his bad hand, and he stepped around and got in between Mama and Stump and reached out his other hand and put it on top of Stump's head. Mama reached across Pastor Chambliss and touched Stump on

54

the shoulder and it looked like they were all praying, but after they stood like that for a second Stump started jerking around like he wanted to get away from them. Pastor Chambliss got up behind him and held his Bible and wrapped that ugly arm over Stump's shoulder like he was giving him a bear hug. He reached out with his left arm to keep Mama away from Stump, and she took her hand off his shoulder and backed away until I couldn't see her. I couldn't stand seeing Pastor Chambliss wrap his arm around Stump, and I couldn't help but be mad at Mama for letting him do it.

Pastor Chambliss just held Stump and held him and it looked like he was hugging him from behind and he wasn't ever going to let him go, even though Stump was trying to get away because he hadn't ever liked folks touching him and holding him like that. All the people in there held their hands up in the air, and then they started singing again after somebody got to banging away on the piano, but I couldn't hardly hear nothing except that air conditioner right up against my head. My arms were getting so sore and tired that I was afraid I was going to fall. I couldn't find Mama's face, but I saw her hand reach out and take Stump's, and he was fighting so hard with Pastor Chambliss that Mama could just barely hold on to it. Pastor Chambliss had both arms around Stump now, and he was holding on to him real tight with his Bible pressed right up against his chest, and they rocked back and forth like they couldn't stand up, and all of a sudden they just fell over and I couldn't see them at all no more because they were laying out on the floor.

Mama reached down and tried to get Stump to stand up, and it looked like she was pulling on his hand, but Pastor Chambliss wouldn't let him go and Mama cried and looked like she was hollering for him to turn Stump loose. I felt Joe Bill tugging on my jeans so hard that I was scared he was going to yank me out of that window and I wouldn't be able to see a thing.

'What are they doing to him?' Joe Bill said, but his voice was just barely a whisper and it sounded like he was running out of breath and he had to force out the words. 'Jess,' he said. 'What's he doing to him?' I just kept watching Mama, and I didn't say nothing to Joe Bill because seeing her cry got me crying too and I didn't want Joe Bill seeing me do that.

Another man came up on the stage and kneeled down, and I figured he was helping Pastor Chambliss hold Stump still, but I couldn't see nothing except Mama crying and trying to hold on to Stump's hand. It looked like she was still hollering for them to get up and leave him alone.

'Jess, we better go,' Joe Bill said. I felt him behind me pulling on my shirt, but I didn't turn around and I didn't get off my tiptoes.

'They shouldn't be doing that to him,' I said.

'Jess,' he said. His voice sounded like he was about to cry. 'We got to go. He's all right.' He didn't say nothing after that, and I turned my head to ask him to put his hands under my feet to boost me up so I could see Stump, but Joe Bill was gone. When I looked across the field, I saw him hightailing it toward the woods, and I watched him run through the high grass with his untucked shirttail flapping out behind him.

I looked in the church again and saw Mr. Gene Thompson standing right up on stage too, and he had his arms locked around Mama and she was crying and fighting with him, but he wouldn't let her go. I still couldn't see Stump or Pastor Chambliss either, and I looked around and around but it was only a little crack and I couldn't see everything in there. I dropped down and ducked under the air conditioner to the other side where Joe Bill had been standing and I got up on my tiptoes and raised myself up onto my elbows so I could look in again, and when I did I saw Stump laying on the stage and Pastor Chambliss and that other man laying on top of him. Stump's feet were kicking like he was trying to get away and a couple other men left their chairs and walked up on the stage and put their hands on him and touched him and somebody was just banging away on the piano and just about all of them had their eyes closed except Mama and Mr. Thompson. She was staring at them where they were laying on Stump and holding him down and touching him and she was crying and hollering for them to stop. Stump kicked his legs around like he was trying to run sideways on the floor, and Mama screamed so loud that I could hear it over that piano and I could hear it over the air conditioner and all those people singing.

For a second I forgot where I was and I

hollered out, 'Mama!,' and when I did she jerked one of her hands up over her head and busted Mr. Thompson right on the lip. He let her go and raised his hand and touched his mouth to see if there was blood coming out. Mama got down on her knees and started pulling all them people off Stump, and he sat up as quick as he could and she hugged him to her and rocked him back and forth and all those men just sat there on the floor and stared at Mama and Stump like they didn't know what to think. Mr. Thompson looked down at Mama, and then he whipped his head around and his big, yellow eyeballs looked right through that little crack like he was staring straight at me.

I figured everybody in the church'd heard me holler out for Mama, and when I leaned back to drop myself down I felt somebody behind me and they put their hand over my mouth and pulled me backward out of the window. I reached out for the window ledge, and I felt a chunk of that old wood break off in my hand. Whoever it was behind me tackled me, and we fell back into the high grass. The sun hit me right in the eyes, and I couldn't see and I was crying and I couldn't catch my breath because somebody'd put their hand over my mouth and it was keeping out all the air. Then it felt like something heavy was resting on my chest. I closed my eyes and tried to scream, but then, when I opened them, I saw it was Joe Bill sitting on top of me.

'Be quiet, Jess,' he said. 'Be quiet.' I tried to roll over on my stomach so I could get up and run, but he wouldn't get off me. 'Be quiet, Jess,' he said again. 'They're just trying to help him.' I was scared to death, and I was crying so hard that I couldn't even breathe. I laid there fighting with him on top of me, and before I knew it I was up and running for the trees.

I ran all the way across the field and into the woods, and I kept running until I was dizzy and had to stop to catch my breath. I looked around for Joe Bill, but I didn't see him. There was a tree beside me, and I reached out and held myself up to keep from falling over, and then I leaned my back against it. I heard something crashing through the trees behind me, and I knew it was Joe Bill coming to find me. I put my hands on my knees so Joe Bill wouldn't see me crying, and when I did I saw my hand had blood on it and I had it all over my blue jeans and it was on my shirt too. I turned my hand over and saw that a splinter half as long as my middle finger had gotten stuck down in the fat part of my hand right below my thumb. All of a sudden it hurt so bad that I couldn't even think about touching it. I just stayed bent over with my other hand on my knee and I stared at the splinter and watched a drop of blood run through my palm, down my fingers, and into the leaves. I tried to clear my head and think about something else besides what I'd seen them doing to Stump. I heard Joe Bill running through the woods behind me.

He stopped running, and I heard him panting like he was out of breath. I turned my head so he wouldn't see me crying, and I tried to make a fist to hide all the blood, but that splinter was so big that it wouldn't let me close my fingers. A drop of blood had landed on my shoe and was running off the side into the dry leaves.

'It's all right, Jess,' Joe Bill said. He couldn't hardly talk because he was so out of breath. 'They were just laying their hands on him,' he said. 'They were trying to help him.' I looked up at Joe Bill. I saw that he was crying too.

3

When I dipped my hand into the river, the water was so cold that it almost took my breath away. I let my wrist go limp, and I swished it back and forth like a brook trout flicks its tail in shallow, rocky water, and I watched the blood leave my hand and move into the river like red smoke drifting up from a fire. I took my other hand and cupped water into it and splashed it over my face to keep my eyes from getting too red and swollen from all the crying. I didn't want Miss Lyle or Mama or nobody else up at the church to know I'd been crying because I didn't want them asking me nothing about what we'd been doing.

Joe Bill sat by the water on top of a rock a little piece down the bank with his arms locked around his knees. He looked out at the river. Neither one of us had said a word since we came out of the woods and snuck back down to the riverbank. I stared at his back for a minute, and then I stood up and shook the water off my hands.

'You know we can't tell nobody about this,' I said to him. 'We shouldn't have seen that. We weren't supposed to see anything.'

'I know,' Joe Bill said.

I thought about what I was saying, and then I pictured those men lying down on top of Stump, and in my head I heard myself holler out for Mama. I stood up and turned away from Joe Bill before I started crying again, and I untucked my shirttail and wiped my eyes with it. I tried to keep my right hand from touching my shirt any more than it already had so I wouldn't get more blood on it.

'We never should've gone up there,' I said. I looked back at Joe Bill. He turned his face toward me, and he looked like he might start crying again too.

'I think they were trying to help him,' he said. 'Mr. Thompson told us it was Stump's special day. Maybe they were trying to heal him. Maybe they were laying their hands on him so he could talk.'

'He couldn't breathe!' I screamed at him. 'He was trying to get up and run because he couldn't breathe, and they wouldn't get off him! They might have been trying to kill him!'

'They weren't,' Joe Bill said.

'How do you know?' I hollered. At that second I thought about telling Joe Bill about what else I'd seen: Pastor Chambliss with no shirt on, standing over the rain barrel and staring down at Stump. But then I thought about how Joe Bill hadn't ever kept a secret in his whole life, and I was already worried about what he was going to tell people about what we'd just seen happen inside the church.

I got down on my knees again and dipped my hand into the water. The splinter had gotten a little softer once I'd gotten it wet, but it still hurt too bad for me to close my fingers and make a fist to hide it from Mama. I cleaned the blood off my hand and splashed more water on my face. Farther down the river, I heard Miss Lyle hollering for all the kids to quit playing and head up the path to the road, and I knew church had let out and it was time to go home. We sat there and listened to her calling for us.

'I reckon we should go,' Joe Bill said.

'You can't say nothing, Joe Bill,' I said. 'You can't say nothing to nobody. I mean it.'

'I won't,' he promised.

He turned and ran down the riverbank to where Miss Lyle and the rest of the kids were. I thought about running after him, but then I looked down at my hand and I felt it throb every time my heart beat. I figured I'd better just walk instead.

* * *

By the time I got back down to where we'd had Sunday school, Miss Lyle had taken the rest of the kids back up the path and across the road to the church parking lot. I walked up the path and stopped at the top and looked across the road. The parking lot was full of people. Heat waves came up off the asphalt and it looked like a mirage, like everybody over there was at the bottom of a swimming pool and I was standing on the edge looking down at them. I thought about what a mirage must look like in the desert after you've gotten yourself lost and you ain't had nothing to drink and are just about ready to die. I reckon at that point your mind can trick you into seeing just about anything it wants you to see.

Some men stood with their hands in their pockets and talked to each other out by the road. A couple of them had that Brylcreem combed into their hair, and they smoked cigarettes and stood back and watched the rest of the people in the parking lot. I looked around, and it didn't take me no time at all to find Mama and Stump because they had a whole crowd of people standing around them. They were all talking loud and laughing, and some of the women hugged Mama and a few people bent down and talked to Stump like they expected him to say something back to them. When he didn't even look at them, they just smiled and stood back and stared down at him and talked to Mama some more without taking their eyes off him. Mama smiled like she loved hearing what they had to say. Stump looked toward me where I was standing across the road, and even though I knew he was probably looking out at the river behind me, I felt like he was staring me right in the eyes.

I looked up and down the road, and then I went ahead and crossed to the other side and walked into the parking lot. The heat waves shook in front of me like a flame coming up out of a cigarette lighter, and for a minute it looked like every one of them people in the parking lot was on fire. The men smoking out by the road saw me coming, and they finished their cigarettes and dropped them on the pavement and put them out with the toes of their boots. They stared at me when I walked past. I knew they were looking at the blood on my shirt, probably wondering what in the world had happened during Sunday school that could've gotten me so hurt. I acted like I didn't see them, and I kept walking toward Mama. A few of the women standing with her saw me coming, and they tapped her on the shoulder and pointed at me. She turned around, and when she saw me she put her hands on her hips and waited until I got close enough for her not to have to raise her voice.

'What happened?' she asked, but before I could even answer, Pastor Chambliss walked over through the crowd and stopped right in front of us. He looked down at me, and then he reached out with those smooth, pink fingers and lifted up my hand to get a good look at it. He held it there like he wasn't going to let it go.

'Well, look here,' he said. 'The good Lord can heal with one hand and harm with the other.' He smiled. 'That's the power of an awesome God.'

One of those women standing by us said, 'Amen.'

I tried to pull my hand away, but he held it tight and I couldn't get it free. He looked over at Stump and reached out to touch him too, but Stump moved closer to Mama like he was trying to get away from him. Pastor Chambliss smiled.

'Y'all coming back for the evening service?' he asked Mama.

'I reckon we can,' she said.

'You should,' he said. He let go of my hand

and nodded toward Stump. 'And bring this one with you. The Lord ain't finished with him yet.'

★ ★ ★

'Now, tell me again,' Mama said. She backed Daddy's truck out of the parking space and pulled out onto the road. The truck shook just a little bit when she put her foot on the gas pedal to get us going. Stump sat in between us and stared straight ahead like we weren't even sitting there in the truck with him. I kept the hand with that splinter in it propped up on my knee so nothing would hit it. It had already started to turn red, but at least it wasn't bleeding anymore.

'What do you want me to tell you?' I asked her. It was hot inside the truck, and Mama rolled her window down and the air came in and blew some crumpled-up papers around on the dashboard. I thought about rolling my window down too, but I didn't want all that wind in my face.

'I want you to tell me again about how you got that big old splinter,' she said. 'I want you to tell me one more time how you done it.'

I looked in the side mirror just before we went around the curve up toward the highway. I could see the church in the mirror behind us, and there was still a bunch of people standing around outside in the parking lot. I saw Mr. Gene Thompson talking to some folks out by the road, and I swear I saw him turn his head like he was watching us drive off toward the highway.

'Me and Joe Bill were skipping rocks after

66

Sunday school,' I said. 'Right after Mr. Thompson came and got Stump. I found an old board and was hitting rocks like baseballs. Joe Bill was pitching. I wasn't holding it tight enough, and it slipped a little in my hand and that's how I got it.'

Mama looked at my hand, and then she looked back at the road. I heard her sigh.

'That board must've been awfully dry and rotten for it to have given you that kind of splinter.'

'It was,' I said. She was quiet for a second and I tried to close my fingers again, but the blood had started to scab up and get real stiff and it was even harder to make a fist than it was before.

'Jess,' Mama said.

'Yes, ma'am?'

'Are you telling me the truth?'

'Yes, ma'am.'

'If I call Joe Bill's mama and ask her to talk to him about it, you think he's going to tell her the same story about that bat?'

'It wasn't a bat,' I said.

'You know what I mean,' Mama said. 'Is Joe Bill going to remember it just like you told it to me?'

'Yes, ma'am,' I said, but I knew he wouldn't tell it like that because he didn't know nothing about what I'd told her. I knew that if I told the truth about how I'd gotten that splinter then I'd have to tell the truth about what I saw them doing to Stump, and then I might've found myself telling her about how the rain barrel got broken and about how pink and wrinkled Pastor

67

Chambliss's body looked when he came around the corner of the house with no shirt on. I sat there and looked out the window and thought about that, and it made my neck feel hot and I could feel my heart beating hard and I felt the blood pumping in my hand like my heart was jammed up under that splinter. I wished I could go back and stop myself from seeing all the things that I'd seen in the past two days, but I knew there wasn't no way that I could undo any of that now, no matter how bad I wanted to.

Mama put on the brakes at the stop sign at the top of the hill, and then she gave it some gas and we turned left onto the highway and headed toward home. Once we got going faster, the wind blew into the window even stronger and it flipped open the pages of her Bible where she'd sat it up on the dash. I looked at those pages while the wind turned them, and I saw that just about every page had Mama's handwriting on it. She rolled her window up and then she reached out and closed her Bible and squeezed it down into the seat between her and Stump.

'Jess,' she said again.

'Yes, ma'am?'

'There's something I need to talk to you about.' I turned and looked out my window again because I didn't want to look at her when I already knew what she was going to say. I knew she was going to ask me about Mr. Gene Thompson telling her that he saw me and Joe Bill spying on them in the church, and then she was going to ask me why I lied about how I got that splinter. I tried to think about whether or not I should just go ahead and

68

tell her about it all so I wouldn't have to worry about it no more, just so I knew for sure that I'd finally done the right thing. I figured Joe Bill was in the car with his mom and dad on the way home from church right then, and he was probably telling them all about us seeing Stump inside the church anyway, and his mama had probably already called over to the house and talked to Daddy and he was going to be waiting for us on the porch when we pulled up in front of the house. If Joe Bill didn't tell his mom and dad, then he'd tell Scooter for sure, and who knew what would happen after he did that.

I put my good hand on the dash and leaned forward in the seat so I could look past Stump and see Mama. I wanted to think of exactly what I should tell her about what all I'd seen, but when I looked at her I saw that she wasn't even mad. She smiled like she was happy even though she had tears in her eyes.

'We had us a healing in church today,' she said. She looked over at me, and I watched two big tears run down her cheeks, and then she wiped her face and looked back at the road. I leaned back in my seat and felt light-headed because my heart had been beating so fast just the second before and now it felt like it had stopped cold.

'What do you mean?' I said.

'We had us a healing,' she said again. She wiped a tear from her cheek. 'This morning, during the service, Pastor Chambliss invited the deacons down front and they all laid their hands on Christopher and prayed for his healing.' I heard her reach out and pat Stump's leg, and I looked over and saw her give it a little squeeze. 'I tell you what,' she said. 'God answers prayer. We've had us a miracle.' I thought about what Joe Bill had said about them trying to heal Stump by laying on him and putting their hands on him, and then I thought about how Stump had tried to stand up and run away while they were doing it and how much watching it all happen had made Mama cry.

'How do you know there was a miracle?' I asked her.

'Because he spoke,' she said. 'He said the only word he's ever said, and he said it this morning in church with the deacons laying their hands on him and praying for our family.'

'What did he say?'

' "Mama," ' she said. 'He called out for me, and he said it. He said, 'Mama." '

I lay my head back on the seat and felt my skin get cold and numb like all the blood had been drained out of my body. I closed my eyes because I was afraid I might throw up if I even opened them to look around. My hand wasn't even throbbing anymore, and it was like I'd already forgotten about that splinter. None of us made a sound, and all I could hear was the hum of the tires against the road.

'Are you sure it was him?' I asked her.

'I know it was,' she said. 'I know it was because other folks heard him too. They were laying their hands on him, and you know how much he doesn't like that, and I guess it just got to be too much for him and that's when he

70

hollered out for me. It was so loud in there with the music going and all that praying, and they were on him, and I swear if it hadn't been the Lord's work I wouldn't have been able to hear him. It was a miracle.'

'But what happens if he doesn't say a word ever again?'

'He will,' she said. 'The Lord ain't going to give us this gift just this one time and then take it away. That ain't no kind of mercy.'

'But how do you know what God's going to do?' I said.

'I just know,' she said.

'But how? Maybe God doesn't want Stump to say nothing else. You tell us all the time that nobody can ever know God's will.'

'That's right,' she said. 'You can't. But the Lord doesn't play no tricks. Evil plays tricks, and there ain't no room for evil in this family.'

I kept my head back on the seat and swallowed hard even though I knew I wasn't swallowing nothing but air, and I tried to keep myself from getting sick. I felt my forehead start sweating because I knew that Mama would tell me that I was evil for being the one who hollered out for her and then letting her believe it was Stump. It didn't even matter whether she knew it was me or not, I felt evil just the same. She rolled her window back down like she was done talking, and that air coming in felt good against my face, even if it was hot and dusty.

'What do you think Daddy's going to say?' I asked over the sound of the wind pouring into the truck.

'We ain't going to tell him yet,' she said.

'Why not?'

'Because he'll need to see it for himself,' she said. 'He ain't going to believe in miracles no other way.'

'Why wouldn't he believe it?'

'Because he don't want to.'

I closed my eyes and thought about Daddy having to see a miracle to believe in it, and then I thought about mirages again, about how miracles might be like that sometimes. It was like Mama was lost in the desert and had gotten so thirsty that she was willing to see anything that might make her feel better about being lost. I knew that she needed to think she heard Stump holler out for her, even if I knew he didn't, and I wondered if it was a sin to think any less of a miracle just because you know it ain't real.

I looked down at my hand and I thought about trying to slide that splinter right out, and I took my finger and felt where the end of it stuck out of my palm. The rest of it was right there just beneath my skin like a branch that's frozen just under the surface of a pond in the wintertime.

'Quit messing with that splinter,' Mama said. 'You're just going to work it down in there deeper, and then I won't ever be able to get it out.'

* * *

Mama pulled off the highway and drove down the Long Branch Road toward the house. Up ahead, my daddy's tobacco fields sat on the left-hand side of the road, and I could see where he'd started to cut and stick the burley and hang it upside down to dry. It looked like somebody had come and pitched little, green teepees in the field as far as you could see. He'd come along in a few days and pick up those sticks full of burley and toss them onto the sled before hanging them in the barn.

The rows of burley that hadn't been cut and stuck yet were tall and thick, and when me and Stump took a mind to hide out we'd run out into the field like somebody was chasing us, and then we'd pretend like nobody could ever find us. I liked to imagine that one day in the late summer Daddy would be out working in the field sticking the tobacco, and he'd come up a row and look down and find me and Stump still hunkered down and hiding out.

'Is this where y'all have been?' he'd ask. He'd look over at Stump, and Stump would smile just a little bit. 'What are you smiling about?' he'd ask.

Mama turned left into our driveway; it was gravel and full of holes, and we bumped along and kicked up gravel dust until we got around the corner and saw the house sitting back up in the holler. I looked for Daddy on the porch just in case Joe Bill's mama had called him, but I didn't see him. But then I looked to the left of the house, and I saw Daddy standing outside by the barn and he had a shovel in his hand with something hanging off the end of it. When we got closer I could see it was a big old snake.

'What in the world,' Mama said.

'It looks like a snake,' I told her.

'It sure does,' she said and sighed loud enough for me to hear her. 'He certainly does.'

She parked the truck in front of the house, and I opened the door and hopped out onto the driveway.

'Come on, Stump,' I said, and I ran past the front of the truck across the yard over to where Daddy stood by the barn. I could hear Stump running behind me. Daddy wore an old blue Braves cap with the white 'A' on it and an old button-down shirt and blue jeans. His work boots were unlaced, and his jeans were tucked down inside them. I stopped in front of him and caught my breath and looked at that snake. It'd been chopped just below the head, and its neck was bent like it was looking at us funny. Blood and guts hung out where it'd been cut.

'What kind of snake is it?' I asked Daddy.

He smiled. 'A dead one.'

'For real,' I said. 'What kind is it?'

'Look here,' he said. He turned the shovel over and dumped the snake out in the gravel, and then he leaned the shovel up against the barn. The snake was a yellowy-brown color with black stripes running all the way down its body. It must've been four feet long and as big around as my arm. Daddy kneeled down beside it and picked up its tail. 'Come take a look at this,' he said.

Me and Stump walked over to where Daddy had a hold of the snake's tail, and we both squatted down to get a better look at it. Daddy shook it back and forth, and it sounded like a

74

dried bean pod when he did it.

'Is it a rattlesnake?' I asked him.

'A timber rattler,' he said.

'I ain't ever seen one of them around here before.'

'I haven't either,' he said. 'Not in a long time.'

'Jess!' Mama hollered from the front porch. 'Come on in here and let me take a look at that hand.'

I walked across the yard and went up the steps and found Mama in the kitchen. She'd lit a long wooden kitchen match, and she held the flame under a little sewing needle, and then she laid the needle down on a napkin and shook the match until the flame went out. She lit another one and held it under a pair of tweezers and then shook that one until it went out too.

'All right,' Mama said. She reached out and took my right hand by the wrist and held it in front of her. 'You need to sit still.'

'It's going to hurt, isn't it?' I said.

'I hope not,' she said, 'but you never know with those old bats. They can give you some awfully bad splinters.'

'It was a board,' I told her.

'That's right,' she said like she'd forgotten.

She held the needle in between her fingers and took the tip and started picking at the skin around the splinter. I expected it to be burning hot, but I couldn't hardly feel it because my skin was already sore and raw from the splinter being in there for so long. I watched that needle, and I kept waiting to feel it prick me.

'What's that going to do?' I asked her.

'It's going to loosen it up,' she said. 'We want it to slide right out of there. Otherwise, I'll end up having to yank on it.'

'It looks like it would come out right now,' I said.

'It's a whole lot deeper than you think it is,' Mama said. 'That skin around it is nice and tight.'

She picked at it with that needle a little bit longer, and then she laid the needle down on the napkin and picked up the tweezers. There was a little bit more of that splinter sticking out of my hand now, and Mama took the tip of the tweezers and closed them around it and gave it a tug, but that splinter wouldn't even budge.

'I can feel it down in there now' I said. 'It seems like it ain't going to come out.'

Mama grabbed hold of it again, and this time she broke off the long part of it where it was sticking out of my hand.

'Shoot,' she said. I looked and saw that there wasn't no more of the wood to grab on to. The rest of it was still stuck down in there, and it looked like a long, skinny freckle spread out just beneath my skin.

'How you going to get it out now?' I asked her.

'We're going to have to dig it out,' she said. She picked up that needle again and dug around and tried to pop that splinter up through my skin. It was hurting so bad that it made my eyes water.

'That really hurts,' I said.

'Well, we need to get it,' she said. 'It ain't good for you just to leave it in there.'

'There ain't that much of it left,' I said. 'I can't even feel it in there anymore.'

Daddy opened the screen door from the front porch, and him and Stump walked into the house and came into the kitchen. Daddy leaned up against the counter and crossed his arms and looked at me and Mama where we sat at the table. Stump walked through the kitchen, and I heard him go down the hall to our bedroom.

'What are y'all doing?' Daddy asked.

'I'm trying to get this splinter out of your son's hand,' Mama said. 'I already got most of it, but there's still a little bit down in there that I can't get ahold of.'

Daddy walked to the table and looked over Mama's shoulder at my hand. He squinted his eyes like he was looking at something way far off in the distance.

'There ain't hardly nothing there, Julie,' he said. 'He'll be all right.' Mama stopped picking at me with the needle and sighed.

'That's fine to say, Ben,' she said. 'But it needs to come out. There ain't no use in leaving it in there if I can get it now.'

'Is it going to hurt you to leave it in there, Jess?' he asked.

'No, sir,' I said.

'He's fine, Julie,' Daddy said. I lifted my hand out of Mama's and looked at my palm up close. A little bit of wood still hid down in there, but it wasn't sticking out like it was before. 'Hey, Jess,' Daddy said, 'I need you and your brother to bury that snake for me. I don't want that thing laying out there and rotting. No telling what kind of animals it'll bring up out of the woods if it just sits there.' Mama turned around in her chair and looked up at Daddy where he stood behind her. Daddy looked at her. 'I went ahead and lopped its head off,' he said. 'It ain't going to hurt them.' He looked at me. 'But you remember, Jess,' he said, 'even a dead snake will strike until the sun goes down.'

'That ain't true,' I said.

'All right,' he said, smiling. 'If you don't believe me, that's fine.'

'He's already got one splinter today,' Mama said. 'He doesn't need to be shoveling nothing with that hand.'

'He'll be all right,' Daddy told her.

'Where should we bury him?' I asked.

'I don't know,' he said. 'Somewhere out there behind the barn will be fine. Y'all don't have to dig it too deep — maybe just a couple feet.'

I stood up from my chair and walked down the hall to our bedroom to get Stump.

'Hold on,' Mama said. She got up too and followed me down the hall, but she walked past me and went into the bathroom and I heard her open the medicine cabinet and move stuff around on the shelves. I walked into me and Stump's room and found him sitting on the bed with his quiet box in his lap. He looked up at me, and then he picked up the top where it sat on the bed beside him and put it back on. He stood up from the bed and carried it toward the closet and stood on his tiptoes and slid it back onto the top shelf. Then he just stood there looking into the closet like there was something else he wanted to find.

'Daddy wants us to bury that snake,' I said. He didn't turn around. 'He wants us to go out there and do it before something carries it off.' I heard Mama leave the bathroom and walk toward our room.

'Hold on, y'all,' she said. She walked into the bedroom with some gauze pads and some tape and some first-aid ointment in her hands. 'Sit down on the bed here, and let's see what we can do,' she said. 'After that y'all need to get changed out of them church clothes.' She looked at my shirt where that blood had dried all over the front of it. 'I don't know what we're going to do about that,' she said.

★ ★ ★

I scooped the rattler's head into the shovel, and then I scooped up its body. I carried the snake out in front of me real slow so I wouldn't drop it, and I walked behind the barn down toward the creek, where the shade kept the ground damp and soft. The snake's body was so long that it almost drug along the ground, and I had to raise the shovel to keep it from catching on something and getting pulled off.

'It'll be easier to dig down here,' I told Stump. He walked along beside me and stared at the snake. At the bottom of the hill I stopped and dumped it out into the grass a little ways away from the creek. It was quiet down there, and I thought about how if I had to be buried I'd want it to be in a place just like this. All the graveyards

79

around here are up on the tops of mountains or set right into the hillsides. Daddy said they put them up high because of the rain. He said if you put a graveyard in the bottomland then you'd better be all right with seeing coffins float down the road after a big storm. I figured it didn't really matter what happens to you after you die, and, if I had my way, I'd rather be down here by the creek where it was shady and nice and cool instead of up on top of some hill where there ain't even any trees to block out the sun. Nobody's going to want to visit you up there in the summertime when it's hot.

I dug the shovel's blade into the ground, and then I turned the handle up toward the sky and jumped on the top of the blade with both feet to force it down as far as it would go. The dirt was soft and loose, and the blade sunk in easy. I raised the first shovelful of thick, dark dirt and saw a couple of earthworms wiggling around in it.

'Look here, Stump,' I said, and I moved the shovel over to where he could see it. He'd squatted down by the rattler and was poking at it with a stick like he was afraid it might just come alive and snap at him. He raised his head and looked at the worms where they wiggled around in the shovel, and then he went back to poking at the rattler again. I dropped the dirt right beside the snake's head and scooped up another shovelful.

I kept digging up and dumping out the dirt until I'd made me a hole about knee-deep and big enough around to hold two snakes without them even touching each other. I stopped and put one foot up on the top of the blade and looked at my hand where Mama had put a gauze pad on my palm and wrapped tape around it. The tape had started to come loose, and the pad was just about soaked through with dirt and sweat. I undid the rest of the tape and tossed it into the hole, and then I lifted up the gauze and looked underneath it at my hand. The skin around the splinter was white and wrinkled like I'd kept my hand in the bathtub for too long, and I took the gauze pad all the way off and tossed it down into the hole beside the tape so my hand could get some air and dry out. I switched hands so I could hold the shovel with my left, and I put my right hand on top of the handle so it wouldn't rub against the wood. I scooped up the snake's head and dropped it down inside the hole. It rolled down the side and stopped right in the center. Stump stood up and looked down at it.

I looked over at the rattler's body where it lay on the ground by Stump's leg, and I walked over to it and stared down at the little rattle on the end of its tail. I bent down and touched it, and then I picked it up and stood up straight. I shook it and listened to the sound it made.

'Look here, Stump,' I said. He turned around and watched me hold the snake. I rattled its tail. 'Listen to it,' I said. 'This would be the last thing you'd hear if one of these boys snuck up on you.' I made a hissing sound and rattled the snake's tail again. I laughed and walked toward the hole to drop it in down inside with the head, but just when I reached out my arm and got ready to let it go, the bloody stump where the head used to be reared back and struck me on the inside of my arm. It made a soft, squishy noise when the snake's guts smacked up against my skin, and for a minute I thought the blood it had left behind was mine. I screamed and dropped the snake into the hole and fell back onto my butt and covered up the inside of my arm with my hand. I looked up and saw Stump standing over the hole and staring down into it. 'Leave it alone,' I said. 'Don't touch it.'

I stood up and wiped the snake's blood off my arm and onto the back of my blue jeans. Then I walked over to the hole and stood beside Stump and looked down inside. The snake's body was crawling around down inside there, and I could just barely hear that rattle going on the end of its tail. It looked like the head had come alive too, and its mouth was opening and closing and its tongue was sticking out. We stood there and watched it for a minute, but then I started wondering if there was any way it could climb up out of there, and I picked up the shovel and started covering the hole over with dirt.

★ ★ ★

Once I had the snake buried, me and Stump walked down to the creek. I kneeled down in the soft mud and washed the snake's blood off the inside of my arm. Stump walked a little piece down the bank and squatted down and started turning over rocks and looking for salamanders. I

82

could hear his hands splashing around in the water and cleaning the dirt off them. I looked down at my own hands, and then I looked up at Stump where I could just barely see his back through all the ferns that grew along the water.

'Do you think we should've said a prayer or something?' I hollered at him. I waited for a second, and then I heard a splash and I knew he'd done turned over another rock. 'I don't think we should've either,' I said to myself.

I wiped my wet hands off on my jeans, and then I stood and walked through the ferns to where Stump had squatted down by the creek. I sat down on my butt beside him. He had both his hands in the water, and he was digging into the mud and pulling it up by the fistful and looking at it up close to see if it had anything in it. You could find you some awfully good rocks doing it like that. I knew his pockets would be full of them if he found any.

'Mama thinks you talked in church today,' I said. Stump rocked backward onto his behind too and crossed his legs and sat Indian-style. He wiped the water off his hands and onto his knees, and then he looked up into the trees like there was something up there he expected to see. 'Hey,' I said, trying to get him to look at me. 'Hey,' I said again. I reached out and touched his arm, and he looked at me for just a second, and then he raised his head back toward the trees. 'It was me,' I said. 'It was me she heard. Me and Joe Bill were outside, and we saw what they did. I was too scared to say anything because I knew how mad Mama would be at me for watching when I wasn't supposed to.' He turned his head and looked up the hill back toward the barn. 'I'm sorry,' I told him. 'I should've said something to Mama on the way home, and I should've tried to stop them from doing what they did. I shouldn't have let it happen.'

Stump looked at me like he just might've been listening to what I was telling him, and then he stood up and walked away from the creek and up toward the hill. I didn't watch him as he went, but I could hear the ferns swishing against his legs when he walked through them. I sat there alone for a little bit, and I thought about how it was this time, two days before, that me and Stump had been coming up the hill from the creek when we stopped underneath Mama and Daddy's open window. I pictured Stump climbing up on top of the rain barrel to see in, and I remembered the feeling I had when I saw Pastor Chambliss come around the corner of the house and reach down and touch Stump. I still felt his fingers on my hand where he'd held it tight to get a good look at where that splinter had gone right in. I imagined Chambliss laying his hand on Stump, and then I imagined the weight of all those men pushing down on top of him. I knew that me and Stump had both seen things we would have been better off knowing nothing about.

*　*　*

I heard Mama hollering for us to come in and I knew that meant she had our lunch ready. The

84

ferns were all mashed down from where Stump had walked through them, and I followed the trail he made up to where I'd buried the rattler. The dirt was still soft, and I walked around on top of it to get it good and packed down, and then I picked up the shovel and set off up the hill to the barn.

I leaned the shovel against the wall behind the barn door, and I looked up at the rafters where I knew my daddy was going to be hanging the tobacco once he'd finished sticking it and bringing it all in. When I left the barn and stepped out into the sunlight, I saw Stump up beside the house. He was on his knees in front of the rain barrel turning the spigot back and forth. There wasn't no water coming out because there wasn't any in there.

'Nothing's going to come out,' I told him. 'It's still broke, and if I was you I wouldn't be messing with it because sooner or later Daddy's going to find out.' We were standing under their window again. It was open, and I could hear them talking all the way from the kitchen. It sounded like they were arguing about something. I looked up at the gutter spout where it was supposed to run down inside the barrel, but it was all bent up and torn loose. 'You'd better use the hose,' I said. He gave the spigot another couple of turns, and I walked over to the hose pipe and turned it on. I washed off my hands one at a time, and I left it running and sat it down in the grass. 'Here,' I said. 'Here, use this.' Stump shimmied over on his knees and picked up the hose and took a sip of the water, and then he rinsed his hands. I went around to the back of the house and opened the back door and walked down the hallway to the kitchen.

'Well, he's the one that called me,' I heard Daddy say. 'It ain't like I called him, Julie. He's been back for a while, and I didn't even know about it.'

'Why'd he even come back? It sounds like he ain't but a couple of miles away, so it's not like he's been dying to see you. It ain't like he's made any effort at all to meet your family.'

'Maybe that's what he's doing now,' Daddy said.

'Yeah, right,' Mama said. 'He probably needs money.'

'He did mention that he's thinking about selling the old place,' Daddy said.

'What a surprise,' Mama said. 'Well, if he asks you for any money, then you'd better tell him to get in line behind me.' I heard her sigh.

'Who are y'all talking about?' I asked. Daddy stood with his hands on the back of one of the chairs and leaned out over the table and stared down at it where Mama had already started setting out the food. He looked at me, and then he looked at Mama where she was rinsing off a head of cabbage in the sink. He smiled at her just a little bit like he was in trouble for something that he wasn't going to take very seriously. Mama just looked away from him and picked up a big knife and sat that head of cabbage down on the counter and started chopping away at it.

'Nunya,' Daddy said. I knew what joke he was

86

playing, but I went along with it anyway.

'Nunya who?' I said.

'Nunya Business,' Daddy said. I walked to the sink and poured a little water into my cup, and then I turned around and leaned against the counter and took a long drink. Mama rolled her eyes and walked past Daddy down the hallway to the bathroom. I heard the door shut, and then I heard it lock. Daddy looked over at me.

'Where's your brother at?' he asked.

'He's with Nunya,' I said. Daddy smiled and reached out and floated a soft, fake punch onto my jaw and wiggled his fist against my face. I felt his wedding ring on my cheek when he did it.

'That's a good one,' Daddy said. He smiled. 'With Nunya.'

* * *

Mama sat a plate full of slices of cold ham in the center of the table, and she'd made pintos and coleslaw with corn bread. I took my fork and picked up a slice of ham and dropped it on my plate, and then I mixed my beans and my coleslaw together and crumbled my corn bread over it, just like Daddy did. It was quiet except for the sound of the silverware hitting on the plates while we ate.

'Where'd you find that snake?' I asked Daddy. He cut himself a piece of ham and stabbed it with his fork.

'I just found him inside the barn door,' he said. 'It's like he was sitting there waiting on me.' He put the ham in his mouth and chewed on it.

87

'Mmm!' he said. 'This is just about the best ham I've ever had.' Mama looked up and stared across the table at Daddy like she was a little bit mad at him, but when I looked back at him I saw he was crumbling his corn bread over his beans like he didn't even know she was thinking about him.

'I don't know what I'd do if I looked down and saw a big old snake waiting on me,' I said. 'It makes me think I probably should have a BB gun.'

'What do you think a BB gun's going to do against a snake like that?' Daddy asked me.

'I'd shoot it,' I said. 'I'd shoot it before it bit me.'

'There ain't no way you're getting a gun,' Mama said.

'That thing would've had you by the thigh before you could even give that gun a pump,' Daddy said. He reached under the table and grabbed my leg, and I jumped when he did it because it surprised me.

'I just think I need a BB gun,' I said.

'There ain't no way,' Mama said. 'One gun's one too many in this house.' She stood up and walked over to the refrigerator and opened it and leaned inside and took the butter out of the door. When she did, Daddy dropped his fork and acted like he was pumping a shotgun and he aimed it at her backside. I laughed, and when she turned around we both went back to eating our lunch. Mama came back to the table and sat down and sat the butter by the corn bread.

'Jess,' she said, 'me and your brother are going

88

to the prayer meeting tonight after supper, and you're going to have to come with us.'

'Why?' I asked.

'Because your daddy's got plans this evening,' she said. 'He's having company over.' She looked at Daddy, and then she took her knife and carved out a slice of butter and dropped it on Stump's corn bread. Stump picked it up and took a bite, and the butter ran down off his chin. He picked up his napkin and wiped it off.

'I don't need nobody watching me,' I said. 'It ain't like I'm a baby.' I looked over at Daddy. 'I bet Stump don't even want to go back to church tonight anyway. Me and him could just stay here.' Daddy crumbled more corn bread over his pintos and then reached across the table for the bowl of coleslaw. He spooned a helping onto his plate and sat it back down.

'Listen to your mother,' he said.

'Christopher,' Mama said. 'Do you want some coleslaw?' Mama picked up the bowl and held it over Stump's plate. She waited, and I knew she was hoping he might say something. Daddy sat his fork down and chewed his food and looked across the table at her. 'Christopher,' she said again. She waited another second, and then she sat the bowl down on the table and picked up her fork.

★   ★   ★

Daddy was standing on the porch and sipping a glass of water when we left for the evening service. The sun was on its way down, and even though it was September and I knew the leaves would start dying soon, it was still awfully hot outside. I rolled the window down in the truck and leaned out and waved at Daddy. He waved back and stood there and watched us until we went around the corner of the driveway.

'I need to tell you boys something,' Mama said. She looked over at me and Stump. 'Your grandpa's coming to see Daddy this evening, and he might still be here when we get home.' She looked back at the road, and I stared at the side of her face. I hadn't seen him since I was real little, back when he used to live out in Shelton where my daddy grew up. Mama'd told me I should call him Grandpa if I ever saw him again because it would make Daddy feel good.

'Where's he been?' I asked.

'Lots of places,' she said.

'Why'd he come back?'

'I don't know.'

'Is Daddy mad at him?'

'Not anymore,' she said.

'But he used to be mad at him?'

'Yes.'

'Why?'

'Because he didn't used to be a good person.'

'But he's good now?'

'He wants to be,' she said.

★　★　★

Mama pulled into the parking lot and parked the truck in one of the spaces along the side of the church. Around to the right of the truck I could

90

see people lining up and talking. I couldn't see Pastor Chambliss, but I knew he was standing there in the door and greeting folks and shaking their hands as they went inside. Mama had brought some pens and pencils and some drawing paper with her in a little folder, and she picked it up off the dash and handed it to me.

'Here you go,' she said. 'I want you to stay in the truck, and make sure to keep the windows down so you don't get too hot. You can open the door if you need to, but I want you to stay inside here.'

'Is Stump staying out here too?' I asked.

'No,' she said. 'He's coming inside for the service.' She opened her door and stepped down from the truck. She waved her hand at Stump, and he climbed down too.

'I want to go with y'all,' I said. 'I don't want to wait out here.'

'Well, you're going to have to tonight. Maybe you can go with us next Sunday morning.'

'But I want to go tonight,' I said. I tried to stop my voice from sounding scared. *I can stop this*, I thought. *I can stop it from happening again. What happened this morning.* I could feel my heart pounding in my chest, and I knew my voice probably sounded like I might start crying, no matter how hard I was trying not to. I couldn't keep my mind from picturing what I'd seen them doing to Stump that morning. Mama just stood there with the truck door open, and she looked over the hood toward the front of the church like she was thinking about whether or not she should let me go with them.

'I don't think so,' she finally said. 'Not tonight, but maybe next Sunday.' She slammed the door shut and took Stump's hand. They walked around the back of the truck to the other side. Mama looked into my window. It was open about halfway. 'Stay inside the truck,' she said. 'Service shouldn't last too long.'

'Please let me go too,' I said.

'No,' she said. 'Come on, Christopher.' They turned and walked toward the front of the building. I watched them go, and then I rolled my window all the way down and got up on my knees and hollered after them.

'Wait!' I yelled. Mama stopped and turned around and looked at me. She held on to Stump's hand and he stood right behind her, and behind him I could see across the road where the path began that led down to the river. I looked at Mama and thought about what all I could tell her that would keep Stump from having to go in there again: that me and Joe Bill had seen what they'd already done to him that morning, that it was me and not Stump who'd hollered out her name when those men started piling on top of him, that Stump hadn't ever said a single word in his life and probably never would. I knew that earlier that morning in church Stump would've screamed for them to stop if he'd been able to, and I knew that if I would just open my mouth and say what all I'd seen I could make sure nobody would try to hurt him again.

But I was too scared to say any of those things, and I just stayed there in the truck with the window down and stared out at Mama. My fingers closed tight around the door of the truck, and I felt that little bit of splinter where it was still stuck down in my palm.

'What is it?' she said like she'd lost all her patience with me.

'Can I go too?' I asked again. 'Please.'

'No,' she said. 'Stay in the truck. We'll see you when we let out. It shouldn't be long.' I sat back down on my butt and watched them as they walked away and got in line in front of the church. The people in line in front of them turned around, and a woman hugged Mama and a man looked down and said something to Stump. Some other folks got in line behind them, and after a while I couldn't see them and I knew they'd gone inside.

The sun sunk down behind the trees in back of the church, and there was just enough light for me to do a little drawing. I picked up the folder off the dash and opened it and looked at the sheets of blank typing paper, but then I closed it and sat it back up on the dash because I knew I didn't feel one bit like drawing. I got as comfortable as I could, and I laid my head back against the seat and closed my eyes and listened for the river across the street, but all I could hear was the music striking up inside the church: the guitar first and then the drums, then the sound of people singing. It reminded me of what all had happened and what all I'd seen. I felt myself starting to drift off to sleep, and I imagined getting out of the truck and sneaking back behind the building and getting up on my tiptoes and propping my elbows on the ledge and looking through the air conditioner into the church.

That was the last clear thought I had because I knew there wasn't no way I was going to do it. Even in my dreaming I knew I'd already seen more than I ever wanted to.

★ ★ ★

I heard voices somewhere out there in the dark, and then the driver's-side door opened and I felt somebody climb up into the truck. I opened my eyes all the way and looked around, but it'd gotten to be nighttime and I couldn't hardly see a thing. I sat up in the seat and expected to feel Stump in there beside me, but I didn't. I knew for sure there was somebody sitting behind the steering wheel because they'd slammed the door shut and I heard them with their hand in their pocket like they were trying to get something out. They struck a lighter, and I saw it was Mr. Stuckey, and he held Mama's keys over the flame like he was trying to get a good look at them. He was about as old as Daddy, and he wore a button-down shirt and he had his hair slicked back with Brylcreem. He found the right key and let the flame die. I heard him put the lighter back in his pocket, and then he cranked the truck.

'What are you doing?' I asked him. 'Where's my mom?'

'She's going to meet us over at Miss Lyle's house,' he said. He put his arm across the seat and turned his head and looked out the back window and backed out of the parking space and pulled around in front of the church. The door to the church was open, and the light from inside shone out into the parking lot. There were all kinds of people standing out there, and some of them had their hands over their faces like they were crying.

'What happened?' I said.

'We're going to be there in just a second,' Mr. Stuckey said. 'Your mama's going to be there waiting on you.'

'What happened?' I asked again.

He kept going and pulled right through the parking lot and drove out onto the road away from the highway and put his foot hard on the gas pedal. I turned around in my seat and got on my knees and looked out the back. I could still see the light from inside the church shining out into the darkness, and the people looked like shadows moving around in the parking lot. Two men were carrying somebody out the front door of the church to where a car was waiting. They put whoever it was inside the car and shut the door, and then they went up to the front seat and got in. The last thing I could see was their headlights turning on.

'Who's that?' I asked. 'Where's Stump?'

'Turn around here,' Mr. Stuckey said. I felt his hand on my back.

'Where's my mom?' I asked again.

'Turn around here and sit down,' he said. 'We'll be there in just a second. She'll be waiting on you.'

Clem Barefield

4

I've been sheriff of Madison County since 1961; it'll be twenty-five years next month. My granddaddy was a sheriff too. He worked out of Hendersonville, North Carolina, about an hour and a half south of here on the other side of Asheville. But places like those might as well be a world away. My daddy was an apple farmer in Flat Rock over in Henderson County. I reckon I grew up thinking I had to be like one of them, and I suppose I chose right. *Serve and protect,* I thought. That kind of thinking is what brought me up into these mountains. When I was sworn in as sheriff I replaced Jack Moseley, who was just fifty-seven years old, not an old man by any means, but maybe that's just my own thinking after turning sixty myself. Before I took this job I asked Jack why he was leaving it, and he told me that he'd just gotten bored. He said didn't much ever happen up here in Madison County, nothing much exciting anyway. He said he found the brook trout and his grandkids to be more interesting. He said I'd see. Said I'd get bored too, like he almost looked forward to hearing me tell him about it. But he died of a heart attack not long after I took the job, and I never had the chance to tell him just what I thought about this part of the country, these people.

But one thing I can say about people up here is that they're different from folks in Buncombe or Henderson County or any other place in these mountains. Most people up here claim they've got Irish or Scottish or some kind of blood in them, and I think that's probably true, especially if you listen to the folks who'll drive up here from the universities to tell you all about the culture they say's disappearing. Then they'll go and knock on cabin doors looking to get Jack tales on their tape recorders, snoop through barns, flag elderly men down from tractors to ask them to sing a couple of the old-time reels.

I'd always heard that it's a different world up here, and sometimes I wonder if it might just be. When I first came over from Henderson, I'd drive through this county and see signs and markers for towns like Mars Hill and places like Jupiter and all kinds of things like that, and I'd think, *Jesus, Clem, how'd you end up here?* But I'll be damned if it's not beautiful: these green fields where farms line the ridges and the spaces in between hide dark hollers and deep coves where the sunlight might not ever reach. Like I said, I've spent almost twenty-five years working this county, but I can guarantee you there's places I've never seen, places that would seem just as strange to me now as they would've when I first stepped foot in Madison County. I've gotten right used to feeling that way, and sometimes, after you've lived in a place long enough, it becomes harder and harder to pick out the things about it that once seemed strange, even if most folks still consider you an outsider after two and a half decades just because you weren't born here and raised up knowing everybody's business.

But if I could talk to old Jack Moseley, I'd tell him that I haven't been bored, even after all these years. Of course there've been particulars about calls and cases I can't quite remember even when I try, but that's due more to my years on the job than any kind of boredom. On the other hand, I've had those calls, those couple of cases that I won't ever be able to forget no matter how hard I try or how old I get to be. This here is one of those.

★ ★ ★

I'd just closed the sliding glass door and stepped onto the deck when I heard the kitchen telephone ring. It was a hot Sunday evening in early September, and, just like I do every day after dinner, I'd gone out to the deck to smoke my one cigarette of the day and listen to the crickets get started up for the night.

I shook a cigarette from the pack and fished the lighter out of my pocket, and once I had it lit, I turned and looked through the glass in time to see Sheila answer the telephone. She looked back at me where I stood in the floodlight by the door, and she listened to the voice on the other end of the line, and then she rolled her eyes. She raised her hand and motioned for me to come inside, and then she pointed to the telephone and mouthed the words 'It's for you.' I decided to make a show of her not letting me smoke in the house anymore, and I raised my cigarette up to where she could see it, and I shrugged my shoulders and smiled. She sat the phone on the counter and walked across the living room and slid the door open.

'I hate to interrupt your exercise,' she said, 'but you've got a telephone call.'

'Who is it?'

'It's Robby,' she said. 'Again.'

'Good Lord,' I said. 'What does he want now? Can't you take a message?'

'Doesn't look like it,' she said. 'Sounds like an emergency.' I flicked the end off my cigarette and dropped the butt into my breast pocket.

'It's always an emergency,' I said. 'Especially with him.'

'I told you he was nervous. And too young. You should've thought twice about deputizing him.' I walked into the house, and when I passed Sheila I squeezed her hand.

'I wanted to deputize you,' I said. 'I just couldn't get you to carry a damn gun.'

'We spend too much time together anyway,' she said, smiling. 'Answer the phone.' I picked up the receiver and leaned against the kitchen counter. I made a show of clearing my throat like people do when they're about to give a speech.

'Hello,' I said.

'Sheriff, it's Robby down at the office. I just had a 911 call come over from Ben Hall up on Long Branch Road. He says his son's been killed.'

That was about the last thing I expected Robby to call and tell me on a Sunday evening, and I stood up straight and put my hand in my pocket and raised my eyes to Sheila's. It looked like she was waiting for me to tell her something funny that Robby might've said, but the longer I looked at her the more her face changed to resemble the same concern she probably saw on mine. 'What happened?' she whispered. I lowered my eyes and looked at the tiles on the kitchen floor. My fingers fumbled with the lighter in my pocket.

'How'd it happen?' I asked.

'He don't know,' Robby said. 'His wife left the house about six thirty this evening to take their boys to church. And then, about eight o'clock, he got a call from Adelaide Lyle telling him his son was over at her house and that he'd died. He asked her what happened, and either she didn't know or she wouldn't say.'

'Did it happen at her house?' I asked.

'No, sir. It happened at the church.'

'Which one of his boys is it?'

'It's the older one,' he said. 'The slow one. The one they call 'Stump.''

'I'm going to head over there now,' I said. 'Won't take me but a second to get things together here.'

'All right,' Robby said. 'Ben Hall's on his way there right now. Sounds like his daddy's back in town, like he might be going to drive him.' When I heard that my stomach dropped to the floor, and for a second I thought I might lose the dinner I'd just finished eating a few minutes before. 'Sheriff?' Robby said. I looked at my watch. It was almost fifteen after eight. I knew I wouldn't beat Ben and his daddy there, even if I left right then.

'I'm here,' I said, 'but I'd better get going. There ain't no telling what Ben will do to those church folks if any of them are at that house when he gets there, especially if his daddy's with him.' I didn't notice that Sheila had left the room until she walked back into the kitchen carrying my hat in one hand and my holster in the other. She laid them on the counter beside me.

'Miss Lyle's address is 1404 River Road,' Robby said. 'About two miles past that church on the right. You know where I'm talking about?'

'I do,' I said. I undid my belt and slid my holster onto it.

'You reckon I should meet you there, Sheriff?' he asked.

'You might want to think about it,' I said. 'I might could use the help.' I hung up the phone and finished fastening my belt.

'What's happened?' Sheila asked.

'Ben Hall's oldest son's been killed out at that damn church,' I said. 'And it sounds like they've moved him to Adelaide Lyle's house out there on River Road.'

'Why would they take him there?'

'Would you want a dead boy lying around inside your church when the law gets there?'

'You think he died at the church?'

'I think so,' I said. 'There wasn't no reason to move him otherwise.' I put on my hat and turned and walked down the hallway to the front door

101

where the keys to the cruiser hung on a hook by the light switch. The front door was open, and I looked out through the glass in the storm door and for a moment I watched the yellow lights of what were probably the last few fireflies of the summer move through the darkness of the front yard. I took the keys off the hook and flipped the floodlights on, and all the fireflies disappeared. In the storm door's reflection I could see Sheila standing behind me at the end of the hall.

'Guess who's back in town?' I asked her.

'I heard you talking to Robby,' she said. 'You think he'll be with Ben?'

'It sounds like it,' I said. I looked into the glass and watched her ghostly image fold its arms across its chest and lean against the wall behind me.

'Please be careful, Clem,' she said. 'Don't let any of this get out of hand. There's no use in anybody getting hurt, especially you.'

'I'm not planning on anything getting out of hand,' I said, but as soon as I said it I knew good and well that sometimes you can't account for the bad things that happen.

5

I climbed into the cruiser and turned on the lights and the siren and drove along the top of the ridge before taking the road down toward Marshall. I knew there were hollers in places below me where it had been dark for almost an hour, but up here on the ridge the sun was struggling to be remembered and I could see red and gold still lighting up the sky in the distance on the Tennessee side of the mountain. I remembered the half-finished cigarette in my breast pocket, and I dug it out and pushed in the lighter on the dash. When it popped, I lit up and rolled down the window.

I smoked what was left of that cigarette and thought about how our son, Jeff, was still alive the last time I responded to a call about Ben Hall. Jeff was about sixteen years old then, maybe seventeen, and the boys were probably juniors at the high school. My son had been friends with Ben for a long time, and I'd known him just about his whole life, but then again so had everybody else, especially after he started making a name for himself on the field. Ben was probably the best football player to ever come out of this county. He'd played left tackle, and he was a big boy too, bigger than any of his teammates, bigger than just about any lineman he ever faced. He got a scholarship to Western Carolina and spent half his freshman year riding the bench and realizing that they made bigger boys than him in other parts of this country. They put him at linebacker near the end of the season, and he did pretty well: played in a few games, did a little partying, got into some trouble, and came home that summer after his grades had fallen so low that he couldn't keep his scholarship. There wasn't no way his piece of shit old man could get himself together enough to pay his tuition so he could go back in the fall, so Ben just hung around Madison County, got married to a sweet-looking girl named Julie, and he'd been here ever since.

One night when they were in high school, I'd gotten a call around ten o'clock about gunshots in one of the new developments out by the interstate, and I left the office in Marshall and headed east on 25/70 toward Weaverville. There are so many neighborhoods out that way now that I couldn't even tell you which one it was with any certainty, but back then there wasn't but a handful, some without any houses built in them yet, a few of them without paved roads.

I turned my lights off and rolled down into one of those developments and instantly noticed how dark it was once I'd left the main road. After a second I realized it was because somebody had gone through and shot out all the streetlights. The busted glass looked like huge pieces of broken eggshells had been gathered into little piles and left on the sides of the street. At the end of a cul-de-sac I saw an old Camaro parked with its lights out. I recognized it as belonging to a friend of theirs Jeff and Ben called 'Spaceman,' and after all these years I can't remember that boy's real name, probably because that nickname suited him so good. I parked and killed the engine and walked the rest of the way to the car. I found the three of them sitting on the ground, leaned up against the Camaro's back bumper, Ben holding a still warm .22 rifle, and two bottles left in a twelve pack of Michelob sitting on the ground in front of them. The rest of the bottles had been busted, and the glass was scattered all around them. I knew they were good and drunk when Jeff looked up at me and smiled like he wasn't one bit surprised to see me standing there in front of them.

'Well, hey, Dad,' he said.

'Y'all know I could arrest all three of you, don't you?' I told them. I leaned over and took the gun from Ben and checked to make sure it was empty.

'Yes, sir,' Jeff said, suddenly somber. The other two didn't look up at me.

'But I think it would be better for me and worse for y'all if I just took you home so we can let your folks know what you've been up to tonight. Tomorrow morning we'll come back down here and get all this glass cleaned up. And then we'll find out who y'all need to pay to replace these streetlights.'

'Man,' Spaceman muttered. I loaded them all into the cruiser and drove up out of the dark, empty development and back toward the county. Jeff sat in the seat beside me, and I could smell the beer on his breath, and I tried to predict what Sheila would say to him, and to me, about all this. I looked in the rearview mirror through the metal screen that divided the front and back seats, and I saw that Spaceman had laid his head back on the seat and his eyes closed. Ben stared out the passenger's-side window. I turned my eyes back toward the road.

'My dad's going to kill me,' Ben said, almost to himself. I looked in my mirror again and tried to catch his eye, but he was still staring out the window.

'I think you might need it this time,' I said. 'Drunk and disorderly. Discharging a firearm. Destruction of property. You might need a little killing.' Ben closed his eyes and leaned back in his seat just like Spaceman had.

'Y'all don't understand,' he said. 'He's really going to kill me. Y'all don't know what it's like.'

Ben Hall was already six foot two by then, maybe six foot three, and his daddy was just a little guy, maybe five nine, but I could see fear in Ben's face and I could hear it in his voice. I'd seen his eyes blacked up a couple of times, and I knew that whatever beating his old man had put on his wife that drove her to leave him he'd also put on Ben more than once. I just couldn't believe a boy that huge wasn't big enough to put a whooping on a man that small. I reckon I understood then just what Ben was up against, and I sighed loud enough for all of them to hear it.

'Well, maybe y'all should just stay at our house tonight,' I said. 'We can figure all this out in the morning.'

'Yes!' Spaceman whispered to Ben like he was celebrating an eleventh-hour reprieve. Even Jeff seemed to relax in the seat next to me, as if knowing that having his friends at our house would stall whatever punishment was coming his way. It got quiet again.

'Putting it off ain't going to make no difference,' Ben said.

★ ★ ★

Sometimes I think that I might've let Ben stay the night with us not because I was afraid of what his daddy would do to him if Ben came home drunk just like his old man did every night but because I was afraid of what Ben might finally do to his daddy with that license that alcohol can give a man. I wasn't ever afraid of Ben Hall, but I think I might've been a little afraid of what he was capable of doing to other people, including his daddy.

It was the memory of that night, especially the look of what I took to be fear or maybe anger in Ben's face, that put me ill at ease as I drove out to Adelaide Lyle's house. The thought of Ben confronting some of those folks from his wife's church with the knowledge that they might be in some way responsible for his son's death made me worry that all those years' worth of beatings would come to a head in a violence that Ben couldn't predict, a violence he'd have no interest in controlling. My fear wasn't founded just on the fact that he was a big boy who'd had to develop a tough streak or because his drunk-ass daddy had come back to Madison County and was likely headed over to Adelaide Lyle's house with him. I was afraid because I knew that church, and I knew the man who ran it as if he thought he was Jesus Christ himself, and some of those people who went to that church believed in Carson Chambliss like he might just be.

People out in these parts can take hold of religion like it's a drug, and they don't want to give it up once they've got hold of it. It's like it feeds them, and when they're on it they're likely to do anything these little backwoods churches tell them to do. Then they'll turn right around and kill each other over that faith, throw out their kids, cheat on husbands and wives, break up families just as quick. I don't know exactly how long Carson Chambliss had been living in Madison County the first time I ever ran up against him. And I'm not saying this fanaticism started with him, because I know it didn't. That kind of belief has been up here a long time before I arrived on this earth, and it's my guess it'll still be around for a long time after I'm gone. But I've seen his work firsthand, and I still can't put my finger on what it is and why it affects folks like it does. Ten years ago I saw a man set his own barn on fire while his family just stood out in the yard and watched it go, just because he thought it was the right thing to do.

In my mind that barn's still a burned-out spectacle set against a darkening sky. The neighbors had all left their houses in the cove and followed the gravel road down to Gillum's land, where they were facing the grassy rise atop which that barn sat with the bright orange light flickering inside. I'd followed the smoke down from the highway, and I was driving slowly past the fence when some of them turned to look at me like they hadn't ever seen the law before. But most of them kept their eyes on the barn where it was swollen with smoke from a season's worth of crop burning. What looked like fog rolled the length of the pasture and picked its way through the barbed wire fence. The cruiser's windows were down, and the air was tobacco-sweet.

Gillum and his two daughters were standing in the yard watching the barn. His wife had gone into the house to save herself from watching it burn and to put off the accounting of loss that would follow. I still picture her inside a too-warm room with closed windows and doors, where she busies her hands and pays no mind to the smoke drifting through the yard and the sound of the boards burning and popping loose from the barn's frame. If she'd have pulled back the curtain, she'd have seen me walking through the yard toward the smoke where Gillum was standing with their daughters and waiting for it to be done.

'What's happened here, Gillum?' I asked him. He didn't take his eyes from the barn, but his right hand left his pocket and touched the shoulder of his oldest daughter. She was maybe thirteen, and she jumped like electricity had suddenly passed between the two of them. Her face looked sad and scared, and she moved closer to her father. Gillum looked at me, and then he looked back at the barn.

'I'm just taking care of something, Sheriff,' he said.

'I noticed the smoke from the highway and thought I'd better come down,' I said.

'Everything's fine.' He was quiet, and I listened to the fire spreading itself inside the barn. Whispered voices rose below us where the people had gathered to watch down by the fence.

'Gillum, you've got a season's worth of tobacco drying in that barn. I know better than to think it's fine.' Before I could say anything else, his youngest girl looked up at me.

'I seen him run in there,' she said. She looked at her daddy, and he reached down and took her hand. She leaned her head against his leg.

'What's she talking about?' I asked. Gillum didn't say nothing, and the girl just looked at me. Then she tilted her head back and looked at her daddy again.

'Who'd you see in there?'

'She says she saw the Devil come running down the road,' the oldest girl said. 'She says she saw him run into the barn.'

'Is somebody in there?' I asked. Gillum's gaze left the barn and turned toward the ground. Up the hill in front of him, the flames had dispatched with the low beams and moved upward along the crossbeams toward the pitch. The eaves were beginning to burn. The roof would catch next.

'Libby Clovis took sick awhile back,' Gillum said. 'Bob tried to wait it out, but her fever just wouldn't break. He rode her over to the county hospital, and they looked her over and couldn't find nothing to do for her. He was close to riding her into Asheville when she got worse, but her mama wanted him to send for the preacher. He told me he figured it couldn't hurt.

'Libby's mama brought out a preacher from Marshall named Chambliss, and Bob said that preacher closed himself up in the bedroom with Libby. He said he could hear all kinds of carrying on behind that door. Sounded like the furniture was getting smashed to bits, like the bed was being lifted up and down off the floor.'

I turned and looked down toward the people gathered in front of the fence. In the back I saw the tall, gaunt figure of Robert Clovis bringing an unlit cigarette to his lips. Our eyes locked, and he looked away quickly. He struck a light, and his washed-out face was framed briefly against the darkening road that fell away behind him. I turned back toward the fire.

'Who's in that barn?'

'It's not for me to say just what it is,' Gillum said. 'But Bob told me Chambliss called the family into the bedroom late this afternoon and asked them to all join hands and pray. Bob said they stood there and held hands and prayed, but he kept his eyes open and looked around. He told me it left her body suddenly. He said everybody in the room saw it: the preacher, Libby's mama, him. They saw it leave her body and run out of the house like a shadow. Whatever was in her is in my barn now, and I mean to be rid of it tonight.'

'You think the Devil's in your barn?'

'Like I said, it ain't for me to say just what it is. I just know it's there.'

'I don't know what your daughter thinks she saw, but I hope that barn's empty when this fire burns out.'

'You ain't going to find a man's body in there,' he said. 'I can promise you that.'

Most of the folks in the group by the fence had gone home, and it was full dark when the north side of the barn collapsed and took part of the roof with it. The sound of splitting wood was followed by a shower of glowing embers that fell like snow onto the lawn. Flakes of warm ash floated toward us, and I felt them blow across my face and I brushed them from my shirt. The noise of the collapsing roof startled Gillum's youngest daughter, and she started to cry.

'Take her into the house,' he told the oldest.

She picked up the little girl and carried her toward the house, where faint lights burned behind curtained windows. I watched them go until the darkness swallowed them. When I turned I realized that Gillum was gone, and I searched the yard until I saw his shape moving away from me toward a small well house. I stood watching his retreating figure and suddenly realized that people were moving past me in the darkness. The neighbors who'd left earlier had returned, and many of them were carrying aluminum buckets and plastic drums. They walked quietly through the yard.

I found myself following the group up to the well house, where someone handed me a bucket and I stood and waited for Gillum to fill it with water from the hose. Behind me I could hear the hiss of the hot ground being cooled as bucket after bucket was dumped onto the smoldering grass. The pump inside the well house clicked on, and the low hum competed with the noise of the fire and the sounds of the feet shuffling in and out of the line.

When my bucket was full, I carried it toward the fire where the others circled the barn and soaked down the grass along its perimeter. A few had even climbed a piece up the hillside and were tossing buckets of water into the trees. The only light came from the fire, and the darkness around me moved with the sound of falling water. I carried the bucket by the handle, and in its swinging the water overflowed the sides and wet my pants and my boots. I moved slower until I felt the heat of the fire on my face, and I stopped and stood beside another man and carefully soaked a strip of grass at my feet.

I went back to the line, where Gillum refilled my bucket, and I worked my way around the barn, soaking down the grass and trying not to inhale the sour smoke from the treated lumber. The earth grew wet until my feet were sloshing through the grass, but I continued to refill my bucket and follow the others clockwise around the barn. I poured the water methodically in straight lines until the grass was no longer steaming. I looked to my right and saw a man in a baseball cap beside me with a cigarette in his mouth. He was using both hands to dump the water from his bucket and trying in vain to blink the smoke from his eyes. I walked back to the well house, where Gillum was still standing and filling emptied buckets. He was talking to someone; when I got closer, I saw it was Robert Clovis.

'I'm going to help you put this back up,' I heard Clovis say. 'I can't help but feel responsible for it.'

'There's no need for that,' Gillum said. 'We can see to that tomorrow. I just want to make sure I don't lose nothing tonight that I can't get back.'

'I'm sorry,' Clovis said.

'There's no need,' Gillum said. Clovis waited until his bucket was full, and then he walked back toward the barn. I stepped forward and held my bucket before me, and it grew heavy as the water from the hose began to fill it.

'I appreciate your help,' Gillum said. I looked up at him and nodded my head, and then I turned to follow Clovis back to the barn, but I stopped when I saw that the fire was slowly burning itself out and the field was already full of inky silhouettes moving against the darkness.

6

That night, while Gillum's barn smoldered in the wet grass, Carson Chambliss suddenly showed up on the radar of the Madison County Sheriffs Department, and he'd been there ever since. He didn't seem to have any connections to the area, and there wasn't any family in this part of North Carolina that I could find. I called on a couple folks around here who I trusted, who I knew could keep their mouths shut about these kinds of things, and I found out he'd come up from north Georgia: Stephens County, about three hours southwest of here. It took a few phone calls, but it wasn't hardly a day or two before I was on the phone with Sheriff Tyrie Nicks in Toccoa, Georgia, asking him if he'd ever heard of a man named Carson Chambliss.

'Good God,' he said. 'Who hasn't heard of that son of a bitch?' Nicks said Chambliss always told folks that he was a mechanic, but all Nicks had ever known him for was being arrested on little charges like petty theft and possession of marijuana and controlled substances. 'I'd had my eye on him for a long time,' he said, 'but he had to go and blow himself up for us to have something that would stick.'

'What do you mean?' I asked.

'He cooked meth,' Nicks said. 'And he moved like a squatter back and forth between shacks and abandoned trailers and we couldn't ever catch him. And then one morning we had an old house explode about ten minutes outside Toccoa. It was Chambliss, what was left of him anyway.'

'Was he hurt bad?' I asked.

'You ain't never looked at him up close, have you?' he asked me.

'No, Sheriff,' I said. 'I haven't.' The truth was that at that time I hadn't laid my eyes on him yet. I couldn't have picked him out of a crowd of two men.

'Well, that explosion took off something like forty percent of his skin. It almost killed him. They had to graft big old pieces from his legs and his back. He must've worn a gas mask or something over his face while he cooked it, because you can't quite tell it just by looking at him. But his chest and the right side of his body are just awful-looking. If you saw him without clothes on, you'd swear he was a danged mutant.' He sighed like he was about to tell me something he either shouldn't or didn't want to. 'You want to hear the messed-up part?' he asked.

'I sure do,' I said.

'He had him a sixteen-year-old girl in that house when it exploded, a runaway from Mississippi. She died a week later from her burns. Her folks drove up here from Jackson and took her home. It was just a sad story all the way around.'

'What happened to Chambliss?' I asked.

'We tried to get him on second-degree murder, but you know how it is, Sheriff. His court-appointed suit got it argued down to involuntary manslaughter, and the newspaper made that poor girl sound like a conspirator. They only gave him three years. I think he might've served two.'

'That don't seem right,' I said.

'It wasn't right,' he said. 'But like I told you, you know how it is.' It was quiet for a second, and I thought he'd finished telling me all he knew about Chambliss. Then he cleared his throat. 'You want to know something else? After he got sent to the Allendale Pen down in Alto, he was explaining away those burns by telling folks that God had done it to him. He told them that the hand of God Almighty had come down and set his body afire to purify him from the sins of the world.'

'But what about the meth explosion?' I asked. 'What did he have to say about that?'

'He said that was how God chose to do it.'

'And what about that girl?'

'He didn't ever mention her, not after he got to the pen anyway. It was just like she'd never existed,' he said. 'But let me tell you this, and you ain't going to believe it when I tell you, but the warden told me he couldn't hardly keep that man from setting himself on fire once he got inside the pen. Warden said Chambliss started up some kind of cult called the Signs Following. He said they'd hold services right there on the spot, wherever they felt moved: the chapel, in their cells, out in the yard. He said they'd speak in tongues, heal each other, talk about the Devil like he lived next door. But the thing was, once they got going, they'd pull out anything flammable they could get ahold of and light it on fire and run their hands over it, hold it right up to their faces: shaving cream, cologne, cleaning spray. He said if you confiscated lighters and matchbooks to try and keep them from setting that stuff on fire, then they'd up and drink it. But not a single one of them psychos was burned or ever got sick. He said Chambliss got him a little following together and there was nothing outside of solitary confinement that could keep those folks away from him.

'He couldn't get nothing out of Chambliss that would explain why they were carrying on like that, but one of his followers told him that it was in the Bible, that Jesus told the disciples that after he was gone they'd be able to do all kinds of dangerous things without getting hurt, he said it would be a sign of their righteousness. I didn't believe him until I got home and opened up my own Bible and did a little searching, and there it was, right there in Mark. Just like they said it would be.' I heard his desk chair squeak, and I imagined Sheriff Nicks leaning all the way back, his boots up on the desk, crossed at the ankle, his hat resting in his lap.

When he mentioned the book of Mark, my mind suddenly recalled the new sign out by the front of Chambliss's church. I recalled the exact verses on it: Mark 16:17–18. I hung up with Nicks, and when I got home that night I took

Sheila's Bible out of her nightstand and flipped through the pages until I found the verses and whispered as I read them out loud: 'And these signs will follow those who believe: In my name they will cast out demons, they will speak in new tongues; they will pick up snakes with their hands; and when they drink deadly poison, it will not hurt them; they will place their hands on the sick, and they will get well.'

Things became clearer to me once I read that. A bad burn from a meth house explosion in north Georgia becomes a sign of holiness and power in western North Carolina. It was all in who told the story, even if that story involved a dead young girl from Mississippi. I suddenly understood the kind of mind that could convince Gillum to set his barn on fire, and I suddenly understood why a group of folks would hide behind newspaper-covered windows while they worshipped, and I finally realized what was in those little crates they carried in and out of that church on Wednesday nights and Sunday mornings. But other than suspicion, what did I have? What could I do? Arrest a man for exercising his religious freedom? None of it was a reason to knock on church doors, interrupt meetings and services. But now, this time, it wasn't a sixteen-year-old runaway but a thirteen-year-old mute boy who was dead, a boy who couldn't have told Chambliss 'yes' or 'no' or 'stop' even if he'd wanted to. This time, I knew it was different.

★　★　★

Nothing I saw at Adelaide Lyle's surprised me when I stopped at the top of her yard and turned off my engine and then my lights. I reached into the dash and found my badge and pinned it to my shirt, and then I opened the door and stepped out and looked into the yard where the front porch light lit up the whole scene. It was just what I thought I'd find.

A couple of beat-up and bloodied men still wearing their church clothes, Adelaide Lyle and two other old women out there seeing to their wounds. Out by the road Ben Hall had his head down on the hood of what must've been his daddy's old truck, and there was Jimmy Hall himself, who'd somehow become an old man since the last time I'd seen him, sitting on the porch steps and smoking a cigarette like nothing had happened. Above him, at the window by the front door that looked out into the yard, stood Ben Hall's youngest son, his mother, Julie, right beside him. When she saw me, she turned and walked away.

Like I said, none of what I saw that night surprised me, but what did concern me was what I didn't see. I didn't see Carson Chambliss, and I knew there had to be a reason why.

Jess Hall

7

Miss Lyle had met me and Mr. Stuckey at her door, and then she took my hand and led me through the living room, where Mama was lying on the sofa with her eyes closed. Miss Lyle told me to sit as quiet as I could right there at the dining room table and wait for my daddy. It felt like an oven inside her house with no breeze coming in, even though she went around opening all the windows after I'd gotten in there and sat down. After she'd done that she went back into the living room and sat down in a chair beside the sofa. It was dark in her house, and there wasn't hardly any lights on except for a lamp in the front room and the bulb hanging over the table where I was sitting and waiting. Mr. Stuckey stayed out on the porch after I came inside, and a few minutes later I heard a car come driving down the road and stop, and then I heard a door open and shut and the car drove off. I knew that whoever was driving that car had come by to pick him up.

I leaned back in my seat and looked into the living room, where I saw a little bit of light coming from under the door to the kitchen. There were people in there, but I hadn't seen them yet. I could hear the voices of a couple of old women whispering. I could smell the coffee they'd started brewing in there too, and I figured they didn't even know I was here, and even if they did they had probably forgotten all about me with Mama lying on the sofa over there in the front room crying like she was and Miss Lyle sitting next to her in that chair whispering, 'Now, now,' and rubbing Mama's back.

Outside, another car was coming slow down the road in front of the house, and I heard the tires crunch on the gravel when it pulled into Miss Lyle's driveway. I heard the car doors open and slam, and then I heard footsteps in the gravel. I prayed it was Daddy coming to get me, and I sat there and listened hard. Whoever was out there shuffled their feet slowly through the gravel like they'd never make it inside. I couldn't hear them in the driveway anymore, and I knew they must've been coming up the porch steps one step at a time.

The door creaked open in the front room and a man's voice said, 'Addie.' It was quiet for just a second after that, and then Mama started crying again even louder than she was before. I knew that whatever made her cry had just been brought into the house because I heard somebody walking across the wood floor in the front room like they were struggling to do it, and I turned around in my chair and looked toward the front room and waited to see what it was. Two old men from the church shuffled into the dining room, and they stopped walking and looked at me where I sat at the table. They were carrying Stump. He had his head leaned forward and his eyes closed like he was asleep, but I knew he wasn't sleeping, and I knew without knowing for sure that I'd seen these same two men carrying him out of the church as me and Mr. Stuckey drove off in Daddy's truck. I wanted to say something to them, but my jaws were shaking and I couldn't get my mouth to open. I could feel tears running down my cheeks.

'Alton,' one of the old men said. He held Stump under his arms and looked at the other man.

'What happened?' I finally asked, but I was crying so hard they probably didn't even understand what I'd said. I couldn't hardly see them with all the tears in my eyes. 'What happened to him?' I asked, but it came out worse than it had before.

'Alton,' the man said again. The one named Alton held Stump's legs and just stared at me. When he heard his name, he looked at the man calling him. They shuffled across the floor to the bedroom on the other side of the table. It was so quiet that I could barely hear Mama crying in the next room, and I knew she had her face buried in one of the sofa cushions. I knew those old men had laid Stump down on the bed because I heard the springs creak. I could hear them in there whispering too, and then I heard the door shut. A second later I felt somebody's hand on my shoulder.

'Son,' a voice said. I looked up and saw the old man named Alton standing over me. His eyes were bright blue and sad-looking, and his face was tan and wrinkled. 'I'm sorry, son,' he said. He squeezed my shoulder just hard enough for me to barely feel it.

'Alton,' the other man said. Alton gave my shoulder another squeeze.

The two old men walked through the front room and opened and closed the kitchen door without making a sound. After a minute I could hear them whispering to the old women who were already in there. I heard the pot tap against their cups when they poured the coffee, and then I heard somebody put the pot back on the stove. I leaned back in my chair as far as I could, and I looked around the corner into the front room. All I could see was Mama's feet, but I could tell that she'd turned over on her side with her back to Miss Lyle. Miss Lyle still sat in that chair by Mama.

I crossed my arms and put them on the table and laid my head down on them. I breathed hard and tried to stop myself from crying, and I knew my breath was probably fogging up the wooden tabletop and I knew it was making my face get wet and hot, but after a bit I knew it was wet from my own tears.

⋆　⋆　⋆

When I looked up, Miss Lyle stood right by the table and I wondered how long she'd been there.

'Jess,' she said, 'can I get you something to drink, maybe some milk or a little something to eat?'

My mouth was dry as a cotton ball and I was

thirsty, but I shook my head no anyway because I just wanted to sit there and wait for Daddy without having to talk to nobody. Miss Lyle stood there looking at me like she was waiting for me to say something else.

'I don't want anything,' I said, and then I put my head back down on the table. I knew she was still standing there looking at me.

'You let me know if you need something,' she said. I looked up, and she was still there. She put her hand on my head and then used her fingers to brush my hair. 'Your daddy's going to be here real soon, but don't be afraid to tell me if you need anything.'

She turned and walked through the front room, and I watched her open the door to the kitchen. She held the door open for a second, and I could see a little table in there and some of them old people sitting down with their coffee cups. Alton and the other old man who'd carried Stump into the house leaned against the counter with their arms crossed. They all looked at Miss Lyle when she came in. She let the door close behind her and I couldn't see nothing after that.

I pushed my chair away from the table as quiet as I could, and then I got down real slow and walked over to the doorway and took a look into the front room. Mama still laid on the sofa with her back to me and I could hear her breathing, but I could tell she wasn't asleep. A voice came from inside the kitchen that was louder than all the others, and I could tell it was Miss Lyle. She sounded like she was angry.

'I don't care why he was in there,' she said.

'He shouldn't have been. Not tonight and not this morning either. No way.'

'But, Adelaide,' one of those old women said, 'I know what I saw this morning, and I know what I heard. It was a miracle.'

'We all heard that boy speak,' the man named Alton said. 'Every one of us heard it.'

'Well, that don't matter now, does it?' Miss Lyle said. 'It don't matter one bit what y'all heard in there this morning. All that matters is what happened tonight, and I can tell you that you'd better be ready to talk about it once the sheriff gets here.' It got quiet after that, and I pictured Miss Lyle with her hands on her hips staring at those old women and those two old men until they looked away from her. I could hear somebody running the water in the kitchen sink, and then it sounded like somebody's footsteps were coming across the floor toward the living room.

I turned and crept back into the dining room and walked to the other side of the table and stopped at the bedroom door where those men had laid Stump on the bed. Nobody had opened the kitchen door yet, and from that far away I could just barely hear them talking in there, and I could hear the curtains stirring in the dining room from the little bit of breeze that came in the open windows now. I put my hand on the knob, and I turned it real slow and hoped the door wouldn't make any noise, and then I walked into the bedroom and closed the door behind me just as quiet as I'd opened it.

It was dark and hot in there with the windows

closed and the curtains pulled shut. When my eyes adjusted to all that dark, I found where just a little bit of moonlight was trying to get through the windows over the bed, and in that light I could make out where Stump laid in the middle of the bed with his arms by his sides. His face was turned away from me like he was asleep or just lying there and staring at the wall. I couldn't see him as good as I wanted to, so I walked closer to the bed until I stood right beside him. The bedspread was a white quilt, and with him laying on it his face looked pale blue in the light coming through the curtains. Some buttons were tore off his shirt and it was pulled open and I could see his chest. I just stood there and stared at him, and then I crawled up onto the bed so I could look at his face. There was a speck of dried blood on his lip like he might've bit it by accident, and his eyes were closed like he hadn't woke up yet, and I thought about waking up in the night and looking over at him and watching his mouth puff out air while he slept. At night the house used to be so quiet that I could hear him breathing soft beside me. Sometimes I'd lay there and listen to him for what seemed like forever, and before I knew it I'd be asleep again. But I didn't want him to be asleep like this on Miss Lyle's bed with the moonlight outside shining on the curtains of this hot room and Mama crying on the sofa with Daddy on his way. I wanted to tell him, 'Wake up, Stump,' but I didn't say nothing because I was afraid to see that he wouldn't hear me.

I got up on my knees on the bed beside him,

and I pulled back the curtains behind the bed and pushed the window open to let some air in. I looked outside. The moon shone bright, and I saw our truck and the other cars parked in the driveway in front of the house. I left the curtains pulled open, and then I looked down at Stump where the moonlight spread across his face. I lay down beside him and stared up at the ceiling while the breeze moved through the curtains over the bed. I thought about how it felt just like sleeping in our bed at home, and for a minute I imagined that Mama hadn't come into our bedroom to wake us up yet.

I closed my eyes and thought about me and Stump lying out in the ferns down by the creek where the sun that came through the trees was still bright on his face. There was an old green frog croaking somewhere along the creek, and his voice sounded like a loose banjo string, and I knew if I didn't keep an eye on Stump he'd take to looking around for that frog until I'd have to get up and go hunting after him. I tried my best to keep my eyes open, but sometimes the water gurgling in the creek can sound like people talking, and I listened to them talk until I drifted off to sleep in all that warm sun, and when I woke up I saw that Stump had fallen asleep too, and it could be late now with the light out of the trees and the air turned nice and cool. I looked at his face until he blinked his eyes and looked up to where the sunlight faded in the treetops and smiled.

'We better get on home,' I whispered.

There was a noise like an old car driving fast

down the road, and I laid there with my eyes closed and listened. I heard footsteps running through loose gravel and a screen door slamming shut and the sound of my daddy's voice come through the walls in a room far away from us. The knob turned on the bedroom door, and I wished it was Mama coming to wake us up even though neither one of us was asleep, and I opened my eyes into that soft moonlight with Stump still laying right there beside me.

'Jess,' somebody said. I looked up and saw Daddy standing in the doorway holding out his hand to me. I couldn't see his face because he was looking away into the other room where the lights were on. I wanted to tell him about what I'd seen, about how they'd carried him out of the church, that he was in here on the bed with me, but the way Daddy stood there made it seem like it was too dark and quiet for me to say anything at all.

I climbed down from the bed and walked over to Daddy where he stood in the doorway still looking into the other room, and he took my hand in his and it was rough and dry and he led me into the dining room, and then he was in there with the door closed and I heard him dragging a chair across the floor toward the bed.

I walked over to the window in the dining room and pulled the curtains back a little and looked outside. It was completely dark out there, but I could make out the shapes of the cars in the driveway and the little trees and the bushes around in the yard. Something caught my eye out by the road, and I looked and saw somebody standing there smoking a cigarette. I watched that glowing orange tip move from their mouth down to their side, and then back up to their mouth again. I couldn't tell who it was out there, so I walked over to the switch and turned the lights out on the chandelier over the table and the dining room went dark. I walked back to the window and pulled the curtains back again and saw an old, beat-up truck parked out by the road in front of the house where a man stood smoking a cigarette and leaning up against the hood. I knew he must be the man Mama wanted me to call Grandpa. He had his cap pulled low and he looked at the ground, and even though I couldn't see his face good he still didn't look one bit like I thought he would. He tossed his cigarette into the gravel and rubbed it out with his boot. Then he folded his arms across his chest like he was waiting for something to happen, and he turned his head and looked in the direction of the ridge on the other side of the road.

The house had just about gone quiet now, and I could barely hear Daddy through the bedroom door where he was sitting in that chair by the bed and whispering something to Stump. I stared out the window and tried hard to hear what Daddy said, but he was whispering too quiet. But then I heard Mama stirring on the sofa like she was turning over, and I heard Miss Lyle scoot her chair a little closer. I imagined Mama's face as she opened her eyes and blinked at Miss Lyle like she'd been sleeping and she'd just woke up from a dream. Outside the man

Mama said to call Grandpa turned his face away from the ridge and looked down the road and coughed and spit something into the gravel.

I let the curtain close, and I sat down on the floor and put my back against the wall. I folded my arms over my knees and I rested my head to hide my face, and then I sat there and thought about what Daddy might be whispering to Stump in the next room, and I cried and cried and I just couldn't get myself to stop.

★ ★ ★

The bedroom door opened, and from where I sat on the floor I could look under the table and see my daddy's boots walk across the floor. He walked around the room past the chairs until he stood right in front of where I was sitting. I didn't look up at him, so Daddy squatted down and put his hand on my head.

'Hey, buddy,' he said. 'Hey, Jess.'

I finally looked up at him, and I figured my eyes looked good and swollen with all the crying I'd done that day. Daddy looked at me, and then he pulled me to him and I put my face in his shirt. I could smell him now, and he smelled like he always does, like the barn and his own sweat from the collar of the shirt he's worn while he worked in the field, and for just a minute I felt better because he smelled like him and that meant he was finally there with me. He put his arms around me and hugged me tight. He stood up straight and picked me up and kept on hugging me, and I figured if somebody was watching us it would look funny with my legs hanging so close to the ground, but I didn't say nothing because right then I liked the way it felt for him to hold me. I kept my face pressed up against his shirt collar, and he carried me through the dining room past the table and into the front room.

Mama was sitting up on the sofa now with both her feet on the floor. Miss Lyle had gotten up out of her chair, and she sat on the sofa right beside Mama. When Daddy carried me in, they were both already looking up at us like they'd been expecting us to walk in and it had taken us too long to do it. Mama and Daddy just looked at each other.

'I called the sheriff, Julie,' Daddy finally said to her. 'Why hadn't nobody called him yet?'

Mama and Miss Lyle just sat there and looked up at him, but they didn't say nothing. Daddy waited for Mama to answer him.

'Chambliss tell you not to call?' Daddy asked her.

'Ben,' Miss Lyle said, 'why don't we just wait until — '

'Chambliss tell you not to call him?' Daddy asked Mama again.

'Yes,' Mama whispered.

There was the sound of another car coming down the road, and Daddy carried me over to the screen door and we both looked out. The moon wasn't giving off enough light, and Daddy felt around on the wall right inside the door until he found a light switch, and when he flipped it the floodlights came on in the front yard. An old red truck pulled into the driveway behind ours; I could see three men sitting in it. When I looked close, I saw that one of them was Mr. Gene Thompson, and the other two were the men I'd seen smoking out by the road that morning who'd had all that Brylcreem in their hair. The man Mama had told me to call Grandpa had already lit up another cigarette, and he was leaning up against the front of his truck. He didn't even turn around to see who'd pulled up in the driveway. Mr. Thompson and those men sat in the truck for a minute like they were trying to decide if they should get out or not, but Mr. Thompson finally opened the door and then the driver opened his and they all got out and started walking up the gravel driveway toward the house. The two men I didn't know were about as old as Daddy, and they still had on their church clothes. Mr. Thompson was walking behind them. His lip had a little bloody scab on it from where Mama had busted it that morning when she was fighting with him and trying to get him to turn her loose.

Daddy put me down and pushed me toward the sofa where Mama sat. He looked at Mama and Miss Lyle.

'Y'all lock this door behind me,' he said. 'They ain't coming in here.' He went to step outside, and Miss Lyle stood up and walked toward the door.

'Ben,' she said.

Daddy turned around and looked at her, and through the screen I could see Mr. Thompson and those men coming up the driveway.

133

'You lock this door,' he said.

Daddy turned and pushed the screen door open and walked down the porch steps into the yard. The door slammed behind him. Mama hollered out his name and stood up from the sofa and reached for me, but I was too far away for her to catch me and she didn't even hardly try. Miss Lyle watched, and then she closed the front door and turned the lock. I couldn't see nothing then, so I went over to the open window on the right-hand side of the door and pulled back the curtains.

'Jess,' Mama said, 'come here and sit down.' I acted like I didn't hear her. 'Jess,' she said again. Miss Lyle stood behind me, and we watched Daddy walk up to Mr. Thompson and those two men. Mama sat back down on the sofa behind us, and I heard her whisper something under her breath, and I knew she was talking to herself and maybe she was even praying.

Those two men I didn't know stood in between Daddy and Mr. Thompson, and I could tell they wanted to get by Daddy and go up the porch steps and into the house, but Daddy wouldn't let them.

'Y'all ain't going in there,' I heard him say. 'Ain't no reason to be out here in the first place. I've already called the sheriff, and he should be here any minute.'

One of the men tried to go right around Daddy anyway, and Daddy put his hand on the man's chest and stopped him. The man looked down at where Daddy had put his hand on him, and he slapped it away and kept on walking toward the house. When he did that, Daddy hauled back and punched him right smack in the face and the man's hands went up to his nose and he stumbled backward into the gravel and fell down right in front of our truck. Before he even hit the ground that other man had ahold of Daddy and they were down on the ground in the yard and wrestling and kicking up grass. Daddy finally got on top of the man, and when he did he started punching him in the face. Mr. Thompson stood behind Daddy and yanked on Daddy's shirt and tried to pull him off. I could hear him hollering for Daddy to stop, but Daddy just kept on punching that man like he couldn't even hear Mr. Thompson.

The man Daddy punched first was on his knees in the gravel, and his nose was busted and bleeding and the blood ran down his face and neck and onto his button-down shirt. He tried to wipe the blood off his face with the back of his hands, but it just kept on pouring out of his nose. He looked over to the yard where Mr. Thompson was trying to pull Daddy off the other man, and he put his hand down on the ground like he was about to stand up. I heard somebody hollering my daddy's name, and I looked up at the road and saw my grandpa running down through the grass toward the house. The man on his knees looked up too, and when he did my grandpa swung his leg and kicked the man right in the face just like he was kicking a ball. The man's nose made a sound like a tree limb snapping in two, and his head whipped around like it had come loose from his neck. He fell onto his back in the gravel, and he just laid there and I could see his chest puffing air like he'd just finished running as fast as he could and he couldn't catch his breath. His arms and legs moved around through the gravel like he was trying to make a snow angel right there in the driveway, but he didn't try to get up again.

My grandpa pushed Mr. Thompson up against the side of our truck, and Mr. Thompson stayed there and watched my grandpa try to get Daddy up off the man he was hitting.

'Ben,' I heard my grandpa say. 'That's enough.' My daddy's fist was covered in blood, and his shirt was turned red from the man's bloody face. 'Stop it, Ben,' my grandpa said. He got Daddy up on his feet, and my daddy shook loose like he was going after Mr. Thompson now. 'Goddamn it, that's enough,' my grandpa said. He wrapped his arms around Daddy and tried to keep him from getting away. Daddy got free and turned around and pushed my grandpa in the chest.

'Get off me!' he screamed. 'Don't you *ever* touch me! Ever!' Daddy pushed my grandpa again, and then he turned around and faced the house and when he did I could see that he was crying. He put his hands over his eyes, and I saw they had blood all over them. He walked out toward the road where my grandpa's truck was parked. My grandpa just stood there and watched him, and then he turned and looked at Mr. Thompson.

'Y'all need to go,' he said. 'There wasn't no reason for you to have come out here to start with.'

Miss Lyle stepped away from the window and unlocked the door and opened it and looked outside.

'Wait, Gene,' she told Mr. Thompson. 'Let me get something to clean them boys up. After that y'all need to leave. Ben called the sheriff, and he'll be here real soon. He don't need to see any of this. It's just going to make it worse than it already is.'

Miss Lyle closed the door and turned around and walked across the front room toward the kitchen. I could hear her in there opening and closing drawers and running water in the sink. She must've told them old people what had happened outside because I could hear them fussing and I could hear the sound of their chairs being pushed back from the table. Mama still sat on the sofa. When I looked at her, she stood up and walked over to me at the window. She pulled me to her, and I hugged her around the waist. We stood there and looked out at the yard where Mr. Thompson helped those men stand up and checked to see how bad they'd been hurt. Daddy was almost out of the reach of the floodlights at the top of the road, but I could see him leaning his head down on the hood of my grandpa's truck, and his shoulders were shaking like he was crying. My grandpa stood in the center of the yard. His back was to us, but I saw him reach into his shirt pocket and pull out a pack of cigarettes. He shook one out and lit it and looked out at the road like he was watching Daddy too.

★ ★ ★

Daddy was still out there when the sheriff pulled up with the red and blue police lights spinning on top of his car. He parked behind my grandpa's truck and turned off the lights and got out and left his door open, and then he leaned in and picked up a cowboy hat where it had been sitting on the seat beside him. He put it on. I could see him good with the light coming from inside his car. He was about as old as my grandpa; his cowboy hat was white, and his brown button-down shirt was wet where his armpits were sweating. The little silver star on his chest shone when the light caught it. He left his arm propped up on the car door, and he just stood there and looked out at the yard.

Miss Lyle and two of those old women were out there with wet washcloths wiping the blood off those men's faces. Somebody had given one of those men a sandwich bag full of ice, and he was holding it up to his nose.

'I think it's broke,' I heard one of those old women tell him.

My grandpa sat on the porch steps smoking and watching Daddy out at the road. When Mama saw the sheriff, she walked through the dining room to the bedroom where Stump was still laying on the bed and she closed the door behind her. Before she left she told me to stay inside. I asked her if Daddy was crying, but she just told me to leave him alone and not bother him. I figured she'd never seen him cry either and it had probably scared her too.

I heard the sheriff walking through the gravel, and then I could just barely see him moving like a shadow until he stepped into the grass and the floodlights hit him and made that little star on his chest shine. While he walked he looked over his left shoulder out at the road, where I knew my daddy was standing.

'What in the hell happened here?' the sheriff asked. He said it like anybody who wanted to could try and give him an answer. Mr. Thompson looked up at him and pointed out to the road where Daddy stood by my grandpa's truck.

'We just came out to extend the sympathy of the church,' Mr. Thompson said. 'We came out in the spirit of faith and fellowship, Sheriff, and that man attacked us.'

The sheriff looked at Mr. Thompson, but he didn't say anything to him, and then he walked over to the man who held that bag of ice on his nose. The sheriff reached out and picked up the hand that held the bag and he looked close at that man's face where it was busted. He squinted his eyes like he was concentrating on what he was looking at, and then he looked over at Miss Lyle where she was trying to get the other man's face to stop bleeding. The man Miss Lyle was working on had his eyes almost swollen shut, and there was a big, bloody cut under one of them. The sheriff let go of the man's hand and the bag of ice dropped back on his nose. He let out a groan like he'd just been punched again.

'Well, I'm sorry if y'all came all the way out here and got your feelings hurt,' the sheriff said. 'But that man's just found out that he's lost his son, so I ain't planning on doing nothing about this little disagreement tonight.' He looked at Mr. Thompson. 'But if you three want to give me a statement about what happened up at y'all's church tonight then I'll be glad to take it.' Mr. Thompson looked over at those two men he'd brought with him, and then he looked back at the sheriff.

'We don't know nothing about it,' Mr. Thompson said.

'You knew enough to come out here and bring these two boys with you,' the sheriff said. 'And I find it funny that you don't know nothing now. Maybe after you saw the law you forgot what drove you to come out here, and that's fine. There's nothing I can do about that tonight. But I'd suggest you head back to Marshall and tell Chambliss and anybody who'll listen that I expect them to be ready to talk as soon as I get things settled tonight.' He stood there like he was waiting for Mr. Thompson to say something, and then he turned away and started walking toward the house.

'I suppose Pastor will talk if the Lord leads him,' Mr. Thompson said. The sheriff stopped and turned around in the yard and looked at him.

'Then you'd better pray to God he's led,' the sheriff said.

'I can't rightly say what Pastor will do, Sheriff. I'm sure you've heard the good Lord works in mysterious ways.'

'So does the law,' the sheriff said. 'You tell Chambliss and the rest of your people that I'll be around to see them.'

The sheriff turned to walk up the porch steps, and when he did my grandpa looked up at him. The sheriff stopped and held up his hand to block out the glare from the floodlights, and then he stared hard at my grandpa. My grandpa stared right back at him. It was quiet except for the sound of the slow footsteps crunching in the gravel where Mr. Thompson and those two men were walking out to their truck.

'So you're back in town,' the sheriff said to my grandpa. He lowered his hand, and the light hit him in the eyes again. He looked from my grandpa up to me where I stood behind the screen door.

'You figuring to stick around this time?' the sheriff said.

'We'll see,' my grandpa said.

'I guess we will,' the sheriff said. My grandpa stood up from the steps real slow to let the sheriff pass. Then the sheriff opened the screen door and I moved out of his way too. He took off his cowboy hat and held it down by his side.

'Where's your mama at?' he asked me.

'In the bedroom,' I said and pointed to the next room.

I watched him walk through the front room and into the dining room, and I heard his boots on the hardwood floor, and then I heard him open the bedroom door.

'Mrs. Hall,' he said. He closed the door quietly behind him.

I looked outside and saw my grandpa standing at the bottom of the porch steps. He had his foot propped up on the bottom step, and he was looking up at me. It was the first time I'd gotten a good look at him. He had gray hair curling out from under his baseball cap, and he had gray whiskers too. His eyes were just as blue as Daddy's, and his nose was crooked. I heard voices coming from the road, and my grandpa turned around and looked out into the darkness at the top of the yard.

'Mr. Hall,' Mr. Gene Thompson's voice said from out in the dark, 'Mr. Hall, I want you to know that we're all sorry for your loss.'

'Stay away from my family,' Daddy said.

★ ★ ★

I was sitting by myself on the sofa in the front room when Miss Lyle came back inside the house. Her hands were full of washcloths that were soaked through with blood. She walked right past me toward the kitchen.

'This is all just a mess,' she said to herself as she went by.

I heard the bedroom door open off the dining room, and I heard the sheriff's boots walk across the floor. He stepped into the front room and looked over at me on his way to the door. He put his cowboy hat back on and looked out the screen door. I heard my daddy and my grandpa talking quietly out in the yard, but they stopped talking when the sheriff opened the screen door and walked out onto the porch. He walked down the steps, and I heard him moving through the grass toward where I figured my daddy and my grandpa were standing.

I could just barely hear all three of them talking, but they were being too quiet for me to understand exactly what they said. But then I heard somebody raise his voice like he was mad.

'That ain't your decision to make.'

'It ain't yours either,' the sheriff's voice said.

'It's all right,' said Daddy's voice. 'He'll run him home. It's all right.'

'You sure?' the sheriff asked.

'Yeah,' Daddy said. 'I'm sure.'

'Can you take care of that boy?'

'He's my grandson, ain't he?'

'I reckon so,' the sheriff said.

8

It was hot and smelled like sweat in my grandpa's truck, and there were papers and stained napkins and balled-up cigarette packets tossed all over the floorboard. The truck's windows were rolled down all the way, and I watched Daddy and the sheriff walk up the porch steps to go back inside Miss Lyle's house. Mama was waiting on the other side of the screen door for Daddy. My grandpa put the key in the ignition and started his truck. When the engine fired up, it sounded like pieces of old metal were beating against each other under the hood.

'Are my mom and dad not coming with us?' I asked.

'No, they're going to stay with your brother,' he said. 'Just for tonight.' He pulled his pack of cigarettes out of his shirt pocket and shook one out, and then he pushed in the lighter on the dash to get it hot. 'I'm going to carry you home and stay the night at your house, if that's all right with you.' He looked at me and tried to smile. The lighter popped, and he pulled it out and brought the orange glow up to his face. When he lit up his cigarette, I saw that his fingers were twitching. He went to put the lighter back, but his hand shook so bad that he couldn't hardly get it in. I heard it tapping against the dash until he finally fit it back in there.

He left the cigarette burning in the corner of his mouth and pulled the gearshift down. He put his arm across the back of my seat and turned his head to back into Miss Lyle's driveway so he could turn his truck around.

The moon looked like it might've been hiding somewhere behind the clouds and the road was dark except where his headlights shined, but his truck was old and his headlights weren't as bright as the lights on my daddy's truck, even though my daddy's truck was a pretty old one too. I couldn't hardly see a thing except for what was right out in the road in front of us. His truck was so old that the insides of the doors had started to rust. When Daddy saw rust like that, he called it 'car cancer,' and I'd heard him say that if you get it inside your truck you might as well give up hope and let it die. I reached out and touched the rust with my fingers, and it crumbled into my hand. I wiped my hand on my blue jeans and saw that it left a dusty brown stain.

'This is an old truck, ain't it?' my grandpa said, but I didn't say nothing back to him.

We rode alongside the river and I looked through the windshield down past the other side of the truck, and I could just barely see the water shining in between the trees in that little bit of moonlight. I thought about me and Stump and Joe Bill skipping rocks this morning, and then I

145

thought about how long ago it seemed that we were all together down there on the bank. Through the trees I could see the lights from Marshall twinkling farther down the river. I knew we'd pass the church soon and if I wanted to I could look to my right out my window at it when we did, but I decided that I didn't want to. I just stared straight out at the headlights, but I knew when we passed the church just the same.

My grandpa took the road up to the highway, and I felt us climbing the hill and I heard his old truck pulling hard like it was straining to make it. When we stopped at the stop sign at the top of the hill, an ambulance turned off the highway and passed us and headed down toward the river from where we'd just come. The ambulance didn't have its emergency lights on or its siren blaring, and I noticed how slow it was driving. I looked out the back window and watched its taillights disappear into the darkness at the bottom of the hill. When I turned around again, I saw that my grandpa was staring at it in his rearview mirror. He sat there just looking at it for a second longer, and then he put his foot on the gas and we turned left onto the highway.

★   ★   ★

'Your daddy and me took a walk in his fields this evening,' he said. 'There's a lot of burley tobacco to be brought in. A lot of work that's needing to be done.' He sat there, and I could tell he was trying to think of something else to say so it wouldn't be so quiet while we drove.

146

'Mr. Gant helps Daddy do all that stuff,' I said, just to let him know that Daddy didn't need him around all the time just because he'd decided to come back and surprise Daddy all of a sudden. I felt him look over at me, but I stared straight ahead at the road.

'Did you know that when your daddy was your age me and him used to work tobacco together?' I shook my head no. 'Well, it's true,' he said. 'I used to have me some burley patches, and I'd take your daddy out in the field with me when he was about as big as you. Now there's a whole mess of tobacco in your daddy's field, and I'm the one helping him.' I felt him look over at me again, and I turned my head and looked out my window and watched the rocky sides of the mountain whip past the truck in the darkness.

'We're going to need some help getting that burley in and getting it hung up in the barn,' he said. 'Would you be interested in helping?'

I didn't answer him. Instead I laid my head back on the seat and closed my eyes and pictured me and Stump hiding out in the barn and spying on Daddy and Mr. Gant like we used to before Mama caught us and whipped us for doing it. Daddy and Mr. Gant have got the sled full of burley, and they're carrying it inside the barn where it's hot and dusty and dark. I like the way our barn smells, and with the burley hanging up in there and drying it takes to smelling sweet and I like it even more. I watch my daddy and some other men climb up the beams toward the ceiling and they wait up there until Mr. Gant starts jerking the burley off the sled. It's so quiet with none of them doing nothing but breathing heavy and passing those sticks of burley up, up, up toward Daddy. I think about looking up to see Daddy way up high off the ground, and I think about how if they'd let me help them my hands would get good and sticky from the tar and I'd try to pick it off my fingers while I waited on Mr. Gant to hand me another load so I could pass it on to somebody else until it ended up in the rafters with Daddy. I opened my eyes and took a quick look over at my grandpa.

'You'd be a big help if you've got a mind for working,' he said. Then he said, 'Let me see your hand.'

'Why?' I asked.

'Just let me see it,' he said. I held out my left hand, and he took it in his. His fingers were tough, and the skin of his palm felt thick and hard. He rubbed his thumb over my palm, and I felt his hand jumping and his fingers twitching like he couldn't keep them still. 'You've got them,' he said. 'I figured you would.' He let go of my hand, and I put it back in my lap.

'Got what?' I asked.

'Farming hands,' he said. 'You got hands just like your daddy. Yes, sir,' he said, 'just like him.'

He turned the knob on the radio and tuned it in to old-timey country music.

'You can put it on whatever you want,' he said.

It only took me a second of listening to the song before I knew it was Patsy Cline. Daddy used to play her records all the time and try and

148

get Mama to dance with him. He said a sweeter, sadder voice never came out of the mountains. I listened to her sing, and I heard that it was a sad, slow song, but I didn't change it. I wasn't interested in listening to nothing else.

★   ★   ★

'You want a cold drink?' my grandpa asked me. He'd pulled off the highway into the parking lot in front of Messley's store and stopped the truck under the little roof by the gas pump. I shook my head no because I didn't want him thinking he had to buy me something just to get me to talk to him.

'I'll get you one just in case,' he said. He opened the door and got out and slammed it shut. The driver's-side window was rolled down, and he folded his arms and rested them on the door and looked in at me. 'What kind of drink you want?' he asked.

'It don't matter,' I said.

'You like Sun Drop?'

'It's fine,' I said.

'What about a Nehi Peach?'

'It don't matter,' I said again.

He turned, and I watched him walk out of the light coming from under the roof and across the dark parking lot to the screen door that led inside the store. The fluorescent lights were bright in there, and they made everything right outside the store seem even darker than it was. Some folding chairs and a couple of rockers sat outside the screen door, and I knew Mr. Messley and some other old men would stay outside and talk and smoke pipes and cigarettes all day when it was hot. Daddy said Mr. Messley was so old that his spine had gone crooked and that was why he was so hunched over and always carried a cane. When he sat outside he leaned his cane against his knee, and he kept it there until it was time for him to get up again. When people walked by on their way into the store, they said, 'Hey, Messley,' and Mr. Messley grumbled under his breath because he knew he had to get up and go inside just to see if they wanted anything.

There was a bug zapper plugged in and hanging just under the metal roof by the gas pump, and I sat in my grandpa's truck and looked through the windshield and watched it fry moths and mosquitoes. It glowed purple, and every now and then I heard it zap a bug and I saw a little spark shoot out. I could hear the crickets out in the shadows too, and I listened to them chirping, and then I heard my grandpa's voice inside the store. I heard a loud noise like something had just crashed to the floor, and then I heard Mr. Messley and my grandpa yelling at each other.

My grandpa pushed open the screen door so hard that it slammed against the wall and swung back and slammed shut again. Mr. Messley opened the screen door behind my grandpa and came hobbling outside with his cane like he was chasing him. His face was red and angry-looking, and he was shaking his fist.

'I ain't never done it once on a Sunday!' he

hollered. 'And I sure as hell ain't going to start doing it for you!'

My grandpa walked toward the truck, but he stopped and turned around and looked at Mr. Messley. He stood there and stared at him for a minute like maybe he was thinking about punching him, and I pictured him hollering for my daddy and running through the yard before he kicked that man in the face, and in my mind I watched that man's nose spray blood all over his shirt. But my grandpa didn't do nothing to Mr. Messley. He just stood there and stared at him. The sound of that bug lamp zapping those moths was the only thing I could hear. I couldn't even hear those crickets now. My grandpa opened the door to the truck, and Mr. Messley went back inside. I could see him watching us through the screen door.

My grandpa slammed the door, and it made the whole truck shake. 'Goddamn it!' he said. He punched the steering wheel as hard as he could, and it made the horn honk. 'Goddamn it,' he said again. He put both his hands on the steering wheel like he might try and tear it off and throw it out the window, and his knuckles went white because he squeezed it so tight.

'You better get on out of here!' Mr. Messley hollered from behind the screen door.

My grandpa looked over at him, and then he cranked the engine and pulled down the gearshift and stomped on the pedal. The tires squealed, and we flew out of the parking lot and turned onto the highway and then it was quiet again except for the sound of the engine carrying us up the hill away from the lights of Mr. Messley's store.

All that hollering had scared me, especially after what I'd seen at Miss Lyle's house, and I tried as hard as I could to keep from crying. I didn't want my grandpa to see me, and I turned my head to let the air come in the window and dry my face. I wanted to stop crying once and for all, but I couldn't. I'd just about given myself a headache with all the crying I'd already done.

My grandpa reached over and patted my leg. He had hands like Daddy too, and it felt like sandpaper scratching against my blue jeans. I pulled my feet up into the seat, and I wrapped my arms around my knees to make it harder for him to touch me.

'Hey, buddy,' he said. 'It's all right. I didn't mean for none of that to scare you. Messley's a friend of mine. It's all right; I don't want you being scared of me.'

I quit crying and sat up straight and put my feet back on the floorboard and used my shirttail to wipe the tears out of my eyes.

'I ain't scared of you,' I said.

My grandpa looked over at me, and then he looked back at the road. He got out his pack of cigarettes from his shirt pocket and shook one loose and put it in his mouth. He pushed the lighter in and waited for it to pop.

'You shouldn't be,' he said. 'You shouldn't be scared of me.'

9

My grandpa stopped his truck in front of our house, and he just sat there and looked up at the porch like he hadn't ever seen the house before. I looked past him out the truck's open window to where the shadow of the barn leaned toward the ridge on the other side of the yard. When I looked closer, I saw a bunch of tiny lights flying around in the darkness.

'Look at all them fireflies,' my grandpa said. He looked over at me. 'You want to catch one?'

'No,' I told him. 'I just want to go inside.'

Me and Stump used to catch lightning bugs all the time and put them in Mama's Mason jars, but they didn't do nothing once they were in there except beat their wings against the glass. Then they'd start to smell funny and they'd just up and die before you knew it. Daddy said they died so quick because they didn't have any air down in there, and he showed us how to punch holes in the lids with nails so they didn't get smothered to death. That was just too much work to think about right then and I didn't feel like messing with them, especially without Stump. He was the one who liked catching them anyway. He liked to turn the lights out and sit the Mason jar in the middle of our bed and get down on his knees and look in at it and wait for it to glow. Sometimes I'd get down on my knees on the other side of the bed and look through the Mason jar at Stump's face. It made his eyes and his nose and mouth all different sizes, and after a while looking at him was like looking through a magnifying glass. He'd kneel there by the bed like he was praying and wait for the lightning bug to glow, and when it did I could just barely see him smiling through the glass with that yellow light spread out across his cheeks.

'Your face looks funny,' I'd tell him, but he'd just sit there and watch that lightning bug and wait for it to glow again.

The Christmas before, when I was in the second grade, my teacher, Miss Bryant, taught us how to make Christmas tree ornaments out of nothing but clay and pipe cleaners. She said we should make an ornament for somebody in our family for Christmas to show them how much we loved them. I thought about making a cross for Mama, but it would've been too easy and too skinny and it wouldn't have looked much like anything hanging on a big old tree. I wanted to make a tractor for Daddy, but it was too hard. I decided I'd make me a firefly and give it to Stump since he liked looking at them so much. I rolled out a piece of that clay until it was about as long as my pinky finger and just a little bit fatter. And then I bent two pipe cleaners into the shape of wings and stuck them in the clay before it dried. The next day, after it was all dry, I dipped the bug's tail into some yellow paint. It looked pretty good to me, and Miss Bryant thought so too.

Mama made a fuss over it when I brought it home from school, and then she hung it on our Christmas tree after Daddy'd sat it up in the front room. I showed Stump where it was hanging on the tree, and even though he wouldn't touch it he stood there and looked at it up close for a long time. I reached out and poked it, and it swung back and forth on the branch like it was flying around.

'Does it look like a firefly to you?' I asked Stump, but of course he didn't say nothing.

But it was gone off the tree before Christmas even came. I asked Mama about it, but she said she hadn't seen it. I figured Stump probably took it down and hid it somewhere in our room. He was always hiding things he liked and things that belonged to him. You could open his drawers or look under his pillow and find all kinds of things: rocks, sticks, dried-up flowers, toys he didn't want getting lost or broken. The only things he didn't hide were the rocks that were ours together. We sat them on the shelves in our room that Daddy'd made for us. Me and Stump would look at our rocks together and try and find stuff about them in Daddy's old encyclopedias. I knew Stump wouldn't ever think about hiding any of those rocks because he knew that we shared them. They were ours together.

* * *

The house was dark inside, and I felt around on the wall by the front door until I found the switch and the table lamp beside Daddy's chair turned on. My grandpa walked right to the refrigerator and opened it and started pushing stuff around like he was looking for something. He looked in the freezer too. Then he closed the freezer door and I watched him go over to the counter and look through the cabinets where Mama kept the food.

'You want something to eat?' he asked me.

'I ain't hungry,' I said. I hadn't had nothing since dinner, but I knew I couldn't eat nothing then.

'Well, you need to eat something,' he said. 'I ain't too much of a hand in the kitchen, but you need to eat something.'

He walked over to the cabinet where Mama kept all the plates and the cups, and he opened it and ran his hand over the plates and then he felt around behind them. He opened another cabinet and just stood there and stared up into it.

'Goddamn it,' he whispered. He turned around and looked at me where I stood in the front room just inside the door. 'Your daddy smoke in the house?' he asked me.

'He don't smoke,' I said.

My grandpa turned around and looked at the cabinets. Then he opened one he'd already opened and he looked inside it again.

'Of course he don't smoke,' he said.

I had to pee, and I walked through the kitchen and down the hallway to the bathroom. I flipped the light switch, but nothing happened. I flipped it a couple more times, but the light over the sink still wouldn't come on. It was dark in there, but I still thought about opening the toilet lid and peeing without the lights, but I couldn't hardly see anything and I was afraid of getting it everywhere. I walked back out into the hallway and opened the back door and looked outside. We had to use the privy out back before Daddy had built us an indoor bathroom, and I saw the outline of it across the dark yard. There wasn't no way I was opening that old door and going in there at night without a flashlight and with nobody to hold the door open for me so I could see a little bit by the moon. In this kind of dark it probably had snakes and all kinds of things hiding out in there. I didn't want to ask my grandpa to hold the door open for me because I didn't want him thinking I was a baby, and I didn't even know if I could pee with him standing there watching me anyway.

I closed the back door behind me and stepped to the edge of the porch and pulled my zipper down. Before I started going I turned my head and looked through the door behind me, and I could see all the way down the hall and into the kitchen. My grandpa was still in there looking through the cabinets. He ducked down, and I knew he was looking under the counter. I peed off the porch, and I heard it wetting down the grass. When I was done, I went inside and walked down the hallway back to the kitchen. My grandpa stood outside on the front porch smoking a cigarette. I could smell the smoke where it was coming through the screen. On the kitchen table was a plate with two pieces of white bread with peanut butter spread all over them. My grandpa heard me, and he turned and looked at me through the screen.

'That's about all I can do,' he said and nodded his head toward the table. He watched me pull out my chair and sit down. I picked up a piece of bread and took a bite. He'd put that peanut butter on there thick, and the bread stuck to the roof of my mouth and I had a time swallowing it. I stood up from the table and got me a glass from the cabinet and went to the refrigerator for the milk. I sat my glass on the counter and poured the milk until my glass was full, and then I put the milk back in the refrigerator and carried my glass to the table.

My grandpa flicked his cigarette into the yard and opened the screen door and came inside. He sat down across the table from me. I took another bite of the bread and chewed on it. I could feel him looking at me.

'What grade you in at school?' he asked me.

I swallowed the bread and took a drink of milk. 'Third,' I said. I looked over at him and saw that he was still staring at me. I looked down at my plate and took another bite of the bread, and then I laid my right hand open on the tabletop and looked at where that little bit of splinter was still stuck down in my palm. With my other hand I picked up my glass of milk and took a good, long drink, and then I sat it down and scratched my palm with my fingernail and looked for the edge of that splinter to see if I could feel it. Just a little bit of it stuck out, but it wasn't quite enough to get ahold of.

'What are you doing?' my grandpa asked. I lifted my hand off the table and opened it up like I was waving so he could see it.

'I got a splinter,' I said.

'Why ain't you pulled it out yet?' he asked me.

'Mama tried,' I said, 'but she couldn't get all of it. She said the rest would work itself out.'

'Good Lord,' he said. He stood up from the table and walked past me and opened one of the cabinets and took down one of Mama's shiny metal mixing bowls. He went over to the sink and ran water in the tap, and then he picked up the dish soap and squeezed a little bit into the bowl. It looked like he was fixing to wash a bowl that was already clean.

'What are you doing?' I asked him.

'A trick,' he said. The water from the tap started to steam, and he held the mixing bowl under the faucet and turned the water down to where it was cooler. Suds started bubbling over the top, and he turned off the water and carried the mixing bowl over to the table. He sat it down in front of me.

'This is going to be a little bit hot at first,' he said, 'but leave your hand in there and let it soak for a few minutes.'

'Why?'

'Because if you want something to get unstuck, then you have to get it slick first,' he said. 'That's why.'

I got up on my knees in the chair and sat back on my shoes, and when I did I felt something sting me in the butt. I looked behind me at my shoes and then I looked in the chair, but there wasn't nothing there. I felt around in my back pocket and found that little piece of quartz rock Stump had given me that morning before Mr. Thompson took him inside the church. I sat it on the table beside the mixing bowl.

'What's that?' my grandpa asked, but I didn't feel like telling him about it.

'Nothing,' I said.

I put my right hand down inside the mixing bowl, and at first the water was almost too hot for me to keep it in there, but I did, and after a few seconds I was used to it. My grandpa sat down at the table in the chair beside mine.

'How'd you learn how to do this?' I asked him.

'Well,' he said, 'if you work with wood long enough you'll figure out how to fix a splinter pretty quick.'

'Are you a carpenter?' I asked him.

'I ain't much of anything right now,' he said, 'but I've been a lot of things. I guess I was one of those at one time.'

I heard him lean back in his chair, and I could feel him watching me. I put my chin down on the table and looked at the side of the mixing bowl. I could see my fuzzy reflection in it, and just beside it I could see my grandpa's face. The reflection of that quartz rock sat right in between us.

'You look just like your daddy,' he said.

I sat there with my chin on the table, and I stared at his fuzzy reflection. I thought about how I could tell him the same thing.

10

I brushed my teeth and washed my face in the bathroom with the lights out and my grandpa went back out on the front porch. I didn't like getting ready for bed without Stump. I wanted to see him looking into the mirror beside me, and I wanted to see him brushing his teeth too. I could imagine him standing there, and I could almost feel his elbow touch my arm when he reached out and turned the water off in the sink. I was glad the lights were burned out; it made him easier to see.

But then I thought about him lying on that bed over at Miss Lyle's house, and then I wondered what Mama and Daddy were doing right then and if they were lying on that bed beside him. I remembered how I saw both of them cry today and just thinking about it made me want to cry too, but I was just too tired to do it.

I walked into the bedroom and turned on the light and looked around. The bed was made up just like me and Stump had left it before we'd gone to church that morning. I kicked off my shoes and reached into my back pocket and pulled out that piece of quartz rock and held it in my hand. It was warm. The shelves Daddy'd made for our rocks were just about full, but I walked over to them anyway and looked for a good place to put Stump's quartz. I sat it down beside a piece of fool's gold that we'd found in the creek, but it didn't seem right to leave it sitting there with all the rocks we'd found together, especially after I'd told him that I'd hold on to it for him.

The closet door was open, and when I looked up at the top shelf I saw Stump's quiet box. I knew there wasn't no chance of Mama or Daddy catching me if I got it down and dropped Stump's quartz rock inside. I figured if Stump was watching me from Heaven, then he probably wouldn't care one bit if I did.

I looked into the hallway and saw that my grandpa was still out on the porch smoking a cigarette. His back was turned, and he leaned against the railing by the porch like he was waiting for somebody to come driving up to the house. I tiptoed out into the kitchen and picked up one of the chairs at the table and brought it back into our bedroom and sat it in front of the closet. I stood up on top of it and reached up into the closet and took down Stump's box. I stepped off the chair and sat the box on the bed. Before I opened it I closed the bedroom door and turned out the light. It took a minute for my eyes to adjust, but there was plenty of light from the moon coming in the window. My grandpa coughed outside on the porch.

I lifted the top off the shoe box and saw it was full of folded paper, some rocks, and a couple of sticks, but sitting right on top of all of it was the firefly Christmas ornament that I'd made for Stump. I lifted it out of the shoe box by the paper clip Mama'd wrapped around it to hang it from the Christmas tree, and I wondered what Stump thought about when he looked at the ornament up close; I wondered if he pictured me and him out in the fields chasing fireflies and trying to scoop them up in Mama's Mason jars, or if he ever opened the quiet box and expected that he might find that firefly glowing. I never knew just what he was thinking, especially when he closed our bedroom door and was all alone with his box, but I hoped that firefly I'd given him made the world quieter for him. I sat the ornament down on the bed and walked over to the shelves and picked up Stump's quartz rock where I'd left it sitting beside that fool's gold. I walked back to the box and dropped the rock down inside, and then I picked up the firefly and sat it back inside too. I put the top back on Stump's quiet box and climbed back up on the chair and put it back on the top shelf where I'd found it. I stared at it for a second, and then I changed my mind. I picked it up again and got down from the chair and slid the quiet box under our bed.

I opened the bedroom door as quiet as I could, and when I peeked out I saw that my grandpa was still standing on the front porch, but he wasn't smoking no more. I picked up the chair and carried it back into the kitchen. He must've heard me because he turned around and looked at me through the screen door.

'You ready for bed?' he asked.

'Almost,' I said.

I walked back into the bedroom and took off my shirt and my blue jeans and got into bed in my jockeys. The windows were open but it was still warm outside, and I kicked off the quilt and only pulled the sheet over me so I wouldn't get to sweating during the night. I laid there and stared up at the ceiling and looked at the shadows the moonlight spread out across it. I could hear the crickets chirping outside and some wind chimes tinkling, and way off in the distance I could hear the water running in the creek at the bottom of the hill. Everything was just like it always was except that Stump wasn't there with me. I rolled over and looked at his side of the bed, and I ran my hand over his pillow. It felt cool against my hand after soaking it in that hot water, and I could feel where my skin had opened up a little after my grandpa used his fingernails to grab hold of that splinter and pull it out.

I tossed my pillow onto the floor by the bed, and then I slid Stump's pillow under my head. It felt almost cold against my face, and for a second I thought I could smell Stump's hair. It smelled like the sheets did when Mama hung them to dry on the line outside when the sun was good and hot. I closed my eyes and ran my hand across Stump's side of the bed, and I imagined he'd just gotten up to pee, and I laid there and listened for his footsteps in the hall.

* * *

164

My eyes were heavy and sleepy when my grandpa came into the room. I felt him sit down on the bed, and I could smell the cigarette smoke in his clothes.

'You asleep, buddy?' he whispered.

'No,' I said. He was quiet, and I laid there and waited for him to say something else. I liked the way the smoke smelled on him and it made me wish Daddy smoked too.

'I hate all this happened today,' he said. 'I hate that you're having to go through all this.'

I opened up my eyes all the way and looked down at the bottom of the bed where he sat. The light was on in the hallway, and I could just barely see his face and the outline of his body.

'When are my mom and dad coming home?' I asked him.

'They'll be home tomorrow,' he said. 'Maybe even before you wake up for school. They've got to take care of your brother tonight.' He looked like he thought about saying something else, but he didn't. He probably figured I wouldn't understand. I could've told him that I understood plenty. I could've told him that I understood that the ambulance was on its way to Miss Lyle's house to get Stump and that its siren wasn't on because they knew he was already dead, and I understood that he was probably at the hospital with Mama and Daddy and a whole bunch of doctors trying to figure out what happened to him. He would've known how much I understood if he'd known what me and Joe Bill had seen.

My grandpa reached out his hand and patted

mine through the sheet. 'Good night,' he said. He started to stand up.

'Where've you been?' I asked him.

He stood up straight and looked down at me. 'Out on the porch,' he said.

'I mean, where've you been all this time?' I said. 'How come me and Stump ain't never seen you before?' I knew Mama would get mad at me for asking him that, but she wasn't there so I went ahead and asked him anyway. He sat down real slow and stared at the bedroom door like he was waiting for somebody else to walk through it. He sighed, and I could tell he didn't want to have to answer a question like that.

'Well,' he said, 'if you've really got to know, I've been all over the place. I spent a couple years driving a rig up and down the coast, hung drywall for a while, worked in a mill up in PA.'

'What's PA?' I asked him.

'Pennsylvania,' he said.

'But why have you been gone so long?'

'I just have,' he said. 'I just went away.'

'Why?'

He sat there quiet like he was thinking hard about what he wanted to say next, and then I saw his head turn like he was looking at me over his shoulder. 'Because sometimes we do things we can't take back, and we need to go away and leave folks alone and let them forget us for a while.'

'What did you do?'

'Lots of things,' he said. Then he said, 'Do you always ask this many questions?'

'No,' I said. 'I was just wondering.'

He turned around so he could see me better. 'Where I've been don't matter as much as me being here now,' he said.

I looked away from him toward the window. I thought about how during the daytime I could see my daddy's tobacco fields all the way up to the road from here. I kept looking at the window, but I knew my grandpa was staring at me.

'Maybe sometime I'll take you up to my place,' he said. 'Show you where I was raised up. We'll go up to the old cabin where I was born and where your daddy grew up. Maybe we'll scout the top field for arrowheads. You think you might want to do that?'

'Sure,' I said, and then I thought about how much Stump liked to find him some arrowheads too so we could sit them on the shelves with the rocks we'd already found. 'I wish my brother could go.'

'Me too, buddy,' he said. 'I hate that he can't. But you know what you can do?'

'What?'

'You can keep his memory,' he said. 'That's the best way to hold on to folks. My mama and daddy have been gone so long that I can't hardly picture them, and I have to remember my memories and hope they're true. Maybe I'll see them again someday and they'll be just how I remember them; maybe not, but I like to think so.'

'You mean in Heaven?'

'Yes,' he said. 'In Heaven.'

I laid there and thought about seeing Stump in Heaven, and then I remembered what Joe Bill

167

had said about Stump not being able to sing or talk or nothing. 'Do you think Stump will be able to talk when he gets to Heaven?' I asked him.

'Of course he will,' he said. 'We'll all be able to talk.' He pulled the sheet up around me. 'And we'll all be able to understand each other.' He stood up again, and then he bent down to the bed and made a show of tucking the sheet tight all around me. He walked over and put his hand on the doorknob and stepped into the hallway.

'You want this door open or closed?' he asked.

'Closed,' I said.

⋆ ⋆ ⋆

I laid in bed in the dark and listened to the sounds of the crickets outside and the little noises of the house settling itself to sleep. That's what Mama used to say at night when I heard something that scared me.

'That's just the sound of the house getting settled,' she'd say. 'It's getting comfortable so it can go to sleep too.'

I saw that the kitchen light still burned under my door, and I listened as my grandpa opened and closed the cabinets and the drawers like he was still looking for something. I heard him open the door and go into Mama and Daddy's room too. I turned away from the door and away from Stump's side of the bed and looked out the window.

There was just a little bit of breeze out there, and I could feel it coming in on my face and I could see it moving the branches on the tree outside the window and I could hear it playing on the wind chimes. If it had been daylight, I could've looked out at the field and seen the tops of the burley swaying back and forth. There were still some lightning bugs out there, and I watched their lights wink off and on while they floated through the yard. My eyes got heavy, and before I knew it I was drifting off to sleep again, and when I looked up I was sitting at the dining room table back at Miss Lyle's house. I didn't think there was anybody else there but me.

I heard the screen door slam shut, and I wondered if it was somebody coming inside the house or if it was just somebody stepping out onto the porch. I sat at the table just as still as I could, and I listened hard and soon I heard somebody's footsteps crunching in the gravel. It sounded like they were walking away from the house and down the driveway toward the road, and I wondered where they were going. I wondered if it was Daddy leaving Miss Lyle's to go to the hospital or if it was the sheriff leaving Stump on the bed with Mama, or maybe it was Miss Lyle stepping outside to wipe the blood off those men's faces. I couldn't hear the footsteps anymore, but I knew they hadn't stopped but had just kept on walking until they were so far down the road that I couldn't hear them anymore. I wanted to push back my chair and open my eyes, but I was so sleepy that I couldn't hardly get myself to wake up.

I pushed the sheet off me and rolled over toward the window to try and see where the footsteps in my dream had gone. It had gotten foggy outside, but there was a little bit of soft light coming from the moon and shining down on the field. The way it looked made me think I might still be dreaming. There wasn't nobody out there that I could see. It was just my daddy's field and the moon and the noise of those crickets chirping and the sound of the breeze rustling the leaves and blowing on the wind chimes hanging on the tree outside the window. My daddy's tobacco swayed back and forth in the wind, and I stared out at the field until my eyes got heavy and I felt them going back to sleep. But just before I got them closed again I saw a light burning in the field, and I saw something moving way out in the burley. I tried to open my eyes all the way to get a better look, but I was so sleepy that I could just barely see the light from the lamp at my grandpa's feet where he stood out in the middle of the field under the moon. He had a burley knife in his hand, and he was sticking my daddy's tobacco.

Clem Barefield

11

The best I can remember, I'd had Jimmy Hall in handcuffs three times before my son died: twice for slapping his wife around and once for being drunk and disorderly at the high school football game. I couldn't ever get his wife to press charges on him after I'd come all the way up there to Gunter Mountain to get him off her, and at the football game he didn't do anything but bust out his own teeth falling down the steps up in the bleachers. He was a real piece of shit, and even though he'd come back to Madison County to find his oldest grandson dead, I had a hard time feeling the least bit sorry for him. But I felt different about Ben.

Seeing them together, still father and son, an old man and a young man after all these years, made it hard to believe that I'd once tried to protect Ben Hall from his daddy. It was even harder to believe after he'd made some kind of name for himself on the football field up in Cullowhee, harder still when I thought about my son, Jeff, lying dead on the side of the road back in Madison. I never figured I'd have to protect my own boy from Jimmy Hall too, and I guess there's no way I could've known. But still, when

171

I get to thinking about it, there are times when I want to be pissed at Jeff and pissed at those boys for not having the balls or the sense enough to complain about him showing up to work like that, but then I catch myself. *Slow down,* I think. *You ain't got nobody to be pissed at but yourself for letting Jeff go with him. You knew better than all the rest of them.* And that's true, and I know it. I knew better than that. But for some reason I didn't stop Jeff. I trusted Jimmy Hall with my son when I wouldn't even trust him with his own. And then I get to thinking, *This one's on you, Clem. You ain't got nobody else to blame but yourself.*

I've heard it said before that those who don't learn from the past are bound to repeat it, and I just don't know what I think about that. I figure I don't have too much use for it. The past will just weigh on you if you spend too much time remembering it. It's like putting on a pair of heavy waders and stepping out to midriver where the fishing's best. Those waders will fill with water if you get too deep, and if you're stupid enough to stay out there a while there ain't a damn thing you can do to keep from being pulled under. I think about that sometimes when I recall the sound of my secretary's voice coming across the CB. In my mind it feels like I'm hearing her from deep under the water, something about an explosion on the lines outside of town. I'm right there, listening just below the surface of that water, wondering why this is something I have to hear.

'Is it Jeff?' I asked her.

'I don't know,' she said. 'They don't know who it is. They can't tell.'

'Jesus, Eileen, is it?'

'I don't know,' she said again.

'I'm headed that way.'

'Bill's going to meet you there,' she said.

Eileen didn't even have to say it, because something told me that it was Jeff. I threw on my siren and drove as fast as I could through the snow down Highway 25/70, and on the whole drive over I couldn't keep from thinking about how unfair it would be if it was Jeff. But since then I've learned to just go ahead and take fairness out of the equation. If you do, things stand the chance of making a whole lot more sense.

★   ★   ★

Somebody had moved him out of the road by the time I got there and left his body at the edge of the woods. Bill Owens was standing by him when I pulled up. When he heard my car he turned around, and I sat there behind the wheel and watched his mouth twitch like he was trying to think of the words that could tell me. But I reckon he couldn't find them, so he just took off his gloves and lowered his eyes and pointed out there toward the tree line.

I sat there for just a second longer and watched the snow come down and light on the branches. It was quiet, seems like snow always makes it quiet and it seems like I'm always surprised by that. I knew that when I opened the

173

car door things would change forever, and I reckon it took some building up to it for me to go ahead and do it. I stepped out and walked toward Owens, but I stopped when my eyes hit on what lay under that rhododendron thicket. They'd draped a blue sheet over him, and it was flecked white where the snow had managed to drift down through the branches. The sheet didn't quite cover all of him, and I could see his work boots, and when I looked closer I could see his toes where the rubber soles had burned away. They steamed against that cold air. Me and Owens stood there together in silence and listened to the sound of steam hissing under that sheet.

'You sure?' I asked

'I am,' Owens said. He raised his hand like he was going to touch me on the shoulder, and I can't rightly remember if he did or not. But I remember the sound of his hand dropping to his side when he couldn't think of what to say next. There wasn't anything for him to say, and I knew it. Not a thing he could've done but just stand there with me. He looked down the road, and when he did I turned and saw where a group of boys had huddled up around the ambulance. We were too far away to hear what they were saying, and it seemed like the snow swallowed their voices. It was coming down in big, heavy flakes and making everything white. It couldn't have been no more than fifteen degrees.

'I should ask those boys some questions,' he said. He lowered his head and walked down the road. When he was gone my stomach lurched, and I figured I was about to empty my gut right there on the roadside. I squatted down and picked up a couple handfuls of snow and rubbed it all over my face to keep from getting sick. I could hear footsteps crunching in the snow behind me.

'I'm sorry, Sheriff,' somebody's voice said. I looked up and saw that a paramedic had left the group at the ambulance and was standing right over my shoulder. He looked like he might've been twenty-five, just a few years older than Jeff.

'You haven't called my wife.'

'No, sir.'

'Don't. Make sure nobody does.'

I picked up a few more handfuls of snow and rubbed it down the back of my neck and covered my eyes with my hands. My fingers burned from the cold. I held that snow to my cheeks until my face went numb.

When I stood up, my stomach jumped again and I turned my back to the tree line and spit in the snow. I looked down the road and saw three boys in coveralls and heavy coats smoking cigarettes and talking to Owens. He had a notepad in his hand and looked like he was asking them questions. I wiped my mouth with the sleeve of my coat and nodded toward them.

'Who are they?'

'Part of the crew,' said the paramedic. 'They're pretty shook up. One of them must have pulled him out of the road when he came off the line. He was lying under them bushes when we got here.'

I looked down and saw that the tracks that had

been left from dragging Jeff out of the road were beginning to fill with snow, and my eyes followed them to where his body lay covered under that sheet. The line to the blown transformer ran through the trees overhead, and the wooden pole around the box was scorched black from the explosion. I looked at Jeff's body under the arbor, and then I turned and walked down the highway toward the ambulance. The boys saw me coming and put out their cigarettes in the snow with the toes of their boots. I didn't recognize any of them.

'All three of y'all work on this crew?' I asked.

'Yes, sir,' said a short blond-headed boy. His hair was cropped close and sharp and made his ears look bigger than they probably were.

'Where's your foreman?' I asked.

He didn't have nothing to say to that question, and I faced him and squared my shoulders. His eyes were scared, and he looked like he was about to cry.

'Where is he?'

He looked to the two boys standing behind him for help, but they both lowered their eyes and I could tell they didn't want to say nothing either.

'He left before the ambulance got here,' the first boy said. 'He took the service truck and told us to wait.'

'Was he drinking?'

He wanted one of the other boys to answer that question, but they wouldn't even look at him. One shook a cigarette from a pack and the other kept his eyes fixed on the road.

'Goddamn it, was he drinking!'

'Sheriff,' Owens said. He placed his hand on my arm like he was thinking about pulling me away from the boy, but I shrugged him off and stepped closer.

'Answer me!'

'I don't know,' the boy stammered. 'I don't know for sure.'

I looked down the road where that blue sheet was just barely visible through the trees.

'Which one of you moved him out of the road?' I asked.

'Mr. Hall did,' the boy smoking the cigarette finally said.

I stared at him until he looked away, and then I pulled Owens aside and asked him what they'd had to say. He looked down at his notepad, but I could see that he hadn't written a thing.

'Jeff was on the line working the transformer,' he said. 'They figure something must have made contact, maybe something on his tool belt. It wouldn't let him go. They had to wait for him to come off.'

'Jesus, Bill.' I turned away from him and put my hands over my eyes and then rubbed them across my face.

'I'm sorry,' he said. 'You should go on home to Sheila. I can take care of this.'

'You can't take care of this,' I told him. 'Nobody can take care of this.' I turned to walk back to my cruiser, but I stopped and faced him again. 'I want you to find Jimmy Hall. I want you to radio me when you do.'

When I got back to the cruiser, I sat in the

driver's seat and stared down the road and watched Owens talk to the boys. One of the paramedics had pulled the ambulance around and was backing it toward the woods.

I picked up the CB and radioed the office in Marshall and Eileen answered immediately.

'You okay?' she asked.

'I don't know,' I told her. 'I haven't thought about it yet. I need you to call the house and tell Sheila that I'll be home late.'

'You need to be at home right now,' she said.

'I can't,' I said. 'Jimmy Hall's done run off. I need you to telephone Sheila.'

I put the CB on the cradle, but then I thought better of it. I picked it up and radioed Marshall again. The static of Eileen's voice came back over the line.

'Eileen,' I said. 'She doesn't know about any of this. Tell her I'm running late. That's all.'

It was getting dark, and the snow took on an eerie blue color against the clouds. I sat and watched the paramedics unfold the gurney out of the ambulance and roll it toward the shadows at the edge of the woods. I didn't want to be there when they carried Jeff away, so I cursed myself out loud and turned the car around in the road and drove north toward Gunter Mountain.

★　★　★

Night was full on when I knocked the car into first gear and headed up the mountain. There was already a set of tire tracks in the snow, and I eased the cruiser into them. The gravel heading up the mountain was warmer than the asphalt had been on the road, and I could feel my tires searching the snow for pieces of rock to catch the tread. There weren't any streetlights up there, and the trees rose up out of the darkness on both sides. Even though I couldn't see it, I knew the land fell away sharply on my right and rolled down toward the bottom of the cove. Had it been daylight, I could've searched through the trees and seen farms and houses tossed like shot across the valley floor.

It had been a couple years since I'd been out to Jimmy Hall's place, but I'd been out there enough to know exactly where it was. Ben was up at Western then, and Hall's wife had left him for good about three years before. Things had been quiet until now.

I turned my headlights off in front of Hall's place and pulled into the gravel drive. A light burned in the window, and a wisp of smoke escaped the chimney. I parked the cruiser by the house and opened the door slowly and sat there half out of the car and wondered what I was going to do.

The porch steps squeaked under my boots, and I stopped and listened like somebody else had made the sound. I undid the holster snap over my pistol and knocked on the door. There wasn't any noise from the inside, and I stood there and listened close to make sure. I imagined Hall behind the door with a hand cannon, drunk as hell and holding his breath, hoping I'd leave. I knocked again and didn't hear a sound. I gave the door a try, but it was locked.

I turned the car around in the gravel and headed back out to the road. My high beams fell into the trees across the way, and I could tell by the sagging limbs that the snow was getting heavy. I looked to my right and saw the tire tracks I'd followed coming up the mountain, but just as I was about to turn out of the driveway, I noticed another pair of tracks on the left that I hadn't seen on the way up.

Hot air gushed from the vents in the dash, and I sat there with it blowing in my face and I stared out at those tracks and wondered who could be at the top of that road. I didn't know what the hell I'd do if it was Jimmy Hall up there, but I knew either way I didn't have a choice but to go and take a look.

★ ★ ★

My front fenders made awful scraping sounds as they plowed through the high snow. The ruts were deep, and my car had trouble on the inclines where the snow was packed hard and frozen solid. I held tight to the steering wheel and stared out at the headlights. Every now and then I looked out the windows and searched for tire tracks that led to side roads and switchbacks, but the light in front of my car made the darkness on either side seem that much darker.

I hit deep snow just before the crest of a hill and my car struggled, and I knew if I stopped I'd be stuck for sure, so I eased onto the gas. I didn't know the road at the top bore to the left, and I came over too fast and fought with the turn. My

180

back end came around and threw me out of the tracks, and I slid sideways into a ditch. The car lurched like it was about to tip. I held my breath and waited for the car to flip and the roof to cave in and trap me inside.

But when the car came to a stop, I realized it wasn't going to flip, and I could tell that my right-side tires were a couple feet below the road, and, although I knew it wouldn't help, I pressed hard on the gas and listened as they dug themselves deeper into the gully. The left-side tires kicked up snow and mud onto my windows.

I killed the engine and sat there and stared at the CB. I picked it up and thought about radioing the station, but then I looked out at the tracks. They continued out of the reach of my headlights and climbed farther up the mountain. I shut off my lights and stepped out of the car and onto the road. My eyes adjusted to the dark, and I could see that the snow was deep up here and still coming down. If it'd been fifteen degrees outside of Marshall, then I knew it couldn't be no more than ten up on Gunter. But I figured that if the tracks had been more than a few hours old, they'd have been covered by now. I pulled my coat tight around me and set out walking up the mountain.

★　★　★

I'd been following the tire tracks for about ten minutes when I heard a muffled noise atop a crest in the road. It was a soft sound, and at first I couldn't make out what it was. I slowed down and crept up the hill in the hope that I'd see whoever was up there before they saw me.

Up ahead, parked just off the left side of the road, was the service truck one of the boys at the scene had mentioned. Even though I was a pretty good distance behind it, I could hear that the hushed noise was the sound of country music blaring from inside the cab.

I came up from behind the driver's window and saw Jimmy Hall sitting inside the truck with his head leaned against the steering wheel. I took a second and planted my feet firmly in the snow, and then I flung the door open and grabbed him by the collar and pulled him out. His feet kicked all along the floorboards, and empty beer cans and crushed cigarette packs tumbled out into the snow. A country song blasted from the radio, and I slammed the door and the music throbbed against the windows.

He struggled with me good for a minute, and he tried to pry my hand from around his collar, but he was too surprised and drunk to fight. I drug him around in front of the headlights and forced him to his knees in the snow. I pulled my gun out of my holster and whipped him across the face with the barrel. The sound was dull and heavy, like hitting a tree trunk with a bat. I whipped him again and heard the bridge of his nose crack. Blood came out heavy like tar, and I watched it run into his mouth and down the front of his coat. He chewed on it like it was a plug of tobacco he was trying his best not to swallow. He wanted to talk, but his words sounded like his tongue was thick. He looked up

182

at me and tried to blink the heavy snowflakes out of his eyes.

'It was a goddamned accident,' he finally said. He tried to clear his throat, and he coughed and spattered blood onto my hand and my sleeve. 'It was an accident,' he said again.

I held him by the collar and stared down at him until he quit talking. He rolled his head forward, and his body went limp like he'd passed out. I cocked the hammer on my pistol and put the barrel to his forehead. I raised his face to mine.

Sometimes, when I get to thinking about it, I wish I'd have blown his damn head off right there and left him laid up in the snow with his brains hanging up in the limbs of some old pine tree. I didn't do it, but I'll be damned if I don't think about it every day. Every single day. I'll be damned if I don't think about how easy it would've been just to take care of it all right there.

'Jesus,' he said.

We stayed like that for a while, me standing and Hall on his knees in the snow with the barrel of my gun against his head. It was quiet, but I could hear the heavy flakes light on the tree branches overhead, and I heard the hushed pulse of music coming from the stereo inside the truck. A baying dog wailed in the cove below us.

'Ask those boys,' he whispered.

I lifted my boot and pushed him onto his back and out of the beam of the headlights. I raised my pistol and squeezed the shot into the trees overhead. It rang through the woods and echoed

183

across the valley. A screech owl flushed at the noise and swooped down from the darkness above. I turned in time to see it soar across the road and disappear into the snow-covered boughs of a pine.

Jimmy lay on the roadside breathing heavy. I walked over and stood above him. 'Get up,' I said. He didn't move. I kicked him, but he still didn't move. I put my pistol back in the holster and reached down and grabbed his collar with both hands and pulled him to his feet. He had trouble standing up, and I leaned him against the front fender and rifled through his pockets.

'Jesus,' he muttered. 'I thought you were going to kill me.'

'I ain't decided not to yet,' I said.

I opened the driver's-side door to the truck and took the keys out of the ignition. The radio went off, and the night was suddenly silent and still. I walked a piece up the road and stopped at the edge of the woods and looked into the darkness where I knew the trees were standing. Then I threw the keys as far as I could, and I listened to them ricochet off the tree branches and trunks until the sound of their falling was swallowed by the snow. My eyes adjusted to the dark, and I saw that the road continued a hundred yards up the mountain and disappeared around a bend. Through the trees I could see a few lights shining in the valley. I went back to the truck and found Jimmy leaning against the hood where I'd left him.

I opened the door and pushed him into the truck. 'You can walk home when you sober up,' I said. It was dark and I could barely see him, but I heard him groan as he sprawled his body out on the bench seat. I knew he'd die if he passed out in that cold truck up on that mountain. I didn't find that to be too bad of an option, and I slammed the door to the truck and walked back down the road.

★   ★   ★

The snow hadn't quite filled his tire tracks in, and I walked just between them on my way to the car. It was late, and the lights in the valley to my left were beginning to wink off for the night. I turned my collar up to keep out the snow, and I buried my hands deep inside my coat pockets. The wind picked up and blew through the trees off in the darkness on the right-hand side of the road. The creaking limbs and branches sounded like hundreds of squeaky doors opening and closing in an old farmhouse.

When I reached the car, I opened the door and climbed inside. The seat followed the slope of the car and tilted down into the ditch and made it difficult to sit upright. I slid down the vinyl toward the passenger side and settled my back against the door. I started the engine and radioed the station in Marshall and told them where I was.

'How's the weather up there?' asked dispatch.

I took my finger off the receiver and looked out the windshield. 'I'm sweating my ass off,' I said. 'What the hell do you think it's like?'

The line was quiet.

'I'll send someone up that's got a wrench,' he finally said.

'I'll be here.'

I set the CB back on its cradle and cranked the heat. Hot air poured out of the vents and my face and ears got warm. I held out my hands and felt the blood slowly creep into my fingers.

I watched the windows fog over, and I pictured Sheila in the kitchen at home, reading a book or flipping through a magazine and looking up now and then to check the window for headlights and listening for the sound of a car door being closed. I didn't know how in the world I was going to tell her about Jeff, but I kept forcing myself to remember that I knew the routine: the pause on the steps of a stranger's porch before you knocked on the front door, the awkwardness of answering questions and drinking coffee in the kitchen while you watched a family grieve. I'd broken this news what felt like a hundred times, but now it was my own family, and I'll be damned if I could remember how to do it.

It almost seemed like payback for all the times I'd sat in those kitchens answering questions, thinking about nothing but the hot dinner and the cold beer I was missing, the warm fireplace and the boots I was ready to kick off and leave on the bedroom floor. But now the comfort of those things was far from my mind, and I couldn't think of anything except the fear on Sheila's face while I stumbled through what I had to tell her, expecting any minute to hear Jeff's keys in the front door, the sound of his footsteps coming through the foyer, his body filling up the doorway in the kitchen. His voice saying, 'Mama, why are you crying?'

But the new memory of Jeff's body smoldering on the roadside forced itself into my head and forced out those imaginings, and just below the noise of the cruiser's engine and the steady stream of the heat coming from the vents I could hear the sound of steam hissing beneath that blue sheet. I thumped the back of my head against the passenger-side window and tried to keep the tears out of my eyes.

★ ★ ★

It seemed like hours had passed when I heard the noise of metal striking metal underneath the cruiser. I opened my eyes and saw pale, murky light coming through the fogged-over glass. Somebody's fist beat hard on the driver's-side window, and I slid up the bench seat and wiped away the condensation. Bright light poured through the cleared spot, and I squinted my eyes against it.

Jimmy Hall's face pressed itself against the other side of the glass. Both his eyes were already dark and swollen, and the bridge of his nose was split open and bleeding from where I'd cracked him with my pistol. I sat and stared at him, and I wondered if he had anything in his hands that I couldn't see.

'Pop your clutch and drop it in neutral,' he said.

I was too shocked to move, and I watched him

turn and walk back to his truck, where I lost him in the glow of the headlights. A second later his truck's engine roared and I felt something tug at the front of my car. I killed the engine and put it in neutral and opened the door and struggled out into the snow. The cruiser lurched in the ditch behind me.

'What are you doing?' I yelled over the noise. His headlights hid his face behind the windshield, and I ran toward his truck and beat on the hood. The snow was near blinding, but I could make out his face once I was through the light. He stared at me through the glass. 'I don't want your help!' I hollered.

Behind me I heard the frame of the cruiser groan as the towline popped from the snow and cinched tight under the strain. Hall slowly backed the truck away from me and the high beams hit my eyes again and all I could see was the bright light through the falling snow. I stood and stared into his retreating headlights.

The cruiser's undercarriage breached the top of the ditch, and the frame scraped against the packed snow. I turned just in time to see it loose itself and roll out of the gully and into the road. When it did, the towline swung with it and tore through my pants leg and ripped into my thigh. I fell to my knees. My hand went toward the pain, and I could feel where my pants were already warm with blood.

The engine on Hall's truck geared down, and he put it in park and stepped out onto the road. I scrambled to my feet and saw his silhouette coming toward me in the light. He stumbled past me and bent to the ground and unhooked the towline.

'I had an extra key,' he said on the way back to his truck.

'I didn't need your help.'

'You got it anyway,' he said. He cranked the winch, and I watched as the line slid along through the snow and came to a stop at his bumper. He fastened the hook to the line. 'You broke my nose,' he said.

'I wish I'd shot you,' I told him.

'I don't expect that to change now,' he said.

'It won't.'

'I didn't expect it would.'

He looked up, and we stared at each other and I realized how quiet it was once the roar of the truck and the sound of our voices had died away. I walked to my car and climbed inside and cranked the engine and put it in reverse. My thigh throbbed from where the line had torn into my skin. I heard Hall yell for me to stop, and I turned and looked out the windshield. He stood in the light of my high beams.

'I'm sorry about your boy!' he hollered. I sat and looked at him, and then I turned my cruiser around and headed down the mountain.

*   *   *

When I got home, I parked at the top of the driveway and stared at the house. All the lights were off inside, and it was silent. I stepped out of the car and leaned onto the hood and listened to the engine cool. Snow fell down into the collar of my coat, and my hands felt heavy and cold. A lamp turned on in the bedroom and light slowly flooded the house, and I knew Sheila was inside moving from room to room on her way down the stairs to the door. She stepped onto the porch and called my name, but I couldn't figure out how to open my mouth and answer her.

She walked down the steps, and I watched her silhouette move across the snow-covered lawn against the bright light of the house. She stopped once to pull her robe around her and kick the snow from her slippers. She reached me and looked into my face.

'Where've you been?' she asked, and then she waited for me to say something. She gave me a worried smile. 'You're going to be a snowman soon if you stand out here too much longer.'

I looked down at her and tried to think of what to tell her first, but I felt like I'd been buried deep in the snow and that she'd arrived just in time to dig me out. I opened my mouth to speak, and I felt the cold air on my tongue and saw the heat from my breath rise like smoke before me.

Adelaide Lyle

12

Yes, I remember it all: Elizabeth and Lottie coming over from the church and showing up at my door just after dark on Sunday evening, Julie right there in between them, hardly able to stand up on her own. Them two getting her to lie down on the sofa in the front room and then taking me into the kitchen to tell me what had happened, and me asking 'Why?' over and over, 'Why? Why was that boy in the church again?' I tried my best to keep my voice low so Julie couldn't hear it, but each time the question just got louder and louder because those two women didn't have no answer for me. 'Why?' And then all that fighting out there in the yard.

It wasn't but Tuesday morning, just two days later, that Sheriff Barefield came back to ask me all about them bringing Christopher over to my house after it had happened, and 'Wasn't it you who always watched those kids?' All I could give him was a 'yes' to that question and nothing else, not because I didn't want to but because there wasn't nothing else for me to give. But if I'd have wanted to, I could've told that story from the very beginning, thinking back years and years ago to a night when I trudged up that mountain in the snow because Ronnie Norman's truck wouldn't go no farther. And now the sheriff coming here and sitting down in my kitchen all bucked up like a rooster, staring me in the eyes like there was something else to it, something I wasn't telling him. Something I didn't want to say. Like I couldn't remember the look on Julie Hall's face when that little boy crowned and I lifted the hood from his eyes: eyes as crystal clear as spring water and not a lick of fear in them. Clear like glass and him staring up at me without ever opening his mouth to cry. It seems like it was so long ago, but I remember it all. I may be an old woman now, but I can remember it all. I remember the very night he was born like it was yesterday.

When I heard it, I sat straight up in bed.

'What's that?' I said, and wouldn't you know there wasn't a soul there to answer. Never had been nobody but me, but still there I was sitting straight up in my bed. 'Who's there?' I called like I expected an answer from a voice that hadn't ever been there. I've lived alone just about all my life except for those years up on Parker Mountain with my great-aunt before she sent me off the mountain and down into town.

There wasn't a single time when I was little that I didn't live with her in that old cabin that smelled like dried leaves and lavender in the winter and damp earth and bergamot in the hot summertime. She was a storyteller if there ever was one, and she'd shell beans into a patch quilt she'd spread out across her lap and talk about

192

my dead mama and daddy like they'd just stepped out into the yard to check the sky for rain clouds. My only memory of my mama is a wispy shadow thrown against the cabin wall by candlelight, and in my mind my daddy is a black shadow blotting out the sun in a cleared field. But she brought them back to me and made sure I understood the lives that had come before my own.

Her memory was sharp as a blade. She could remember the exact year of the best burley tobacco crop she'd ever raised, and she could tell you the name and lineage of just about every person up on Parker Mountain, even though most of them folks had less than nothing to do with us. She'd shuck bushel after bushel of corn in the candlelight and tell me the names of all the animals on her daddy's and granddaddy's farms. I'd work alongside her and listen to her talk as far into the night as she'd let me. I was just an itty-bitty little thing, even for my age, and she was the oldest person I knew, and I thought she must have been the oldest person who had ever lived.

It was 1919 the year I left her, the year she made me go. Late spring, and hadn't nothing come up out of the ground fit to eat, and Lord knows we didn't have no cash money and nothing to trade with. There wasn't much to go around for none of us then.

'You need to get off this mountain and down to the city and get yourself set up to a job,' she said. 'We ain't going to last the summer through on what we got, and besides, it's time you lit out on your own. Girls your age been give away by now and laid up with a baby or two and a piece of land all theirs.'

I was fourteen, and I didn't know any better; I just figured she wanted to get rid of me. I didn't know we'd have both probably died had I stayed the summer through.

Now, I had me a choice to make between Marshall, which is the county seat, Burnsville over there in Yancey County, and Asheville. Well, I'd been to Marshall once or twice before and back then there wasn't too much there but the courthouse and a couple of feed stores and the like, and I figured Burnsville wasn't much better than that, and knowing what I know now it would've been a long, tough trip there. I decided I'd go to Asheville, and I can tell you this, and this may surprise you when you hear it, but that's the farthest away from Madison County I've ever been. I ain't never had no reason to go no farther.

* * *

But if I don't remember coming into the city that Saturday evening in the spring with all those trees budding along the French Broad River, that man on the wagon that carried me in from Weaverville pointing to that brown water and saying 'We had us a flood here three years ago,' and then I looked out on the banks and seen some of them market and warehouse buildings all tore up from the river rising like it did and carrying with it all them tree limbs and all that trash and whole heaps of other stuff from downstream.

We came in the city from the north, and if that wasn't the dangdest thing I'd ever seen, taking that cart through the farmer's market on Lexington Avenue and all that food looking like it had just been ripped off the vine and all them chippies there wearing their makeup and their powder and waiting on them farm boys to close up their stands and pack up their wagons and spend a little time with them before lighting back out for the country. We rode right through there, and my head almost fell off with all the looking around I done.

'Where you wanting me to stop?' that man asked me.

'It don't much matter,' I told him. He must've thought he had a real mountain yokel on his hands, and I can't say I much blame him. If I wasn't the greenest thing he'd ever seen, then I don't know what was.

'Well, what kind of work are you hoping to find?' he asked me.

'That don't much matter neither,' I said.

That must've frustrated him because that man stopped that wagon right smack in the center of town with all those cars and trolleys whizzing by and me sitting up there all bright-eyed and scared. He sat there with the reins in his hands and watched me get down and dust myself off and reach up for my little piece of luggage.

'What you figuring on doing now?' he asked me.

'I'm figuring on finding me some work,' I told

him, and it wasn't hardly no time at all before I'd done just that.

That night I found me a bed in a little tenement shack for girls, and the next day I took a job as a laundress taking in wash from the summer folks who stayed in the boardinghouses around the square and uptown in the hotels. And Lord, if those folks from places like Charleston and Atlanta and Savannah didn't have just about the nicest, finest clothes I'd ever seen. But even all that fine fabric didn't make that job no easier; washing is some hard work on your hands. You keep them wet like that for long enough, and you can just about peel off your skin like an onion. It'll give you some soft hands, but Lord if they don't get to hurting you good after you done it awhile. I hated it, but that was about all the work I could find. It was early summer and a good three months before the apple season sprung out there in the south of town and there wasn't no tobacco coming in yet, so washing was about all the work I could get and about all the experience I had with the kinds of jobs folks did in town.

I washed clothes like the devil all summer long to keep my belly full and my back covered, and the first day them tobacco barns on the river opened up I was down there trying to hustle up a little work. They took one look at me, a skinny little girl from the hills, and they said, 'What in the world do you know about tobacco?'

Of course I'd worked burley all my life, and I told them, 'I know more about it on both ends than you do on this one. You let me work for you and pay me a fair take, and I'll show you just what I know.' And let me tell you, there was me at fourteen hustling that market like nobody's business.

'You there,' I might say to some or other seller, 'what in the world did you do, drag that burley through the French Broad on your way here? Y'all going to have to dry that out good before it gets on this scale,' and 'Yes, sir, you got yourself a right pretty crop, and we want to make you a right pretty deal to go with it.' I used to carry on like that just about all the time, trying to get those buyers a good price.

They'd say, 'Where in the world did you learn to talk burley like that?' and I'd go into some or other long windy about being born with a burley knife already in my hand, and I'll be doggone if some of them fellers didn't want to believe it.

But if that wasn't a tough time for folks with all the boys gone off to fight and then bringing that sickness home. It wasn't bad enough the city was about slam full of lungers. You could see them sitting up on the screened porches of some of the sanitariums along the road from town and on the way to the tobacco barns. Folks would try and hide it, but you could tell them right off when you saw them. Just sickly looking and trying their best to hide those little handkerchiefs, those little red spots on the cotton. When the boys started coming home from the war in spells, it got a whole lot worse than it was before. The flu they brought home with them just spelled out disaster, and not only in town neither, and not just in this part of the country. Thousands died, thousands. We ain't never seen the like of it since, and I hope we don't in my day. Whole families just up and dying in only a week or two. Ain't never seen the like of it since.

★ ★ ★

I came home to Madison County that fall after the leaves had turned and were just about off the trees, and on the road up the mountain I guess I had what you might call a premonition.

'Addie,' a voice said somewheres in my mind, 'when you get up there things ain't going to be the same as they was when you left.' And for some reason, and I can't say why, I knew I wasn't going to find my great-aunt alive.

The place was just as still and quiet as it could be — no smoke coming up out of the chimney, nothing but weeds and a shriveled-up crop in the ground. I listened to the wind tumbling through the dead stalks in the field, and I remember that it put me in mind of hearing paper trash blow along the sidewalk in the town I'd just left from. If I'd have closed my eyes I might've thought I was right back in downtown Asheville carrying a heap of dirty laundry down a lamplit street instead of lugging my own little piece of luggage and a purse padded with a couple bills and some loose coins up the hill toward home.

Sure enough, I found her in the bed by the cold fireplace covered up to her neck with all the quilts she'd made. I can't say just how long she'd been dead, but I've seen pictures of those Egyptian kings after they find them in their tombs, and I think it's fair to say she was on her

198

way to that. But she'd took the time to plait her hair, and it's because of that that I can fool myself into remembering that she looked just like a little girl laying there with those tight gray pigtails splayed out on the pillow beside her. If she'd still been alive and it had been somebody else laying there, even a stranger, I think I would've cried just for seeing a dead body. But it wasn't nobody else but her and there wasn't nobody else there but me, so I figured there wasn't much use in all that carrying on.

Then, at that time, I couldn't believe she'd been laid up dead for who knows how long and there hadn't been nobody coming up to check on the old woman and the little girl living on top of Parker Mountain. I found out later that folks had in their minds all kinds of no-count ideas about me and her living up there alone. They said she ran a still out there in the woods and had me out selling liquor to men on the other side of the mountain down near Greenville, Tennessee. The kids up there thought we were witches hiding out and eating the fingers and toes of little boys we caught on the land. With people holding truck in ideas like that, I reckon it makes pretty good sense that they'd stay as far away from us as they could.

I'd always known she wanted to be buried with her people up in the field above the cabin where they'd buried family for years. She'd take me up there on Decoration Day, and we'd sweep the stones clean and clear what grass and weeds there was growing up around them. She'd lead us a little service under a stand of oaks up there,

199

sing songs, say a prayer or two. From that high up you could see the county rolling away from you to the east, and if you turned and looked around the other way you could see the range running clear to Tennessee. It was a right pretty place, and I figured that was where I'd lay her to rest.

Now, I didn't know the first thing about burying a body, and I for sure didn't know a thing about building no coffin. But I did know how to dig me a hole, though, and that's just what I did that next morning on top of the hill. I climbed up there just as the sun was breaking good on the ridge to the east, and I laid into that ground with a pickax and an old shovel. I didn't stop digging until that hole was as deep as I was tall, and even then I knew that it wasn't quite deep enough, but I was just too wore out to keep on.

After I finished I set off down the mountain and stopped at the first cabin where it looked like people were living. When I got close I seen a woman out in the field, and I called out to her.

'Ma'am,' I said, 'I hate to bother you.' I looked on the other side of the field and seen an old man coming up out of the barn. He seemed like he was surprised to see a girl like me walking up the road to his place. That woman looked at him, and then she bent down to her work again. The old man made his way across the yard toward me so slow I thought he might not ever make it.

'What is it you're needing?' he asked me once he was close enough. He had on him an old pair of wire-rimmed spectacles, and through those glasses I could see how worn his eyes looked, like he'd spent his whole lifetime squinting up at the sun.

'I hate to bother you,' I said again. 'I live up the road a piece with my aunt — '

'I know who you are,' he said. I shut my mouth quick, and he just stared down at me. Then he turned his head and spit a brown stream of tobacco juice into the grass beside his boot.

'Well, I just came in from Asheville yesterday evening, and I found her passed away. I'm down here wondering if I could borrow — '

'What took her?' he asked.

'I don't know for sure,' I said. 'I reckon it might have been this flu. But I can't figure out how. I'm sure you know folks up on this mountain here didn't have too much to do with her. I don't know how she could've caught it with nobody stopping by to see her, her not having no friends that I know of.' He looked at the ground for a minute, and then he spit another stream of juice into the grass and rubbed it in with the toe of his boot. 'I need to borrow some tools from somebody so I can fix up something fit to bury her in,' I said.

He looked up from the ground out to where his wife stood in the field. She'd quit working and was looking over at us, like she'd been able to hear us talking to each other from all the way across the yard.

'I've got cash money,' I told him. 'If that's what it'll take, then I'm ready to spend it.' He looked back at me.

'There ain't no need for that,' he said. 'You go on and lay her out. We'll be up there with it in the morning.' He turned, and I watched him walk back toward the barn. The woman was staring at me from the field. I raised my hand to her.

'Thank y'all!' I hollered.

*　*　*

I bedded down in the back room with her still out there in the bed by the fireplace, and that night I had me a dream. I can tell you that I ain't never had such a dream before in my life, and not since have I remembered one so clearly.

It was dusk and I was walking up the hill from down there in the bottomland where the river snakes its way west to Tennessee. In the dream I wore some kind of baptismal robe that was so long that it drug along behind me in that dark, black mud, and I can remember just as plain as day looking down to see where it was still wet around the hem from me being in the river. It looked like I'd only stepped ankle-deep into the water and then changed my mind and walked right out, because in my dream the rest of me was dry and I didn't have no memory of being dunked under that cold water. No memory of any prayers being prayed over me and no ringing in my ears from the testament of faith I'd have likely been expected to share.

I didn't know just where I was at first, but the sun had sunk down below the hill that I was walking toward, and the whole country out there

202

was just as quiet as it could be. It was then, with my back to the river, that I got the sense that somebody was following me, that somebody was right there on my heels going up that hill right along behind me. I stopped walking, and I turned around and I could hear my robe dragging over the grass and I could feel my bare feet stepping on that wet cotton hem. When I looked behind me, there was Jesus. He had on him a blue robe that was as dark as pitch where it was soaked through from the waist down, and I knew he'd been all the way out there in that water just waiting on me, and somehow or another I'd decided not to go out and meet him.

I knew it was Jesus sure enough because he looked just like they always said he would: olive skin, soft brown eyes, light brown hair. But in my dream he was much older than what you might find in a picture Bible or in the paintings that might be hanging up in a church. In my dream he was much older than they let him live to be. I could see the years around his eyes and his beard had patches of gray and white in it, and when he walked toward me from the river he had a little hitch in his step like his hip or his leg was hurting him and giving him a little bit of trouble. I just stood there watching him, and when he got within earshot, he hollered out to me.

'Why'd you stop walking?' he asked.

'Because,' I told him. 'I didn't know you were back there.'

'Yes, you did,' he said. 'You just forgot. But go on, I'm following you now.' I just stood there not knowing what to say, and Jesus waved his hand like he was shooing me away. 'Go on,' he said. 'It's all right. I told you, I'm following you.'

I turned around and faced that hill again, and when I did I felt something heavy in my hands. I looked down and saw that I was holding a plate with a napkin over it that was wet with grease, and when I lifted that napkin I saw that it covered a heap of hot fried chicken. All of a sudden I felt somebody walk past me, and when I looked up I saw it was a woman in a long white robe just like the one I had on, and when I looked her in the face I felt like she was somebody I might've known once upon a time. She held a plate in her hands too, and beside her was a man with a guitar strapped over his shoulder and he held a tambourine in one hand and a jug of something in the other. When I looked around that bottomland, I saw it was plum full of people in robes carrying food and instruments up the grassy hillside in the growing dark, not a one of them saying a word, not a one of them making a noise. They looked just like ghosts or haints, and then it struck me that they might just be angels. Jesus walked right up beside me, and we stood there watching them walk past us and on ahead of us, and I could feel that fried chicken cooling under that napkin and that plate was growing cold against my fingers.

'Go on,' Jesus said again. 'I'm right here behind you.'

I set off walking up the hill even though I knew I wouldn't ever be able to catch up with all them folks, but I knew it didn't matter because we were going to a Decoration Day and I knew they'd have the food set out and the hymns going and the sweet tea poured when I met them at the top of that hill. I looked up there where some of the people were already starting to crest the hill, and there was a woman facing me, and when I looked close I saw it was my great-aunt and she was looking down at me and smiling like she was waiting for me and might just be willing to wait there forever. She didn't look like the tiny, shrunken thing I'd found by that cold fireplace. She looked straight and strong and shiny like a new silver dollar. I knew that I was going to wake up before I got to the top of that hill where she was waiting. Jesus must've known it too, for I felt his graying beard against my cheek and I could hear his breath in my ear where he walked right along beside me.

'Look at her, Addie,' he whispered. 'That's what immortality looks like.'

$$\star \quad \star \quad \star$$

I heard that man and woman from down the mountain driving their wagon out there in the road early that next morning, and I stepped out the door and saw him leading a big brown mare up the hill by the reins. A cart was bumping along behind her, and the coffin he'd made was resting up on top. It wasn't too much more than a rectangular box made from a few old boards, but I can tell you that I was glad to have it.

'Thank y'all for coming,' I said when they stopped in the road in front of the cabin.

'It ain't nothing,' the man said.

'We're glad we could help,' the woman said. He unloaded that box, and I helped him carry it inside where I'd laid my great-aunt out on the bed.

'I'll leave this to y'all,' he said, and he walked past us back outside. The woman helped me lift my great-aunt into the box, and I straightened her dress and smoothed it out. She was so light it was like lifting a little child. I'd unplaited her hair the night before and combed it out the best I could, but it didn't look like her. It was like we were loading up somebody I didn't know to carry them up the hill to the graveyard, and I expected my great-aunt to walk in the door any minute.

'Addie,' she'd say, 'what in the world?'

The woman and I stood there looking down at her where she laid in that box. It was quiet inside there, and I could hear the horse's feet shuffling in the dirt road outside.

'We should leave it open until we get up there,' the woman said. 'Odus will nail it shut then.' She went outside, and I could hear her out there in the road talking to the man. He opened the door and stepped inside.

I helped him carry the coffin out to the cart, and when the sun hit her face I saw for the first time just how bad she looked. Her skin was so white you could almost see through it. He fastened the coffin down on the back of that cart, and the three of us followed the road up the mountain to the graveyard. Once we got up there I helped him unload her, and the woman got the ropes they'd brought to lower her down into the

206

hole I'd dug the day before. The man had brought along a hammer and a little sack of nails for closing down the lid.

He pulled the lid off the sled and he sat it over the top of the coffin, and then he got down on his knees and started hammering it shut. Every time that hammer hit, it echoed up through those oaks with a report that seemed like it would carry forever — a sound like a rifle blast ringing out over the mountains. When he finished, we lowered her down with the ropes, him on one side of the grave and me and his wife on the other. Once we finished, we just stood there looking down into that hole.

'Do you want to say something?' the woman asked me.

'I don't figure there's much to be said now,' I told her. Besides, I knew that what I'd wanted to say to my great-aunt I'd already said to myself, and if she was listening up there she'd have heard it just the same.

After finding her dead and alone, I told myself I wasn't going to die in a drafty cabin with nobody to find me but the critters and maybe some snooping kids. I thought, *Addie, it ain't no way to live up on this mountain alone for the rest of your life; you need to get down to where folks are,* and so I up and left, and I've lived just outside Marshall since '20. I reckon that's been along about sixty-odd years.

13

But I wasn't going to tell the sheriff any of that story because it had no bearing on whatever truth he needed to find. The story he wanted was the story of Christopher inside that church, and that was a story I just couldn't give him. But if he'd have taken the time, I could've told the sheriff about the very moment Christopher's story started, and maybe from there he could have followed it to see how it changed Ben and Julie, how it changed their marriage, and how they ended up where they were.

On the night he was born I laid there in my bed and listened for that noise again, that same noise that sounded like a voice coming from somewhere inside the house. I held my breath and bent my ear, and just when I was ready to blame it on fancy I heard it just as plain as day.

'Who's there?' I called out and waited. I heard that wind driving outside and the patter of that snow against the windows, and then a little voice was signaling me from the front door. I could barely hear it over the wind and the snow, but when I was sure I'd heard it I popped up out of the bed, and how dark that night was with me shuffling across the floor and turning on the switch on the lamp and the light filling up the bedroom and part of the hall.

I stepped into the front room in my bare feet and my gown, and I called out, 'Who is it?'

'Lord have mercy, Addie, it's me,' the little voice behind the door said. 'Now open this door before I'm froze solid.'

I recognized that voice, and I opened the door and the wind just about knocked me down, and here came the snow blowing in with it. Gerty Norman was out there standing in her dead husband's waders with one of her son's work coats swallowing her up. I could barely see her eyes peeking out from where she'd wrapped a scarf tight around her face and pulled a man's winter cap down low on her head.

'Is that you, Gerty?' I asked.

'Who in the world do you think it is?' she said through her scarf. She stomped right past me on her way inside the house with that snow falling off the tread of them heavy waders.

'What would make you want to walk down here in this weather at this time of night?' I asked her. She was slow getting that scarf unwound from over her mouth, and I could see that her cheeks were bright red apples against her face. Her eyes were teary from the cold. When she finally unwound that scarf and took off her cap, her body gave her a good shiver.

'It's Julie Hall,' she said. 'It's time, and Ben's truck can't get her down the mountain. They tried calling Doc Winthrop, but they couldn't get ahold of him. They tried calling you too, but I reckon your phone's out with this weather.'

'Winthrop's probably drunk and laying up in the bed by now,' I told her. 'There ain't no way that man's heading up Gunter Mountain tonight. Not in this snow.'

'Ben asked if you might could see her through, at least until this weather lets up and they can get down the mountain to the hospital. I told him I'd come down here and ask you, but I let him know it's pretty nasty down here too.'

Don't you know I stood there and watched those little red apples disappear from her cheeks and listened to the wind whipping that snow around while I thought about how warm my bed in the next room was.

'Ronnie might can get you up there,' she said. 'His truck's got them big old tires on it, and I wouldn't be a bit surprised if he could drive you clear up that mountain.'

I can say I thought about it awfully hard. 'I reckon I'll go,' I finally said. 'Just let me get me some clothes on.' I turned to go back toward the bedroom and she followed me, and then she walked into the kitchen and went right up to the stove and took those heavy mittens off and held out her hands to warm them. I'd fed the fire before I went to bed, and when she opened the grate I could see them flames just a-hissing and popping in there. I stopped and looked back at her.

'Watch yourself in them waders,' I said. 'That rubber will melt on both you and my floors too.' I knew she was frozen through and couldn't rightly feel how hot that fire was on her.

'I know,' she said, but she sure didn't back away from it.

'Gerty!' I said. She muttered something under her breath about being scolded and made a fuss of stepping back just to rile me.

I went into the bedroom and put on my wool stockings and pulled on two sweaters over my gown. My heavy coat was hanging on the bedpost, and I pulled that on too. I found my gloves and boots and my hat and carried them into the kitchen so I could sit down and put them on at the table. When I walked back in the kitchen, there was Gerty right up against that stove again. I decided that if she wanted to set herself on fire, why, I'd just go ahead and let her.

★   ★   ★

We opened the door and stepped outside, and that wind almost knocked me over again and the snow was just blowing around all over the place. Me and Gerty set out trudging the half mile up the road to her house. It was a climb, I can tell you that. And here we were, two old women out in the snow holding on to each other for dear life and slipping and sliding right along like little kids on roller skates.

'Lord, Gerty,' I said, 'how'd you make it down this hill by yourself?'

'I just done it,' she said.

'You think Ronnie can get up that mountain in this mess?'

'I'm sure he can.'

'What did he say?'

211

'I ain't woke him yet.'

Well, I just about laid down and died right there. I stopped right in my tracks, but Gerty just kept on walking. I hollered after her. 'You're telling me I'm climbing up this hill to get in a truck that you don't even know can get up Gunter, with a driver that ain't even woke yet?'

'That's what I'm telling you,' she hollered back.

'Why didn't you wake him up and ask him if his truck could make it?'

She stopped then and turned around. I could barely see her through the snow.

'Because you know you're heading up that mountain anyways,' she said. I knew she had herself a point there, so I didn't say nothing else about it.

Ronnie had his truck pulled into his daddy's old garage by the house, and I told Gerty I'd be in there waiting on her to get Ronnie out of bed. I bet I sat there ten minutes. I thought I'd be frostbit for sure before that boy got out there with the key to turn that engine over and get that heater running. I saw the light come on in his room, and I pictured Gerty in the house standing by his bed.

'Get up now, Ronnie,' she was probably saying, real soft. She babied that boy, much more than I would've if I'd had any of my own. 'Get up, Ronnie. Miss Lyle's out there getting frostbitten and might be dead before your feet hit the floor.' That's what I would have told him, but like I said, he weren't mine.

But here he came after a while. I turned my

head and saw him stumbling out to the garage through the snow like the walking dead. A big boy, bigger than his daddy was for sure. He had on his coveralls and had pulled his coat over them. He wasn't wearing a hat, and when he opened the door and got into the truck the snow stuck in his hair like popcorn.

'Good morning, sunshine,' I said once he got settled.

'Hey, Miss Lyle,' he said, like a man more dead than alive.

*　*　*

But good Lord, if that weren't a drive. That boy white-knuckled at the steering wheel and me praying to all the angels in Heaven that we wouldn't skid off the road into the creek or the woods or somebody's yard. Anybody who saw us from their windows would have thought we were a couple of daredevil kids out tempting Mother Nature.

That whole drive I sat there looking out at those heavy snow-flakes pounding the wind-shield and thought about Ben and Julie up there in that house all by themselves with their first baby on the way. I never knew Julie's people, and Ben's mama had run off years ago and I can't say I remember her too well. Those kids had them only one daddy between the two of them and him a sorry, disappeared drunk at that.

Julie was just a beautiful girl with that curly blond hair and that fair skin. It's a hard thing to come across skin that fair up in these parts with folks spending so much time working outdoors. But hers was as fair as a baby's, and I figured Ben never let her turn her hand over back then because he loved her so much. He was a good boy, hadn't taken to drinking yet and didn't have quite that same meanness running through him like his daddy did. His daddy was just an awfully mean man. After his wife had run off, I figure whatever meanness he'd had left over he took out on Ben; but they shared their ways just the same.

The worst beating I ever heard of Ben's daddy putting on him was after one of them women down in Hot Springs called him up and told him Ben had been down there to see her. I ain't saying that I hold with that kind of women, but you can't help knowing who you know and hearing what you hear. How she knew how to get ahold of Jimmy Hall to tell him about his own son I can't say, but I figure it's pretty easy to hit upon. Ben was still in high school then and a good-sized boy, a football-playing boy. He even played him a year or two up at Western Carolina. But none of that kept his daddy from working him over for holding with folks like Miss Lillian down in Hot Springs. You'd have thought his daddy hadn't never heard of a boy doing such a thing, but all the folks I know around here thought better than that. They knew Jimmy Hall had always known plenty about those types of women.

It wasn't too long after the sheriff's boy died while working with Jimmy Hall that he dropped off into nothing and left Ben all alone. It was probably the best thing that could have happened to Ben. He tried to be a different man than his daddy, and I can tell you that's good enough for some of these boys up here, but it wasn't for Ben. He wanted to be a good man, a good Christian man. I just think his blood was set against him.

Maybe Ben thought he could run from it, and maybe that's why he took his family off that mountain not long after Christopher was born. Maybe he gave up Gunter for the valleys closer to the French Broad to escape a past that had already marked him with his daddy's closed fist and a strong taste for whiskey.

A few years after Christopher was born and before they had Jess, Ben and Julie moved into a little house with an outdoor privy that had been built down in the holler by a man named Tupelo Gant. Mr. Gant was a childless man who'd built that little place for him and his young wife just a few years after they'd gotten married, and he lived in that house and on that land for years and years and ran him a good little farm. But before he even knew it'd happened, he woke up one morning and saw that he was too old and stubborn to work that burley against the state, and he up and sold that house and the land and took his wife to live in one of them ugly old trailers that were popping up like toadstools all over this county.

When he found that land for sale, Ben moved his wife and his new baby boy off that mountain and out of his childhood home and down closer to the river. Maybe he took leaving his home once and for all as a sign that he was moving back to a time when it was custom to wear a heavy coat and carry you a light to the outhouse in the snow, when it was just a normal thing to be able to walk to work because work was across the yard and in the barn and down in the field. It was expected that men's hands would be good and calloused by reins and shovels and the hands of other men whose lives they knew by the tough skin of their handshakes. Looking back on all that myself, I don't see anything romantic about none of it. I like my inside privy and my washing machine, but some of these young folks are different, and they want times to be hard so they can prove something. Who they want to prove it to I just can't say, but I reckon Ben was one of these young folks, and he believed that he and his family could find themselves a simpler life. Or maybe he was forced off that mountain to this bottomland by his family's history and a fear of its reckoning. It could have been just about anything that made him do it, and I can't say for sure just what it was.

★   ★   ★

The road up Gunter Mountain is a paved blacktop, but it didn't used to be nothing but mud and a little bit of gravel. It was all paved at that time and it still is as far as I know. But Lord if that boy's truck didn't struggle with his tires sliding around in the snow like we were driving on glass, and me sitting there worrying about him carrying that thing clear off the mountain.

'I don't know if it's going to make it up, Ronnie,' I kept saying, but it was like he couldn't hear me. He was hunched down over that wheel and talking to that truck under his breath like he could make it believe otherwise.

'We ain't going to make it, Ronnie,' I finally said. 'You're just going to have to stop and let me out. I reckon I'll have to walk it.'

He just sat there and stared out at them big old snowflakes filling up his headlights.

'My ma will kill me if I let you walk up the mountain in this,' he said. 'I bet that snow's more than a foot deep up here.'

'I don't know if there's anything else to do,' I said. 'No,' I told him, 'I think I'm going to have to walk it. You head on home and go back to bed, and I'll call over to the house when it's done. I'll just meet you right here.'

'My ma's going to kill me,' he said.

'Well, that's between y'all,' I said and opened the door. 'There ain't nothing else for me to do but walk if I'm getting up there tonight. You drive safe getting home. I'll give you a call in a little while.'

I closed his door and set off up the mountain in all that blinding snow.

I was trudging up that road when I remembered Gerty telling me that Ben had tried to call Doc Winthrop to come up here and see about Julie and the baby, and I almost had to laugh out loud when I pictured it. That old coot was probably ten years older than me, and I reckon he'd been drunk just about his whole life. Even though I was raised by my great-aunt, a woman who was a healer if there ever was one, I never had no plans for myself to fall into doctoring folks whenever they took ill or got hurt, but it's a good thing I started when I did because old Winthrop sure wasn't any kind of help a person could set store in. There weren't any ambulances or nothing out here until the hospital came, and what they call a country doctor was about all folks had. Even after all that new stuff came, folks were just as likely to call me or Winthrop or somebody else to help them deliver a baby, set a broken arm, or put a stitch or two in a bad cut.

Just like when Collie Avery took that fall from the top beam of his daddy's barn when they were hanging burley. It must've been a good forty feet straight down. Folks there figured he'd probably broken his back, and I reckon they were right scared to even move him. His daddy called up Doc Winthrop and asked him to come out. He said, 'We ain't going to move him until you get here. Hurry, though, he's in some awfully bad pain.'

Winthrop said he'd be right out, but if those folks didn't wait just about all day with that boy laying there on the floor of that barn going in and out of consciousness from all that pain he was in. His daddy finally got ahold of me, and I went out there to see about him.

'I don't know where that old bastard Winthrop is,' that boy's daddy said when I got there.

That boy of his hadn't broken his back, I knew that for sure. But that fall did crack his pelvis in two, and he spent a good month at a hospital in

Asheville trying to heal it up, and I'll declare he still walks with a limp that'll make you grit your teeth. I don't know if I ever seen nobody in the kind of pain that boy was in after that fall.

And don't you know I found out what had happened to Doc Winthrop when one of that boy's brothers was driving me home that evening. We were going across the bridge over Laurel Creek out there in Summey, and if I didn't look down off the bank and see that old buzzard's truck drove clean off the road into the water.

'Go ahead and pull over up here,' I said to that boy.

He parked on the side of the road, and me and him shimmied down that bank and waded a piece out into the water. We looked in there and seen Winthrop sitting behind that steering wheel just a-snoring like he was at home in bed. You could smell that shine on him or whatever it was he'd took to drinking that day.

'Wake up, Winthrop!' I hollered at him. 'You done drove your dang truck off the bridge.' He opened his eyes real slow, and then he blinked a couple of times and sat up straight and looked around.

'Well, I reckon I did,' he said.

He left it there too. It's a new bridge there now, but if you drive down through Summey and cross over the Laurel and look down over the side you'll see that truck. There's branches hanging over it now and it's almost covered in moss, but I can tell you it's there. He's been dead for years, but his truck's still just sitting

219

there. And I can tell you if you drive down that way and cross that bridge and look over the side you'll see it.

*   *   *

Ben was as white as a sheet when he opened the door, and he looked to be just about scared out of his mind. 'Who drove you up?' he asked.

'Gerty's boy, Ronnie, couldn't make it all the way,' I said. 'I walked most of it.'

'I hate to make you do that,' he said, 'but I'm glad you're here.'

'She in the bedroom?' I asked him.

'Yes,' he said. 'Her contractions are giving her fits. I ain't been able to help her at all.' I'd decided to leave my coat on for the time being, and I went over and stood by the fireplace and held out my hands.

'How far apart are they?' I asked.

'How far apart are what?'

'Her contractions,' I said.

'Good Lord, Miss Lyle,' he said. 'I don't know. I didn't even think to check.'

I turned back and faced the fire and felt that cold leaving my hands and my face. 'Well, you go ahead and put on a pot of boiling water,' I told him. 'Go on and toss some scissors in there and find some string and some towels or whatever you got to clean with. We might be having ourselves a long night.'

I opened the bedroom door real quiet and looked in and saw Julie sitting up in the bed and leaning her back against some pillows. When I

220

walked inside the room, the air coming in the open windows hit me in the face and I almost hollered out for it being so cold in there after leaving the warmth of the fire.

'I had Ben open them up,' she said. 'I can't get cooled off.'

She lay back against them pillows and tried to smile at me. Her face was wet with sweat, and her hair and gown were soaked clean through.

'Good Lord, child,' I said. 'How are you doing?'

'I'm getting on all right,' she said. 'I don't think it'll be long now. I'm glad you're here.' I pulled my coat tight around me and walked toward the bed.

'I'm glad I could come,' I said.

I helped her shimmy down to the bottom of the bed and hollered for Ben to find some more pillows to prop her up. He brought me a little chair, and I sat down at the foot there.

'How far apart are they?' I asked her.

'They're right on top of each other,' she said.

I lifted up her gown and took a look, and that's when I seen that boy's head crowning inside that sac. 'I figure to know why,' I said. 'Y'all about to have you a baby here in no time flat.'

Ben went up there and took her hand, and she started in to pushing and breathing. I watched that little boy's head come through, and I could see then he was going to be born with the caul, and sure enough, he was.

'This boy's born for good luck,' I said. 'Looky here.' I held him in my arms and lifted that little hood from his eyes, and that's when he opened them up and blinked and looked up at me. Ben was standing right over my shoulder when he did it, and I could hear him breathing and it was so cold in there I could see his breath coming out of his mouth like smoke. I could hear Julie crying softly from up on the bed. 'He's got blue eyes just like his daddy,' I said. Ben reached down to take him out of my arms, but I stopped him.

'Not just yet,' I said. 'There's still work to do. Take that piece of string and cut it in two.' He pulled his knife out of his pocket and cut it. 'Now tie one piece around the cord right here. Make sure you get it good and tight.' I motioned to the baby's belly and watched Ben tie a knot. 'Do the same on the other end,' I told him. After he'd done it I told him to get them scissors out of that boiling water and come back in the bedroom. He went in the kitchen and came back with them scissors wrapped in a towel. He looked down at the cord, and then he looked at me.

'All right, Daddy,' I told him. 'Go ahead.'

* * *

Ben closed the windows, and the room got to feeling almost comfortable with the heat coming in from the fireplace in the front room. I'd pulled the chair up alongside the bed, and I sat watching Julie feed the baby. He was making little grunting noises like babies do when they're nursing. I could see that Julie's face looked worried.

'Why hasn't he started crying yet?' she asked.

222

'You got yourself a content little boy,' I told her. 'I wouldn't get to complaining about him being too quiet just yet.'

'Something ain't right,' she said.

'He's fine,' I told her. 'He's a good, strong boy. He's hungry, that's all. Just let him eat. There's plenty of time for crying.' I looked over at Ben where he was standing with his arms folded at the foot of the bed. He was watching Julie. 'He's a good, strong boy,' I said again. But even as I said it, I knew it wasn't so.

After delivering the afterbirth I took it into the front room to talk with Ben about what he needed to do next.

'You can use that same pot you boiled the scissors in,' I told him. 'It don't matter, but you need to boil this here into a tea and feed it to Julie and the baby. It'll be good for them. They're slap wore out, and they need every bit of help they can get. After you get done with it you need to dig a little hole and bury it out in the yard.'

Ben just stood there staring at the afterbirth where I held it wrapped in that towel. His eyes looked like he wanted to say something to me, but he seemed like he couldn't figure out how to put the words together.

'I don't know,' he finally said. He looked up at me.

'What is it that you don't know?' I asked.

'I don't think we're in for that,' he said. 'We're trying to have us a Christian family, Miss Lyle. I don't think we're in for all that old-timey stuff. It don't seem right.'

'Don't seem right?' I said. 'Did I not slap your behind hard enough on the day you were born? Let me tell you that it don't matter what 'seems,' it matters what 'is.' And if I was you I'd get to digging a hole out there in that snow while I had me a pot of water boiling on the stove.'

'That ain't our way,' he said.

'Well, I ain't going to try and change your mind,' I told him. 'But you called me up here to deliver your baby, and I done that the best I could. If you don't want to take my advice, then you don't have to. But like I said, I done the best I could. It's up to you now. Ain't going to be nobody up here but y'all, and you need to start thinking about what's best for your family.'

'I am,' he said. 'And I appreciate you coming up here, and I hope I can repay your kindness sometime.'

We stood there looking at each other for a minute, and then I tossed that towel onto the kitchen counter and went back in to check on Julie. Her eyes were closed, and she was holding the baby in her arms. They both looked to be sleeping. I took my coat off the back of the chair and closed the door softly and walked back into the front room.

'Call down to Gerty's, if you would.'

'I will,' said Ben. 'Let me get some warm clothes on, and I'll walk down with you. Ain't no sense in you going back down alone.'

'I can go back just the way I came,' I told him. 'But I'd appreciate you calling Gerty's boy.'

I set off down that mountain and got about halfway when I looked up to see something coming toward me in the snow, and I slowed down and thought about stepping into the woods until whatever it was had passed me by. But when it got closer I could see it was Doc Winthrop on the back of his old mule coming up the mountain to help Julie. I could've passed by without him even knowing it. He would've got himself all the way up that mountain before he realized that he'd seen him a ghost floating down Gunter in a snowstorm. But I couldn't help saying something to him, even if he was just a drunk country doctor toting a bag of broken old instruments up a mountain in the snow. I waited until we got abreast of each other and I could hear him moaning real quiet and see the smoky breath of his old mule.

'Save that poor beast the trouble, you old sot,' I told him. 'Ain't no reason for you to go no farther.'

I heard him pull on those reins, and that mule came to a dead stop right there in the snow. I kept on walking.

'Shit,' I heard him say.

★   ★   ★

Julie and Ben named that little boy Christopher, but only Julie and the folks at church ever called him that. Ben always called him 'Stump,' and so did just about everybody else who knew him. Julie hated that nickname like it was poisonous, and she always called him Christopher. I never once heard her call him anything else.

But she did tell me that he'd been given that

225

nickname one afternoon when a man from the state had come out to the house to chart Ben's burley. This wasn't too long after they'd moved off the mountain to Mr. Gant's house down in the holler and Ben had took to growing tobacco. I reckon he ended up a right good farmer and a downright state swindler after he got to learning that with a big smile and a few extra dollars them agents wouldn't give him any problems about his overage. But Lord knows that wasn't always so when he first started out.

Julie's story went that this agent had had him the pleasure of jerking up several rows of that burley while Ben just stood there and watched, and now the dusty roots of those plants peeked out from the tailgate of his state truck. He stood by the back fender and charted Ben's patches on his clipboard, and then he just crossed his arms and waited while Ben looked that chart over and read all that paperwork just as slow and careful as he could.

Now, Julie was a beautiful girl, just a fair little thing with her white skin and that blond hair — the kind of girl that's got her admirers and probably don't even know it for all her sweetness. Maybe she caught this man's eye and made him turn his attention from where Ben was looking over the paperwork to where Julie'd bent to her knees in the flower bed to get at the clumps of weeds and bullgrass by the porch. Or maybe that man noticed the little boy that stood right there beside her in the flower bed with just the tips of his little fingers dusting her shoulder like it was something that needed cleaning. I

226

don't know what got him looking, but I figure he looked long enough to see that the boy's deep blue eyes were fixed on the field he and Ben had just risen from on their way back up to the house.

'Hey, fella,' that man said like he expected the little boy's head to turn toward him or his eyes to light on him where he stood by the truck. Of course Christopher didn't move. 'Hey, little man,' that agent said even louder. Now, I've seen some folks get flat-out embarrassed when little ones don't pay them no mind. It ain't a strange thing to feel that way, and I reckon this man wasn't no different.

'That's a quiet boy,' that agent said to Ben. Julie said she stopped pulling up the weeds and turned her head to see Ben and the agent standing in the driveway behind her. The setting sun was just beyond them, and she could only see their outlines against all that light. The man turned toward her. She could barely make out his face in the glare. 'You got yourself a soft-spoken boy there,' he told her. 'A deep thinker. Any little boy who can stand like a stump in a cleared field is a deep thinker.'

He laughed to himself like he was hoping that Ben and Julie would laugh with him, but Ben had finished reading and signing all that paperwork and he just handed over the clipboard and the pen to the agent.

'He's a mute,' Ben said. 'He hasn't said a word a day in his life.'

The agent put the clipboard under his arm and dropped the pen into his breast pocket.

'Now, I didn't mean to say — ' he began.

'What-all burley you took from me better get gone,' Ben said. 'I don't want to hear nothing about it taking root somewhere up the road.' He stood there and looked at the agent, and then he walked past him and crossed the yard toward the barn.

The man looked to Julie where she was still hunkered down in the flower bed. She took her bandana from the pocket of her dress and wiped the sweat off her forehead. I reckon she probably even smiled at him in an unassuming way that made him even sorrier for saying such a thing about her son.

'I swear I didn't mean nothing by it,' the man said. He looked from Julie to the little boy whose eyes had been fixed on the field, but he saw that Christopher's gaze had turned and set itself on the path his father had cut across the yard toward the shadow of the barn.

That child was touched, and I just don't know what else you could call it. He never cried once as a baby, and by the time he was three years old those two kids knew he wasn't ever going to speak. He'd hum sometimes or maybe even grunt when he wanted something, but that was about it. He was quiet, all right, but you couldn't say he wasn't peaceful. He could spend all day sitting still on the porch steps with just his eyes creeping around the yard to take measure of the things resting just out of line with your own gaze: the tree line, the ridge, an earthworm inching itself along through the dirt. I used to sit with him when he was just a little bitty thing, and sometimes I got to believing that I could feel his eyes on me. When I did, I'd whip my head around right quick to try and catch him staring, but I never could. I'd find him instead just sitting there with his eyes locked on a black spread of birds moving in silhouette against a bright sky or else watching the edge of the breeze rustle the dried leaves on the oaks crowding the ridge behind their little house.

It wouldn't have really mattered one bit if Doc Winthrop had made it up to Ben and Julie's house on time because there wasn't no amount of doctoring by a drunk old country doctor or root working by a half-froze old woman that would've helped that boy a bit. I knew that much the very minute I laid eyes on him the very night he was born. But I can tell you that Ben refusing to even think about listening to me set me off, and I thought about it my whole walk down the mountain in that driving snow. You show me a woman who calls herself a Christian up in these parts, and I'll show you a woman who knows how to heal. It ain't unchristian to make do when you're poor, I can promise you that. You just show me a Christian woman up here, and I'll show you a woman who knows what to pick and where to find it. If you don't know how to heal yourself, then you don't know how to live when times are hard. My great-aunt taught me that the best way she knew how, and never once had anybody told me they weren't going to do what was best for them. Not until Ben did that very thing the night his boy was born.

You can find just about everything you'll ever

229

need out there in those woods if you're willing to look hard enough, and if you're poor, you'll look right hard. Wild ginger calms the whooping cough and it's jewelweed for the poison ivy, and if you're going courting you'd best bring your bergamot for your breath and some strong, fine-looking teeth. And me, I find a good pokeweed liniment staves off the rheumatism during a chilly, rainy fall.

Now, I can't say that boiling a tea or praying or healing would have helped that boy none, but I can tell you it wouldn't have hurt him a lick to try, especially if you knew what you were doing and how to do it. But I can tell you there's stuff out there that'll kill you just as quick as you can eat it, and you've got to know what to look out for.

When I was a little girl, my great-aunt told me a story about a band of Confederate outliers who took to starving in the mountains north of Madison. Most of my people were Union, and couldn't none of them have cared less about the war until it crept like a black cloud over the rim of the eastern hills. When it found them, they grew bitter quick at being forced to fight a war that wasn't their own.

She told me the story of those outliers one day while we tended the laundry on the porch of her cabin. I'd spent the afternoon watching her hands dive in and out of a wooden basin filled with soapy water while she rubbed her raw knuckles across the aluminum washing board. I remember thinking that by now the knuckles on more delicate hands would've took to bleeding, and I'd heard stories of women having to rewash baskets of laundry after finding their own blood warmed by the sun in brown smears across drying sheets.

After she'd wrung that water from each piece of laundry, she'd fold it into the basket in my arms until I couldn't hardly carry it down the steps into the yard, where I pinned the underclothes and dresses to tight lines running between two black locust posts. I've got some clear memories of walking the rows of billowing sheets while the image of the porch and the outline of my great-aunt's body stood stamped upon the sunlight. Her soft voice carried down the steps and trailed out into the yard, where it disappeared between the folds of white cotton.

'Those Confederates were starving, Addie.'

I stepped from between the sheets and dragged the basket through the high grass and up to the porch. I stood by her waist and listened and waited for her to pile the heaps of wet clothes into the basket.

'They must've been wandering the hills for days and didn't know no better than to eat that jimson fruit. That stuff can make you crazy until you almost want to die.

'This was back when they used to carry all the baccer into Hot Springs to cart it down the turnpike to the Asheville market. I was in town with my daddy and his crop the day those boys came down from the hills, shooting up everything and carrying on like nothing you've ever seen. I remember that wildness in their eyes, and my daddy told me it was jimson sure enough. He said nothing else could make a man act like that.

'By the time those soldiers were done, they'd shot some folks in town, and the folks they didn't kill had killed all but one of them soldiers. The one who'd survived was a boy from Gastonia who'd caught a bullet in his thigh. Folks said he'd been the only one of them Confederates without a gun, said he didn't even look old enough to handle a rifle. He was about out of his head by the time all the shooting stopped. Some folks in town took him in and cared for him and kept him safe and hid away.

'A few days later a posse of Confederate home guard rolled through looking for those outliers who'd shot up the town, and a few days after that a band of Union came through looking for rebels. But folks kept that boy hid. They weren't going to give him up, no matter who was looking for him. When news came from Raleigh that North Carolina had withdrawn her troops and the war was over and done, they took that boy out to the middle of town and strung him up. They hung him. Just like that.

'I saw that boy's face when they done it. I think I'll remember it for the rest of my life.' She quit her washing, and I watched her wet hand lift a big old grasshopper from the rim of the basin. She tossed it into the air, and I saw its wings open and catch the breeze before it disappeared.

'Why'd they kill him if they thought he was innocent?' I asked.

'Because,' she said, 'he was someplace he shouldn't have been, and sometimes that's enough.' And now, when I think about what happened to Christopher inside that church, I think the same thing.

14

If somebody would have wanted to, after Christopher was born, they could've just stood by and watched Julie and Ben grow apart from each other real slow. It was like a tree had sprung up between them, a tree that was just too thick to throw their arms around. Julie had always been a strong Christian woman, and she got herself believing that her little boy's being touched was a gift from God. But Ben wasn't no mystic about it, and I reckon he saw his own quietness in that little boy, and he loved him all the more because of it. He figured silence marked Christopher as being his son in a way their blood never could.

But that tree that grew up between them was just a gnarly old thing with thick roots that ran deep and wild and tore at the ground until it opened up, and, once it did, Julie found herself clear across a great divide from Ben, so far apart that they couldn't even see each other from where they stood. Julie looked around and saw that she needed her faith to help her understand God's plan for that little boy and for her family. It was like Ben's lack of faith inspired her, and his turning his back on God and the church worked on her belief and made it that much stronger. She never missed a chance to teach her boys a lesson about the Lord, especially after Jess was born. He was a curious thing, and once he lit into asking you questions about God and Heaven and Jesus you'd better have him some answers ready, or it just wouldn't do. But his daddy was somebody different altogether. There were two things that man just wouldn't talk about: his heavenly father and his own daddy. I reckon he figured that once he cut his ties with his earthly father, any substitute, whether holy or not, was going to be judged with the same thorough measure he judged just about everything else in his life.

And the Lord knows that when people don't get what they need they take what they can find, and Julie wasn't no different from most women about such a thing as that. What she found was a Christian family that welcomed her and her two little boys and never asked one question about why her husband wasn't joining the rest of his family on Sunday mornings. I reckon it was just about good enough for her, but I know there were still times when that loneliness for the way her and Ben used to be would come over her, and with it'd come a fear of him that I couldn't ever quite put my finger on. I ain't saying that Ben was the kind of man to hit a woman, because I can tell you that he wasn't. His daddy was, but Ben just didn't have it in him the way some men do. He wasn't the kind of man to let a woman get him riled up enough to go and make a scene and take to swinging his fists. But he was a brooding soul, and I believe the way he carried himself in all that quietness hurt Julie more than an open hand ever could. It got to where those two didn't hardly talk to each other at all, not even about the most important things married folks are supposed to share.

It turns out that the tree I'd imagined growing up between those two wasn't no tree at all. What I took for being roots were actually stories and lies and promises that festered deep into Julie's heart to where there wasn't anything anybody could do to pry them loose. Those thick limbs and branches that kept Julie and Ben from seeing each other when they needed to the most weren't nothing but arms and fingers that held Julie back, covered her eyes, and took her hand and led her to a place she never had no intention of going. Looking back now, it wasn't no tree at all; it was Carson Chambliss.

★   ★   ★

It must have been a year or so before Christopher died that I was out in my backyard gathering my laundry off the line when I saw Julie about as bad off as she'd ever been. It had come up a little rain, and I was trying to get all my laundry in before the sky opened up and took to pouring. On my way out back I looked across the valley and saw the dark clouds gathering in the distance, and I figured they were getting a good wash just a little piece up the road. It wasn't doing anything but drizzling now, but I knew better than to think that it wasn't going to come up a storm some time soon.

I took to unfastening the laundry from the line and tossing it into the basket when for some reason, and I can't tell you what it was, I knew that somebody was watching me. I turned around, and that's when I saw Julie standing up in the corner of the yard by the house. She was standing there in the rain and watching me with her arms folded across herself like she was freezing, but it was a warm summer day, not a bit cool at all.

'Lord, girl,' I hollered up at her. 'You just about scared me to death.' I turned around and went to unfastening the rest of my laundry from the line, but when I looked again I saw that she hadn't moved an inch. 'You all right?' I hollered. She didn't say nothing to that, and she didn't make no move to come down to me either, so I dropped the clothes I was holding into the basket and walked up the yard to where she was standing. When I got close up to her, I could see that her hair was damp and her skirt was wet where it had caught some high grass on her walk over to my place. She had on a pair of rubber boots that were covered in mud up to her ankles.

'You all right?' I asked her again when I got up to the top of the yard where she was standing. She pulled her arms even tighter around her and turned her head and looked up the road she'd just come down. That rain picked up a little then, and I could hear the thunder rumble out over the valley behind me.

'Can you keep me from having a baby?' she asked. She turned her face to me and her eyes looked like she was just terrified to have to ask me a question like that.

'Do you think you're pregnant?'

'If I was, could you keep me from having it?' she asked.

'Why are you asking about that?' I said.

'I just can't have me another baby,' she said.

'Well, Lord, why not?' I asked. 'Having a baby is a good thing, girl. It ain't no reason to be scared.'

'I can't have it,' she said.

'Why not?' I asked.

'Because,' she said, 'I'm afraid it'll happen again.'

'What'll happen?' I asked.

'It'll be like Christopher,' she said.

'Goodness, Julie,' I said. 'That ain't no reason to get rid of it. Christopher's a fine boy, and you know you don't love him no less than you would've if he'd been different. And look at Jess. You got yourself two fine little boys, and there ain't nothing wrong with either one of them.'

'But Pastor said it might happen again,' she said. 'And I think he might be right.'

'What makes you think that man knows anything about having a baby?' I asked. 'He ain't no woman, and he ain't no prophet neither. No matter how bad he wants y'all to believe he is.'

'He just knows,' she said. 'And I believe him when he says it.'

'What's Ben got to say about all this?' I asked her.

'I ain't told him yet,' she said. 'And I ain't going to either.'

'A man needs to be told something like this,' I said. 'I think a father needs to have a say in it.'

'If you're thinking you ain't going to do it, then tell me now so I'll know for sure,' she said. Her eyes dropped to the ground, and her voice was just a whisper. 'I already been trying to stop it anyway.'

'What have you done?' I asked. She turned and looked out over the trees that ran down into the holler behind the house. When she looked at me again, her eyes were full of tears. She tried to say something, and then she stopped herself like she was going to cry.

'I been doing all kinds of things,' she finally said. 'Boiled some water in a pot and knelt over the steam until I couldn't stand it anymore.' She looked back toward the road, and then she looked down at her stomach. She lifted up her blouse with one hand and pulled at the waistline of her skirt with the other. When she did, I saw that her stomach was purple with bruises so dark it looked like she'd dyed her skin with blackberries.

'Lord, girl,' I said. 'Who done this to you?'

'I done it,' she said. 'I threw myself on the edge of the porch until I couldn't stand up to do it again.'

She started crying then, and I went to her and wrapped my arms around her, and when I did her body shuddered like it was too painful to even be touched. She folded her arms across her belly again and leaned her head against my shoulder and took to sobbing.

'It's going to be all right,' I said. 'There ain't

nothing to be afraid of.'

'I was going to drink some castor oil, but I didn't have any,' she said.

'Who told you that would work?' I asked.

'Pastor did,' she said. When I heard that, I leaned back so I could see her, and she stepped away from me and wiped her eyes.

'Pastor told you to do all this to yourself?' I asked.

'He showed me how to do it,' she said. 'And he told me if I didn't get it this month then I should come and see you. He said you might be able to fix it, if you're willing. He said you wouldn't tell nobody either.'

I didn't like Carson Chambliss speaking for me, especially when it came to this kind of thing, especially when we hadn't said more than two words to each other in years and years. And I didn't like a grown woman telling her pastor she was pregnant before her own husband knew and then him sending her out to me after showing her how to get rid of it on her own. Then it dawned on me, and I'll never forget the look on Julie's face when I asked.

'Is this Ben's baby?'

She raised her eyes to mine, and we stood there looking at each other. 'What do you mean?' she said.

'Is this Ben's baby?' I asked again.

'Of course,' she said. 'Whose in this world would it be otherwise?'

'You tell me,' I said.

'If you don't think you're going to do it, then tell me now,' she said. 'I can figure out something else if you won't help me.'

I ain't going to say that I hadn't ever done it before, and I ain't going to say there's not reasons good and bad for that kind of thing, but I knew right then there wasn't no way I was going to do it for Julie Hall, no matter who'd sent her. But I didn't tell her that with her standing out in the rain soaking wet and scared to death, bruises spreading out across her belly like flower blossoms.

'Let's just wait,' I told her. 'Let's just wait another month and see what happens. It ain't going to hurt nothing at all if we just wait. You probably ain't going to show for a while anyway.'

★   ★   ★

But I guess what she'd done to herself must've worked because she never mentioned nothing else about it to me, and she sure didn't have no baby. I waited a couple of months before I asked her about it again, and I could tell then that she didn't want to talk about it at all. We were standing out in the parking lot one Sunday afternoon after the service had let out. I'd brought the children up from the riverbank, and they were all running in between the cars and chasing each other like they always did. Julie was standing and talking to a few of the women from the church, and I waited until she was alone before I went up and spoke to her.

'I reckon you had your cycle,' I said, 'because you ain't been back around to see me.'

'I got it this month,' she said.

'You ever tell Ben?'

'No,' she said. 'Turns out there wasn't nothing to tell. I was just late; that's all.' She turned around and hollered for Jess and Christopher, and then she loaded them up into Ben's truck.

'You come by and see me if you ever need to,' I said. 'It ain't got to be about something like this, but just know you can come and talk to me whenever you need to.'

'Thank you,' she said, 'but I reckon everything's all right now. I'm fine.'

I stood and watched her back Ben's old truck out of the parking lot and drive off up the road. I remember thinking, *There goes a woman who's gone and got herself scared good*, but I just couldn't figure out what in the world could've scared her so bad.

I turned back toward the building to talk to some folks before they left, and when I did I saw Carson Chambliss standing in the door of the church. The sunlight was right in his eyes, and he stood there with a wooden crate in each of his hands. He stared at me without even once blinking. He held those crates down at his sides by the little suitcase handles that were fastened to them; they had chicken wire stapled up around the insides, but he was too far away for me to see what was in there, although I knew well enough what they were.

'How're you, Sister Adelaide?' he asked me.

'I'm fine,' I said. 'I'm just about to leave.'

'We had us a blessed service this morning,' he said. 'And I pray our children did as well.'

'We got along fine,' I said. 'We always do.' He

242

took him a few steps into the parking lot and stopped in front of me, and when he did one of those crates he held bucked so strong I was afraid it would jump out of his hand. He looked down at it for a second, and then he looked up at me. He was smiling.

'That's good to hear,' he said. 'Children are the lifeblood of this church. There ain't no future without them.' He turned and set those crates in the back of Tommy Lester's pickup truck where Tommy had put the ones he was carrying, and then he went around to the other side and climbed in beside Tommy. I watched them pull out of the parking lot and listened to Tommy rev the engine as they took off up the road.

I stood there and watched them go and thought about how that was an awfully strange thing for a man to say who'd go and show a mother how to kill her own.

15

But Julie did come back out to my house. She showed up at my door on Monday evening, the day after Christopher died, and when I saw her standing out there I could tell that she'd been crying.

'You told me before that I could come and talk to you,' she said.

'Well, of course you can, girl,' I said. 'Come on in here.' I closed the door and led her over to the sofa and sat down beside her. It was only the night before when we were doing this very same thing, and it almost brought a chill to my bones, the very idea that we were almost going to relive it together. 'Can I get you anything?' I asked her. 'I got a little bit of coffee left on the stove, or I could heat you up a little water for some tea.'

'No,' she said, 'I'm fine. I just need to get away from that house.'

'Well, Julie, you can stay with me for as long as you need to,' I said. I reached over and put my hand on hers, and when I did she took to crying. She tried covering her eyes with her hands, but it didn't do any good. 'You can bring Jess over here with you too. He might want to be with his mama.'

'I can't,' she said. 'Ben won't let me have him. We've already talked about it. He won't even let me be alone with him, he won't even hardly look at me.'

'He's just trying to get through this,' I told her. 'Same as you. Everybody goes about dealing with things in different ways.'

'But he started up drinking after we got home from the hospital last night. And this morning, after his daddy took Jess to school, the two of them went off to his daddy's house and they've been over there all day. I wanted to pick Jess up from school, but he wouldn't let me have the truck, and I'm afraid he's drinking too much to drive and I'm afraid of what's going to happen. When I tried to talk to him, he just told me that everything that's happened is all my fault.'

'Well, y'all just lost your son yesterday, Julie,' I said. 'Y'all just lost your little boy, and there ain't nothing that can prepare folks for something like that. People say all kinds of things when they're grieving, especially men. This is just one of those things you can't be prepared for.'

'It's not just that,' she said. 'I'm scared of him. I've never seen him like this in all the years we've been together. He's acting just like his daddy did, and I hoped he wouldn't ever be that way.'

'Now, you know that ain't true,' I said. 'You know he's a better man than that.'

'I'd hoped he would be,' she said. 'But he's blaming me for what's happened, saying it was my idea, saying the healing must've been my idea.'

'Well, Julie, you did the best thing you knew to

do,' I said. 'And you know it's not right of Ben to blame you for trying to help Christopher.'

'But it wasn't my idea,' she said. 'It wasn't my idea to do it.'

'Well, who in the world said it needed doing?'

'Pastor,' she said. 'It was his idea. He told me there was something in Christopher that wasn't letting him talk, and he promised me he could get it to leave him alone. He told me to trust him and that I shouldn't even tell Ben about it until after it was done. He said that Ben would understand God's truth eventually, that everybody would see how God had healed him.' She dropped her hands in her lap and sat there staring down at them. 'But I shouldn't have let them do it again last night,' she said. 'Not after what happened yesterday morning.' She raised her eyes and looked at me. 'But, Miss Lyle,' she said, 'I swear I heard him speak. I swear he called out for me with all of them laying their hands on him. I know he was scared, but it worked. The Lord was healing him. I know He was. And Pastor wanted me to bring him back last night so he could finish, but I was scared after what had happened, and I wanted to say something. I wanted to stop it, but I just didn't know how.'

'You really trust him, don't you?' I asked.

'Who?'

'Chambliss.'

'Yes,' she said. 'I do. I do trust him. I know he's a man of God. I know God speaks through him.'

'Julie, like I told you, you can stay here as long as you need to. But I can't have that man over at this house, and I'm asking you to please stay away from him, at least until all this gets settled. Your little boy died in his church, under his hand. I just think it's best if you stay away from there for now. At least as long as you're staying here with me. Can you do that?' She looked down at her hands for a minute like she was thinking about whether she could or not, and I honestly didn't know how she was going to answer. She finally looked up at me.

'Yes, ma'am,' she said. 'I can do that.'

'Good,' I said. 'I just can't have him coming around here. Not after what's happened.'

As I was saying that, I'd already started thinking about how Carson Chambliss wasn't going to like Julie staying with me, and I knew for sure he wasn't going to like me talking to the sheriff on Tuesday afternoon, even if I didn't know anything for certain about what happened to Christopher. Chambliss knew there were other things that I'd seen and heard, other things that I could talk about that might make him look bad or guilty. So I wasn't a bit surprised when Julie came into my room on Wednesday evening after the funeral and told me he wanted me to come down to the church the next day, and I can say that after I did I knew for certain that I'd looked right into the face of evil.

Clem Barefield

16

Adelaide Lyle's skin was thin like paper, and her veins were blue smears across the backs of her hands. I watched them roll over her knuckles where her fingers kneaded the chair against which her body leaned. It was Tuesday morning, two days after they'd brought that boy's body out to her house on the night he died.

'Would you like something to drink?' she asked me. 'Something to eat?' Before I could even answer her, she turned her back to me and shuffled over toward the cupboard and started searching the shelves.

'I'm fine not to eat,' I said, but she kept staring into the cupboard as if she couldn't hear me. 'I'm fine not to eat,' I said again, louder this time to make certain she heard me. She turned around and looked at me for a moment like I'd hurt her feelings somehow, like I'd denied her something by not eating whatever it was she might have been able to pull from that cupboard. I motioned toward the empty seat at the head of the table. 'I just want to talk to you for a few minutes,' I said. 'Just a few minutes. That's all. Shouldn't take too much longer than that.'

She hesitated for a minute, and then she

walked back to the table and pulled out a chair. After she had lowered herself into the chair she smoothed out the tablecloth and interlaced her fingers and left them resting there before her. Her brown eyes were bright and uncertain, and I watched tiny flecks of gold flash across them.

'I need you to tell me everything you know about what happened to Christopher on Sunday evening,' I said.

'I don't know anything to tell you,' she said. 'I wasn't there. I was at home. They brought him here after it happened.'

'After what happened?'

'After he died, I reckon,' she said.

'How did he die?'

'I don't know for certain,' she said. 'Like I told you, I wasn't there. All I know is what folks told me.'

'What did Julie say about it?' I asked.

'She said they were trying to heal him. That's all she said.'

'Where's she at right now?'

'I don't know,' she said. 'But she ain't here.'

'How long has she been staying with you?'

'Just for one night,' she said. 'But she may be staying here a little while longer.'

'Why isn't she at home with her family?'

'Because she says it ain't safe there. She says Ben's taken to drinking and blaming her for what's happened.'

'Why doesn't she feel safe? Has he threatened to hurt her?'

'I don't know,' she said. 'You'd have to ask her about it, but you saw for yourself what he did to those boys who came out from the church on Sunday night.'

'I did,' I said. 'But there's a lot of men who would've done them the same way.'

'Would you have?' she asked.

'I can't say that I would have,' I told her. 'Maybe at one time, yes. But a young man's got more fire in him. An old man like me tends to think about things a little more deeply.' She looked away, and I sat and stared at the side of her face. I knew she could feel my eyes on her. 'Has anybody told you not to talk to me about this?'

'Nobody tells me what to do,' she snapped. 'Nobody ever has. I've been at that church since I was a young woman, and not once has anybody ever told me what to do.' I sat back in the chair and stared at her for a second, and then I looked away and noted the tidiness of her kitchen. The shiny utensils hanging over the stove. The clear glass above the sink through which the sunlight poured.

'I know you've got a mind of your own,' I said. 'And I know it led you to take the children out of that church. And because of that, I know there has to be some good reason for Christopher being in there on Sunday night,' I said. 'I believe they might've told you what it was.'

'Folks told me they were trying to heal him,' she said.

'And how were they doing that,' I asked, 'by smothering him to death?'

'It was an accident,' she said. 'And you well know it.'

250

'Do you think he needed healing?'

'No, I don't,' she said. 'But that's not for me to say, and it's not for you to judge either. You didn't know that little boy. You don't know what he went through with some of those kids picking on him. You don't know what his family went through all these years.'

'I know he's dead,' I said. 'And I know his daddy wasn't there and his mama won't stay put long enough for me to ask her about it. I know that, but it ain't enough to make sense of.'

'You can't make sense of everything,' she said. 'That ain't the job of man.'

'It's my job to make the best sense I can, and I'm more than willing to leave the rest to Him, if that's what you mean. But sometimes I need a little help. That's why I came out here to talk to you.'

'I wish I knew how to help you,' she said.

I leaned forward and put my elbows on the table. 'Has Carson Chambliss told you not to talk to me?'

She stood up quick and pushed back her chair. It made an awful scraping sound as it slid over the hardwood. She walked to the sink and leaned her hips into the counter. Her back was to me, and I imagined her eyes flitting across the grass and scanning the yard while taking full measure of the way the tone of my voice had arched around my words.

'I'm sorry,' I said. I watched her shoulders drop. 'I just want to be sure that folks know they can talk to me. I want them to feel safe because I need to find out what happened.'

251

'I'd tell you if I knew,' she said, turning to face me. 'I can promise you that. I may be an old woman, but nobody tells me what to think or how to do, especially Carson Chambliss.' She folded her arms across her chest, and I watched as she appeared to pull herself inward. Her brief anger softened into a sadness that spread out across her face. Her eyes grew wet.

'I love those children,' she said. 'All of them. I love every single one of them like they're my own. And to lose one of them, especially Christopher . . . ' Her voice trailed off.

I sat and listened to her and watched her eyes fill with tears, but I was somewhere else, listening to my own voice over hers. *She doesn't know what she's saying. She's an old woman and she's never raised her own and she doesn't know what it is to lose one. And she's not a man and she doesn't know what it is to watch a mother grieve.* I stared straight ahead and watched as it all came back to me. The dappled snow on the rhododendron. The silence me and Owens suffered as we stood over Jeff's body, smoke rising from his boots and catching in my nose and in my throat until I wanted to puke. *I could tell her about dreams,* I thought. *About how at night I wake from white-hot sparks hissing from my son's toes while the current holds him on the line. But those are dreams, and there ain't no place for them in the daylight.* Not now, anyway. Not here.

I looked past my own memories, and I tried to picture Adelaide Lyle's face twenty years younger and wet with tears. I figured my arms would grow heavy with her just as they'd grown heavy with Sheila, and that her sadness would work itself into the core of my being and leave a hollowed-out place that couldn't ever be filled. I knew that real loss isn't something you feel after watching a child once a week while his mama sings hymns. It takes a lifetime to build equity in loss. There ain't nothing before that.

'You talk to Pastor Chambliss yet?' she asked me.

'No,' I said. 'You're the first person I came to. But I can tell you that I plan to visit him as soon as I find out where he lives.'

'Well, I might can help you with that,' she said.

'I'd appreciate it,' I said. 'But will you tell me something else?'

'Depends on what it is,' she said. 'Depends on whether or not I know what it is you're asking about.'

'After going to that church for all these years,' I said, 'and after spending all that time with those folks, what was it that led you to take the children out of there?' It grew quiet inside the house, and I caught myself narrowing my eyes and turning my head like I was listening for something I might not be able to hear. 'Was it Chambliss?' I asked. She looked at me, and then she nodded her head. 'What was it exactly? I promise I'm not going to say anything to him. There's no reason for him to know I've even been here.'

I could tell that she was thinking about the promise I'd just made, and I knew she was wondering whether or not I could keep it. And apparently she decided that I could.

'This ain't the first time it's happened,' she said.

'What do you mean 'this ain't the first time'?' I asked.

'This ain't the first time somebody's died from all that carrying on,' she said. 'And as I sit here telling you this, it becomes clearer and clearer to me that I should've tried to keep them from taking Christopher into that church in the first place. I don't know that I could've stopped them even if I'd wanted to, but I didn't even try. And now, here we are.' And then she said a name I hadn't thought about in years and years: Molly Jameson.

17

It took me two days of looking and asking around, but on Thursday evening I headed out to Little Pine Creek in the South Marshall Township, where Chambliss was renting an old farmhouse from a deacon named Phil Ponder. The two-lane road ran along the creek, and the land opened up as I headed down into the cove. You could tell that autumn was bearing down on us because the leaves on the trees atop the ridge were just starting to get notions of color. I drove past the scarred, rocky outcrops until I got low enough to follow the creek on my right. I took a little one-lane bridge across it and headed down a gravel road until I drove into a clearing where a little house and a barn sat way back off the road.

There was an old, broken-down Buick sedan parked in the driveway and an even older-looking coonhound tied up on a chain in the front yard. He howled like the dickens when I got out of the car, and I stood there looking at him until he finished and tucked his tail and sat down on his haunches. After that I put on my hat and looked around the yard. Then I walked up on the porch and saw that the front door was flung wide open. I leaned my head inside the house. It was cool and dark.

'Hello,' I said. I waited a second to see if anybody who may be in the house had anything to say. Right inside a set of stairs led up to the second floor. On my right was a sitting room where one chair had been pushed up under a little table. There were a few books scattered on the tabletop. Overhead a single bulb hung down from the ceiling. All I could see of the room on my left was an old cloth sofa with cushions that somebody had tried to keep together with duct tape. 'Hello,' I said again. I couldn't hear a thing except that old hound dog growling at me out there in the yard.

'You're trying to scare off the good guys, you old mutt,' I told him as I walked by on my way down the porch steps. He quit growling and looked at me hard and cocked his head like he might be trying to figure out what I was saying to him.

I stood there in the yard and watched what was left of the sun fall through the red maples, and I looked up and saw the thunderheads off in the distance. The breeze picked up and stirred the bitternuts and the sweetgums down by the creek across the road. I turned up my nose and caught the reek of that black bank mud and it smelled good, clean and cold, and I thought about the weather coming on and the days growing shorter and shorter. Wouldn't be long before I'd have us a fire going at night in the front room. Then the snow again.

I walked to the side of the house and stood in front of the cruiser and looked out across the yard and considered the old barn for a minute. It was sun-scorched and just about bleached white and appeared to be leaning to one side as if it might tumble over into the high grass. I set off across the yard to have a look. I don't hold with snooping because that'll get you into trouble real fast in this line of work. But I can tell you it doesn't ever hurt to take a good look around when you got the time. Seemed to me like time was about all I had right then.

The barn didn't have a door on it, and I walked up to it and stood just outside it and looked in at all that blackness. I could smell the damp earth of the dirt floor, and I watched the dust motes float up and drift in and out of the light. I stood there and listened to the wind pick up on the ridge behind the barn and tumble down toward me and roll out over the road toward the creek bed in front of the house. I thought I saw something move way back toward the far wall, and I squinted my eyes and took a step inside so they'd adjust to the dark.

'Come on in, Sheriff,' a voice said. 'I heard your car when you pulled up. Forgive me for not coming out to meet you.'

'That's all right,' I said. 'I hate to be a snoop, but I was hoping you'd be out here.'

'Well, here I am,' said Chambliss.

My eyes had finally got adjusted, and I could see the outline of his body, and I could tell he had his back turned to me and his hands were moving like he was working on something. I could feel the wind coming through the cracks in the walls and there was a sound like dried leaves being rustled somewhere in the barn that I couldn't see. He clicked on a little lamp on the table in front of him, and the edges of his body glowed. I wondered if he'd turned it off when he realized I was there.

'I hate to interrupt you,' I said. 'I just wanted to ask you some questions about what happened up at your church this past Sunday night. I just need to get some things cleared up, and then I'll be out of your hair and on my way.'

'What kind of questions do you have?'

'Well,' I said, 'I've just got a couple about that boy we had that funeral for yesterday evening.'

He stopped working and stood there for a second just as still as he could be. Then I saw his body move and he turned to face me. The little lamplight behind him shone all around him. The wind picked up again and whistled through the walls and stirred what sounded like leaves somewhere against the wall of the barn.

'I just realized there ain't hardly no light in here,' he said. 'It don't bother me, but I'll bet you can't see a thing.'

'I'm all right,' I said. 'It ain't like I'm looking for nothing anyway. Just talking.'

'But it's awfully dark,' he said again. 'There's a bulb right above you there on that middle beam. If you don't mind to turn that bulb on, it would let us see each other a little better.'

I looked up toward the beams running over my head and saw an exposed bulb, and I stepped forward and felt around in front of me until I found a little piece of string where it hung down. I gave it a tug, but the light didn't come on.

Chambliss clicked off the lamp on the table, and his voice seemed to rise from the darkness.

'I'm sorry, Sheriff,' he said. 'I think it's got a little short in it. If you'll reach up there and give the bulb a turn, then it'll come right on.'

I stood up on the toes of my boots and ran my hand along the beam until my fingers closed around the dusty bulb. I gave it half a turn and it came right on, and when I looked up at the beam again there was a snake coiled around it with its head reared back like it was ready to strike. My hand snapped back, and I hollered out and fell onto my back in the dirt.

When I looked up, I saw Chambliss standing above me in the light from that bulb, and just over his shoulder I could see where a thick cord of rope with a pulley set to the end of it had been wound around the beam.

'You all right, Sheriff?' he asked.

'I'm fine,' I said as I got to my feet and dusted myself off. 'My mind was just playing tricks on me. That's all. I just thought I saw something that wasn't there.'

I took my hat off and ran my fingers over my head and put it back on. I raised my head and took a good look at Chambliss. His flat-top haircut was streaked with little hints of gray and he was older than I'd remembered, but he looked to be strong, like a man who was used to doing hard work. He had on blue jeans and a spotless blue dress shirt with the sleeves rolled down. His hands were covered in some kind of grease, and I figured he'd been working on something when I found him. I looked over his shoulder and saw that he'd been beneath the hood of an old Chevy. He rubbed at his nose with the back of his hand; the grease left a smear just above his lip.

'What did you think you saw up there?' he asked, smiling.

'It doesn't matter,' I said.

I dusted off the front of my pants and looked around the inside of the barn. It was slam full of rusted old farm implements: a deflated tractor tire with a bent wheel, a couple of broken-down engines hanging on chains from the rafters. There were tools of all sorts scattered all over the dirt. I turned my head to the right, and when I did I saw what must've been hundreds of molted snake skins tacked to one whole wall of the barn, and I realized that the sound I'd heard earlier was actually the wind whipping through the slats in the walls and rustling those skins. It was a sound like a dead cornfield being stirred in a breeze. Underneath those snake skins were stacked dozens of little crates fitted with handles and clasps. I quit dusting my pants and just stood there looking at them. Chambliss followed my gaze to the wall, and then he looked back at me. I heard him laugh to himself.

'You're not afraid of snakes, are you, Sheriff?'

I looked back over at Chambliss. He was smiling again.

'I wouldn't say afraid. Wary. But not afraid.'

He walked over to the wall and ran his fingers through the snake skins. Some of them had rattles on the end, and they sounded like tiny maracas when he jostled them.

'Where did you find all those?' I asked.

'Oh, they're easy to find if you know where to look,' he said. 'I guess you could say I collect them. I like to think they remind us that we can change into something new. That's what the good Lord can do for us when he grants us salvation, Sheriff. He makes us new. All the old, dead life falls away from us.' He looked over at me like he expected that to leave some kind of impression.

'I've heard something about that,' I said. 'And I can see how that would mean something to you as a pastor, especially after what happened to you down in Georgia — that fire and all.' He looked up at me like he was shocked that I even knew about that, much less had the guts to bring it up.

'I don't think I understand what you're getting at,' he said. 'I don't think you understand either.'

'Sure you do,' I said. 'A couple phone calls, and I traced you back to Toccoa real quick. I've just never had a reason to let on that I know about it until now. But like I said, I can see how you'd like those snakes. They shed skin, men shed skin. Skin grows back, sometimes it gets grafted on.'

'I served my time for that,' he said. 'I don't know why you're even talking about it. It's got no bearing on my life here.'

'It might and it might not,' I said. 'But it's funny what you find out about people after a little boy dies. It's funny how it gets folks to talking about things they hadn't talked about in years.'

'What are you getting at?' he asked.

'Does the name Molly Jameson mean anything to you?'

'I had nothing to do with that,' he said.

'Nothing that I could charge you with,' I said. 'At least not right now. But this other, this little boy, that's something else altogether. This thing can't be left out in a garden and forgotten. It's got to have some kind of conclusion.' He must've been telling the truth about that bulb having a short in it, because the light began to flicker off and on, and before I knew I couldn't hardly see anything inside that barn. 'You mind if we talk outside?' I said.

'Not at all,' he said. 'But I need to tell you that I'm attending a prayer meeting this evening.'

'I won't keep you long,' I said. 'I promise.'

★   ★   ★

I walked out into the light of the backyard, and he followed me. That thunderhead was getting closer, and the sky had started to darken even though we had a couple hours of daylight left.

'The days are getting shorter,' I said. 'Seems like every year I forget it'll happen, and every year it surprises me.'

'I know you didn't come out here to talk about the weather, Sheriff,' Chambliss said. He was holding a rag and wiping at his hands. I watched him use it to get in between his fingers.

'I know you know that,' I said. 'And you know I've never given a damn about what y'all do up in that church. I've never passed judgment about how y'all chose to worship, no matter what I heard people say about it. But this is different. Something happened up there on Sunday night, and I need to find out what it was.'

'What happens on Sundays in your church, Sheriff?'

'Mr. Chambliss, I haven't stepped foot in a church in about twenty-five years, and stories like this one here make me think that's been a pretty good decision.'

Chambliss laughed to himself and looked down at his hands and kept wiping at them like he just couldn't get them clean enough.

'A few of the folks I've talked to seem to think y'all were attempting some kind of healing,' I said.

'If I knew who you'd been talking to, I might be able to give you some kind of bearing on the truth.'

'Well, I ain't going to tell you who I talked to, if that's what you're getting at,' I said.

'You know Adelaide Lyle's about out of her mind,' he said. 'You can't trust a word an old woman like that says.'

'You trust her with the church's children, don't you? As far as I know, one of them never died while she was watching them. That boy had a bruise the size of a football on his backside. I don't guess you'd know anything about that, would you?'

'I can't say that I do,' he said. 'Young boys are likely to get all kinds of bruises.'

'That's true,' I said. I turned toward my car like I was thinking about leaving. I even took a step toward the yard, but then I turned around and looked at Chambliss.

'I almost forgot,' I said. 'You ever hear of something called petechiae?'

'No,' he said. 'I ain't never heard that word.'

I put my hands in my pockets and looked down at the gravel. 'That's okay,' I said. 'Most folks haven't.' I looked up at him again. 'And I'll admit that I hadn't heard it either until it showed up in a coroner's report about fifteen years ago.' I took a step toward Chambliss. 'Down in Hot Springs, a man named Chestnut had strangled his girlfriend with a telephone cord and then shot himself in the head. It was just an awful scene in their trailer: blood everywhere. But as bad as that scene was, as bad as it was to see that man's brains blown all over the wall and all over his sofa, nothing bothered me until I saw that woman's face. Her eyes were open, and they looked like somebody had come along and just poured blood into them. I learned from the coroner that they looked that way because her vessels had exploded because her air had been cut off while he was strangling her. It wasn't just her eyes, though. You could see that her vessels had burst under the skin around her cheeks, her neck. I can still see her face, just as blue as a robin's egg, those eyes swimming in blood.'

'Why are you telling me this?' he asked. 'I didn't even live here then. I never knew those people.'

'That's true,' I said. 'You didn't live here then, but you're here now, and I'm telling you this because Christopher had petechiae, just like that

264

poor girl did. But we know Christopher wasn't strangled with a telephone cord. He died from broken ribs — three of them. That's a strange thing to die of, isn't it?'

'I reckon it is,' Chambliss said.

'Well, he didn't die just because his ribs broke. The coroner's report says he died because one of those broken ribs punctured a lung. He died of asphyxia. That means he suffocated, Pastor.

'Now, I don't know what y'all do up in that church that could cause something like this to happen, but I want you to know that it's all going to come out eventually. And I can tell you, the sooner it does the better it's going to be for everybody. If it takes the court and subpoenas and the jail to get you to talk, then that's what it'll take. But this family's got themselves a dead boy and no answers.'

'Are you threatening me, Sheriff?'

'No, I ain't threatening you,' I said. 'But folks get to talking after something like this happens. People get ideas, and they're likely to place blame whether it's deserving or not.'

'Are you one of them people?'

'No,' I said. 'I'm not one of them people. I ain't ready to blame anyone just yet. All I'm doing is looking for facts and trying to make sense of them. But it probably ain't me and my blame that you need to be worried about.'

'Who, then?'

'You must not have seen what that boy's daddy did to those men you sent out there to Miss Lyle's on Sunday night.'

'I have, and it wasn't called for either. I'd like

to think a sheriff offers his people a little more protection and is a little more interested in keeping the peace.'

'I am interested in peace,' I said, 'and that's why I'm here. But I can promise you that you ain't going to have none of it until this is settled. One thing I can't promise you is that that boy's daddy ain't going to come around looking for answers just like me. Only difference between me and him is that I'm bound to uphold the law. He's not going to have any interest in doing such a thing. He hasn't seen the law work for him yet.'

'You think he's coming to kill me or something?'

'No,' I said, 'I ain't saying that, Pastor. We already had us one funeral. I'd like to hold off a while on having another one if we could.'

I heard a crack of thunder way off behind me over the hills. The breeze picked up again and stirred the branches on the trees behind the barn.

'Now, I believe you're a spiritual man, Mr. Chambliss. And I know you like to keep your secrets about what's going on up there in that church, and that's fine with me as long as nobody gets hurt and nobody ends up dead. But there's a family's spirit that needs healing, and I would think a God-fearing man would want to see that it's done.'

'God don't just care for the spirit, Sheriff,' Chambliss said. 'I'm sure even a man like you knows that Christ healed the sick.'

'Yeah, I know He did,' I said. 'But you ain't Christ.' He smiled and looked up at me and narrowed his eyes. 'You call me when you get to feeling like you want to do the right thing. If not, I can guarantee that you'll be hearing from me soon.'

I turned and walked away from the barn and out across the yard toward the cruiser.

'We're all in need of some kind of healing, Sheriff,' he hollered after me.

I opened the door to my car and slid onto the seat and watched him as he walked back toward the barn. The first drops of rain splattered on my windshield. I thought about what he said and realized that I couldn't have agreed with him more.

18

I could smell the pork chops frying in the pan when I opened the door and walked into the house. Sheila was in the kitchen with the radio on, and I walked down the hallway to the bedroom. I hung my belt and my holster on the closet door, and then I unbuttoned my pants and untucked my shirt. I kicked off my boots and left them on the far side of the bed and sat down. I could hear Sheila's footsteps coming down the hall. She stopped at the bedroom door.

'You ready to eat?' she asked.

I turned and looked at her over my shoulder. 'You sure know how to greet a man,' I said.

She smiled. 'Well, come on while it's hot,' she said. My shirt was almost soaked through with the rain, and I took it off and dropped it by the bed. I walked into the dining room in my undershirt and sat down at the table.

'I forgot to wash my hands,' I said.

'It's all right,' Sheila said. 'It won't kill you to eat with dirty hands, not tonight, anyway.'

I forked two pork chops and dropped them onto my plate, and then I spooned some salad out beside them.

'You want a beer?' Sheila asked.

268

'You want a beer?' I asked her back.

She smiled at me and stood up and went into the kitchen and I heard her open the refrigerator, and then I heard the sound of the bottles clinking together. She walked back into the dining room and sat my beer in front of my plate. She sat down and picked up her fork. 'So, what you got so far?' she asked.

I took a sip from my beer and sat it on the table and looked at it for a minute. I watched the sweat run off the bottle onto the tablecloth, and then I picked it up and wiped it down with my napkin. I sat it back on the table. 'Well, I got a dead boy who never said a word in his life, a mama who don't want to say one now, a preacher who's more interested in saving my soul than telling me the truth, and an old woman who's too scared of him to say hardly anything at all. I know it sounds like I got a lot, but when you take a hard look at it it don't amount to much more than jack shit, if it even amounts to that.' I picked up the beer and took another drink.

Sheila smiled at me across the table. 'Something'll break,' she said. 'It always does.'

And by God if she wasn't dead on with that.

Jess Hall

19

After the school bus dropped me off on Thursday afternoon, I left my book bag on the porch by the front door and walked over to Joe Bill's. There wasn't nobody at home at my house, and I didn't feel like being there alone.

I rung Joe Bill's doorbell, and he flung the door open before the chimes even stopped. He stepped out onto the front porch and closed the door behind him like he didn't want me to see what he was doing inside his house.

'Hey,' he said.

'Can you play?'

'Yeah,' he said. 'But you can't come inside. My mom's not home. She doesn't want nobody coming in when she ain't here.'

'All right,' I said. 'What do you want to do?'

'It don't matter,' he said. He turned his head to his left and looked down the road like he was expecting to see someone. 'I was just out in the backyard shooting Scooter's BB gun a few minutes ago.'

'What were you shooting at?'

'Just different things,' he said.

'Can I shoot it?'

'No,' he said. 'I already put it back, and I ain't

270

getting it out again. He'll be getting home from work pretty soon, and I don't want him catching me with it. He'd kill me if he did.'

'Whatever,' I said, but I didn't blame him. Joe Bill was scared to death of Scooter, and I was too. He was fifteen years old, but he seemed a whole lot older to me. He had a fat friend named Clay, and I was especially afraid of him because he was as dumb as a rock and that made him even more terrifying because he'd do just about anything Scooter told him to do. The two of them worked for Joe Bill's daddy down at his garage in Marshall. Joe Bill had sworn that one time he saw his brother talk Clay into eating some broken glass that somebody had busted out of the windows in an old school bus that was parked in the junk lot behind the garage. Joe Bill said Clay thought about it for a minute, and then he picked out a couple of pieces of glass from the gravel and put them in his mouth and chewed them for a while and swallowed them. Joe Bill said Clay's mouth didn't bleed or nothing. I didn't know if I believed that or not, but sometimes I thought I might.

The meanest thing I'd ever seen them do was a few years before when Joe Bill got a remote-control car for Christmas. We'd built a little ramp out in his driveway, and we were taking turns launching the car off into the grass. Scooter and Clay rode up on their bikes and watched us from out in the road. After a minute they came up the driveway and Scooter picked up that car and wouldn't give it back, and then he told Clay to jump up and down on our ramp until it broke, and it wasn't but two or three jumps before it snapped right in two because he was so fat. Joe Bill said he was going to holler for his mom, and when he did Clay picked up a baseball bat out of the carport and Scooter tossed that car up into the air and Clay swung at it like he was hitting a baseball. He busted all the wheels off the car and knocked out the batteries. It landed right in the middle of the yard, and Joe Bill went running over to it and picked it up and looked at it, and then he threw it down and ran into the house.

He left the carport door open and I could hear him crying inside, but Scooter and Clay just rode off on their bikes before Joe Bill's mom came out. I knew Joe Bill wouldn't fess up to crying about that now, but I think I probably would've cried too. That was an awfully nice car just to watch it get broken for no reason.

'Well, what do you want to do?' I asked.

'We could shoot some baskets out back,' he said.

'Okay,' I said.

★   ★   ★

There was a little patch of dirt in Joe Bill's backyard where his daddy had put up a basketball goal, but it really wasn't nothing but a wooden backboard with a rusty old rim nailed to it. The rim didn't even have a net on it. The court was just made of dirt, and when you bounced the ball it looked like brown smoke was rising up off the ground.

272

'You want to play PIG or HORSE?' Joe Bill asked. He tried to dribble the ball between his legs, but he bounced it on his foot and it rolled to the edge of the dirt before it stopped at the grass. He walked over and picked it up.

'Lets play PIG,' I said. 'HORSE takes too long. It'll be dark before we're done.'

'Okay,' Joe Bill said. He took a few steps toward the basket, and then he leaned backward and tried to aim the ball like he was going to throw it over his head behind him. 'Are you watching?' he asked me. 'I make this one all the time.' He looked at the goal upside down and tossed the ball toward the basket with both hands. It rattled on the rim, but it didn't go in. I heard thunder rumble over the mountain behind me, and I turned to look in the direction of the sound, and I saw the clouds had started growing darker. I knew that if Mama was at home instead of at Miss Lyle's, then she would've come looking for me by now, but she wasn't there and there wasn't nobody who knew where I was right then except for Joe Bill.

'It's your shot,' he said.

'You hear that thunder?' I asked.

'The storm's still a long way off,' he said. 'It's your shot.'

I carried the ball and walked away from him toward the woods, and then I turned around to see how far away I was from the basket.

'You can't make it from there!' Joe Bill hollered.

'Want to bet?' I hollered back. I held the ball up to my chin and stared at the rim like I was concentrating on it, and I thought about how far away the basket was. I walked a little closer before I took my shot. The ball rolled around the rim like it wasn't going to go in, and then it dropped into the basket.

Joe Bill caught the ball when it dropped through, and then he walked out to where I was still standing.

'Good luck,' I said.

'Whatever,' he said. He took his shot, but it bounced off the side of the rim. The ball rolled out to him and he picked it up.

'That's a P,' I said. Joe Bill bounced the ball once, and then he held it against his chest and brushed the dust off it. I clapped my hands for him to toss the ball to me.

'I made it,' I said. 'I get another shot.' He bounced me the ball.

'What's it like having a new grandpa?' he asked me. I looked down where my shadow stretched out in the dirt in front of me, and I thought about how to answer that question. I held the basketball against my stomach and turned sideways. It made my shadow look like I was pregnant.

'He ain't new,' I said. 'He's always been my grandpa.' I took a shot from where I stood, but it hit the backboard and bounced off the rim. Joe Bill chased it down and picked it up.

'But you hadn't ever met him before,' he said.

'I know,' I said. 'But that don't mean he's new.'

'Have you asked him where he's been?'

'Lots of places,' I said. 'But I'm not really

274

supposed to ask about it, so don't bug me.'

'I was just wondering,' Joe Bill said. He bounced the ball a couple of times, and then he said, 'What was it like when you went over to his house?'

'It was okay, I guess,' I said. 'It's just a trailer.' I'd had to go out there on Tuesday after school because Daddy said I shouldn't go to the funeral home to see Stump that night, even though I told him I wanted to because I was old enough to do that kind of thing. Mama might could've talked him into it, but she wasn't there to do it. She'd been at Miss Lyle's house ever since Monday, and I hadn't even seen her except once when one of the women from church had brought her out to the house early on Tuesday morning to get some clothes before I went to school. I couldn't go to Stump's funeral either because Daddy said that he didn't want me missing school. He said he didn't even want to go to the funeral home himself because it wasn't going to be Stump laying there anyway. He said Stump had gone off to Heaven and would just be sitting up there watching the whole thing and wondering why everybody was so sad.

My grandpa's trailer sat way back up in a holler over in Shelton. On the way over there he told me it was so far up in there that it almost looked like midnight even in the morning, but when he parked his truck and we got out I realized that I could see everything just fine. His trailer was made out of metal and it had a flat roof and a couple of little steps that led up to the door. I slid my book bag off the truck's seat and slung it over my shoulder, and then I followed him up the steps. It was dark inside there when he opened the door, but then he pulled open the blinds in the front room and went into the kitchen and pulled open the blinds over the sink. The trailer smelled like it had been closed up for a long time, and I could see the dust floating through the light where the sun came in the windows.

'How long have you lived here?' I asked him.

'Just about a month or so,' he said. 'But it's been mine a long, long time. I grew up on this land before I moved up to Gunter Mountain when your daddy was a little boy.' We stood there looking at each other for a second, and then he turned around and opened the refrigerator, and I could hear the sound of bottles clinking together. 'You want something to eat?' he asked me. 'Or a Coke or something?'

'I'm okay,' I said. I walked over and dropped my book bag on the sofa and sat down beside it. The sofa cushion was soft, and I sunk deep down into it and my book bag fell over into my lap. I picked up my book bag and sat it down on the floor and unzipped it and got out my spelling book and a pencil and some paper. I opened the book across my lap.

'You got some homework to do?' my grandpa asked.

'A little bit,' I said. He looked at my book, and then he looked out the window over the sink. He twisted the cap off the bottle of beer he'd taken out of the refrigerator.

'I'll stay out of your hair, then,' he said.

That night, after it got dark, my grandpa made a fire on the hillside behind his house, and we sat out there and roasted hot dog weenies on metal coat hangers. He didn't have any hot dog buns, and I didn't want to eat hot dogs on white bread, so we just dipped them in mustard and ketchup and ate them right off the coat hangers after they'd cooled off. He'd sat a bag of potato chips in between us and brought a two-liter of Coke up there too. He poured some Coke into my cup and then he poured some into his, and then he took a little metal flask out of his pocket and poured a little bit of that into his cup too. He'd stopped drinking beer once it had gotten dark outside, but just before we left the trailer and come up to the hill he'd taken a bottle of liquor down from the cabinet and filled the flask. He put the flask back into his pocket and took a sip of his drink. Then he leaned back and settled himself on his elbows.

'This is what men do,' he said. 'You know?' I lifted my hot dog out of the flames and looked over at him, but I didn't know what to say. 'This is what men have always done,' he said. 'They've always been outside, underneath the stars, cooking their food over an open fire.' He took a long drink. 'That's what the Indians did,' he said. 'The same Indians that used to live on this land, hundreds and hundreds of years ago; they did the same thing you and me are doing now.' He looked over at me. 'You feel like an Indian?' he asked.

'No,' I said. I pulled the hot dog off the end of my coat hanger. It burned my fingertips, and I

277

sat it on my lap so it could cool off before I ate it. I opened the plastic pack of hot dogs and took out another one and stuck it on the end of the hanger. My grandfather put his hand over his mouth and then slapped his lips and hollered and made a sound like an Indian.

'I feel like an Indian,' he said. He elbowed me, and my hot dog brushed against one of the logs on the fire. Sparks rose up out of the flames and drifted up into the dark sky. He laughed. 'You do it,' he said. I put my hand over my mouth and made a sound like an Indian too. 'All right,' he said. 'Now we're both Indians.' He finished his drink, and then he opened the bottle of Coke and poured some into his cup. 'This is what men do,' he said again.

We ate those hot dog weenies and sat out there on the hill by the fire until it had just about burned itself out, and then he let me go up into the woods behind us and find some sticks to put on the fire. I knew that Daddy had told him to make sure that I went to bed on time because I had school the next day, and I knew it was already way past my bedtime by then, but we just sat out there on that hill and looked at the fire.

'You got you a girlfriend?' my grandpa asked me.

'No,' I said.

'You like girls yet?'

'They're okay, I guess,' I said. 'My mom says I'm too young to have a girlfriend.'

'That sounds about right,' my grandpa said. He turned up his cup and drank what was left in it and tossed it into the fire, and then he reached into his pocket and took out the metal flask and unscrewed the top and took a long drink. He wiped his mouth with the back of his hand and let out a long sigh like he was thinking about something he didn't want to think about. 'That sounds like these women up here,' he said. 'They'll cut off your pecker before they'll let you play with it.'

I thought about telling him I didn't know what that meant because I hadn't ever thought about a girl cutting off my pecker, but my grandpa just looked into the fire like he didn't want me to say nothing, so I didn't. He took another sip from the bottle and spit into the fire and the flames shot up a little bit and I could feel the heat from the fire on my face. My grandpa looked over at me and opened and closed his fingers like they were a pair of scissors. 'They'll cut it clean off if you let them,' he said. 'Just like that.' He laughed a little at what he said and I laughed too, and then I lay back on the ground and looked up at the sky and watched little glowing pieces of ash float up toward the stars and disappear.

'It don't surprise me that your mother would say something like that to you,' he said. 'About you being too young to like girls. It doesn't surprise me at all.'

'Why not?'

'Did you ever meet your mama's mama? Your grandmother?'

'No,' I said. 'She died before I was born. I never met her daddy either.'

'I never did either,' my grandpa said. 'He'd been dead for years when her and your daddy met. Her people lived up in Mars Hill, and I didn't know a single one of them. I only met her mama once on the day those two got married up there.' He stopped talking and unscrewed the cap on the flask and took a swig, and then he put the cap back on. 'Your grandmama was a big woman, bigger than you can imagine her being.'

'How big?' I said.

'You know how big a washing machine is?' he asked.

'Yes.' He sat there quiet for a second, and then he looked over at me.

'Have you ever seen a Volkswagen Beetle?'

'She wasn't that big,' I said. 'There ain't no way she could've been.'

'You never saw her,' he said, laughing. 'She was a big woman, biggest woman I'd ever seen. She was a strong Christian too. Mars Hill's a dry town, and they held that wedding in a little Baptist church by a cornfield. It was early in the summer, and that corn was just as bright green and shiny as it could be. Your grandmama's name was Margaret, I think, Margaret Sampson, and she was already sitting right down front when I got to the church. And then, after the wedding, I walked outside where they'd set up some picnic tables with food, and there she was just sitting in the shade under a great big oak tree. I never saw that woman move, and I couldn't ever figure out how she got out there so quick.

'And let me tell you,' he said. 'She sat out there and watched the folks at that reception like she was a hawk. She held the wedding and reception both there at that church and there wasn't going to be any dancing and there definitely wasn't going to be no drinking. I reckon folks knew that before they came. I ain't never seen a woman so intent on getting her way, but that's how she brought your mama up. Religion was important to them. I didn't bring your daddy up that way; I didn't bring him up much of a way at all. But your mama was brought up to be religious, and folks don't change,' he said. 'It doesn't matter how bad you want them to.' I heard him unscrew the cap off the flask and take another drink. 'Sometimes it don't even matter how bad they want to change themselves.'

I thought about that, and then I thought about how much Daddy had changed in just the past few days, and then I thought about Stump sitting up in Heaven watching all the things that were going on down here. I wondered if he'd been watching me and Grandpa sit out there by that fire roasting those hot dogs, and then I wondered if he was watching me right then as I stood on the dirt court in Joe Bill's backyard with Joe Bill trying to dribble the ball between his legs right there beside me. He stopped dribbling and looked up at me.

'Can I ask you something weird?' Joe Bill asked.

'All right.'

'Do you think Stump's in Heaven?'

'Of course he's in Heaven,' I said.

'How do you know?'

'I just know,' I said.

'Was he saved by the Holy Spirit?'

'What?'

'My mom says that's the only way you can get into Heaven,' he said. 'She says you've got to confess your sins and be saved by the Holy Spirit.'

'I guess he was saved then.' I knocked the ball out of his hands and carried it out to where the free-throw line would've been if it was a real basketball court.

'But how do you know?' Joe Bill asked.

'I just think he's in Heaven,' I said.

'How?'

'What do you mean, 'how?''

'How's he in Heaven if he can't talk? How could he have confessed his sins and been saved by the Holy Spirit?'

'I don't know,' I said. 'I just think he's in Heaven. My dad told me he's there.' I remembered how Mama used to tell me and Stump that you'd know you'd been saved when you felt the Holy Spirit move inside your heart. I tried to imagine what that would feel like, but it was too hard for me to think about it out there behind Joe Bill's house with that thunder rumbling out over the mountain and Joe Bill running his mouth.

'Maybe that's why they were trying to heal him,' Joe Bill said. 'Maybe they wanted him to talk so he could confess his sins and go to Heaven when he died.'

'I don't want to talk about that,' I said.

'I wasn't talking about it,' Joe Bill said. 'I'm just saying that maybe that's why they did it.'

282

'You don't know why they did it,' I said. 'You didn't even see it. You ran away. And you don't know what they did on Sunday night either.'

'Neither do you,' he said. 'You weren't in there.'

'You don't even know what you're talking about,' I said.

'Neither do you,' Joe Bill said again. I looked at him and thought about tossing that basketball into the grass and busting him in the nose, but instead I just dribbled it once and then shot it as hard as I could. It bounced off the backboard so hard that the pole shook in the ground. The bail rolled toward Joe Bill's house, and we both stood there looking at it. I wanted to tell him about what I'd seen on Friday afternoon when Stump fell off the rain barrel, but I knew it was too late. I knew that if I was going to tell anybody about that I should've done it before Stump went into the church on Sunday morning, and I definitely should've said something before Mama took him back in there that night. But it wasn't going to make no difference telling Joe Bill about it now.

'Go get my ball,' Joe Bill said.

'You get it,' I told him. 'It's your ball, and it's your shot anyway.' He looked at me for a second, and then he walked toward his house and picked up the basketball. He turned back toward the goal and stood there looking at me like he was thinking about saying something else. I could see the road in front of the house over his shoulder, and I saw Scooter and Clay tearing down the road on their bikes. Gravel dust flew up behind them from under their tires, and I watched as they got closer and closer.

'Your brother's home,' I said.

Joe Bill turned around, and we watched Scooter and Clay pull their bikes into the yard. Scooter slammed on his brakes and slid his back tire around in the gravel. They dropped their bikes in the driveway and walked toward the carport. Scooter saw us standing in the backyard, and he stopped walking and just stood there and stared at us. Clay stopped walking and stared at us too. I didn't know what to do, so I raised my hand and waved at him. Scooter flipped me the bird.

'Fuck off!' he hollered. I heard Clay laugh.

'I'd better go home,' I said. 'It's getting late. It might rain too.'

'If you want to, you can stay a little while longer,' Joe Bill said. He turned and looked at me, and then he looked back up at the house. 'My mom will be home soon. You can wait until she gets back, and then she can drive you back to your house.'

I knew Joe Bill said that just because he didn't want to be left alone with Scooter and Clay without his mom being there. I didn't blame him, and I didn't say nothing to him about it. I wouldn't have wanted to be at home by myself with Scooter and Clay either.

'I'm glad we weren't shooting his gun when he got home,' Joe Bill said. He was still staring up at the house, and I looked down where he held the basketball and I knocked it out of his hands again. 'Hey,' he said. 'It's my shot.'

'I'm taking another turn,' I said. 'That last one

didn't count.' I walked away from the goal to the other side of the court closest to the house. I took a step toward the basket and shot it. I watched the basketball hit the rim this time before it bounced out onto the dirt.

'Almost,' I said.

'Almost ain't close enough,' Joe Bill said. He picked up the ball off the ground and wiped some of the dust off it. 'You shouldn't shoot from so far,' Joe Bill said.

'I'm getting closer,' I said. Something like a bumblebee buzzed past my ear, and I ducked my head and flicked it away. 'What was that?' I said.

'Don't move,' Joe Bill whispered. I looked up at him and saw that he was staring over my shoulder back toward the house. I turned around and saw Clay standing in the backyard by the carport. Scooter was down on one knee beside him with his BB gun pointed right at us. He cocked it and gave it two pumps. He raised it up to his shoulder and took aim at us again. I realized it was a BB that had just buzzed past my ear.

'He won't shoot us if we don't run,' Joe Bill whispered.

I heard Scooter take a shot, and a BB bounced off the basketball. Joe Bill dropped it in the dirt, and his throat made a sound like he was about to cry.

'Don't, Scooter!' Joe Bill screamed.

'Did y'all touch my gun?' Scooter hollered. Joe Bill looked at Scooter, and then he turned his head slowly and looked at me. He had his mouth open, and I could hear him breathing hard. Thunder rumbled out over the mountain behind him.

'I did,' Joe Bill said. He looked at Scooter. 'I took a couple of shots, but then I put it right back where it was.'

'I told you not to touch it,' Scooter said.

'I know,' Joe Bill said. Scooter lowered his BB gun and stared at Joe Bill for a second, and then he looked over at Clay.

'Go get them, Clay,' Scooter said. Clay jumped like somebody had just scared him, and he set off across the yard toward me and Joe Bill.

'Jess,' Joe Bill whispered. 'Run.' I looked from Clay to Joe Bill. 'Run,' he said again. It was a long way across the yard up to the road, and even though I knew Clay was too fat to catch me I was still scared of Scooter running after me, and I didn't know what I'd do if they chased me on their bikes. I also figured Scooter might try to shoot me if I ran off. I felt something land in my hair, and I realized it was raining. It must've surprised me, because I lit out of Joe Bill's yard and didn't stop running even though I could hear Scooter and Clay hollering for me to come back. I swear I even heard a couple of BBs whiz past my ears.

The rain was coming down so hard that by the time I got up to the road my shirt and my shorts were soaked all the way through and I could feel the water sloshing around in my socks. I knew those wet socks would make my toes all wrinkly.

I stopped running when I ran out of breath, and I slowed down and walked up the road toward where it curved around in front of the rock wall below the highway right above me. Water ran down from the highway like a little stream, and it spilled off those rocks like a waterfall. I stood on the side of the road and reached my hand over the guardrail and let the water run through my fingers. It ran in the gully beside the road and then got carried down toward the French Broad. I followed the gully where it ran alongside the road before it headed down the bank toward the river. I stepped out onto the bridge and looked over the side at the river, where it ran faster and louder than it had when I'd walked over it on the way to Joe Bill's house. There were sticks and leaves and stuff in there and I watched it all float toward the bridge before it went under there and came out the other side. I pushed back off the rail and walked to the other side of the bridge and looked over. A car passed by and slowed down when it saw me like it was going to stop. I waved, but it just kept on going. I figured whoever was in there probably wondered what I was doing out there in all that rain.

I started running again once I got across the bridge, and soon I was on the road to my house. Down in the cove the rain ran down the hills on both sides, and I watched it run and I knew it was filling up the creek and floating up all those crawdaddies. In my head I sang a song that Mama taught me and Stump when we were little:

It's raining, it's pouring,
An old man is snoring.
He went to bed and bumped his head,
And couldn't get up in the morning.

Before I knew it, I was headed up the driveway toward our house and the water rolled down through the gravel in little streams, and I knew if I came out in the morning I'd be able to find me some good quartz rocks that had gotten themselves washed up in this heavy rain. I heard the thunder crack somewhere behind me, but I was almost home and it didn't scare me one bit.

When I came around, I saw somebody out in the yard on the side of the house, but it had gotten too dark to tell who it was, but my daddy's truck was parked in front of the porch and I figured it was him. Once I got into the yard, I saw that he was messing with the gutter where the water poured down on the rain barrel. The rain came down so hard that I felt like I was looking at him through an old window screen, and I walked up into the yard and stood by the house and watched him, and I wondered if I should say something. The rain was loud, but I could hear him talking to himself and trying to put that gutter back together where it had broken. His feet slipped in the grass, and he had to get a good hold on the rim of the rain barrel so he didn't fall. I was too scared to say anything because I didn't want him asking me what happened. He looked up from the rain barrel and saw me standing there.

'Where you been?' he asked, but it was raining so loud that I couldn't hardly hear him good enough to know what he'd said. I looked at him, and then I looked at the gutter where it was bent. He quit messing with it and took a step toward me and then lost his balance and almost fell. He grabbed on to the rain barrel and stood up and started coming toward me again. When he got close, I saw his clothes were soaked all the way through just like mine were. 'Where you been?' he asked me again.

'I went to Joe Bill's after school,' I said.

He stared at me, and I saw that his eyes looked like he hadn't been asleep in a long time. It seemed like he couldn't even look at me for being so tired. He pointed behind him at the rain barrel.

'What happened to this?' he said. He waited for me to say something, but I just stood there without saying anything.

He bent down, and I could smell his breath and it smelled like Grandpa's did when he laughed out there on that hillside by the fire. Daddy bent down eye level with me and put his hands on his knees, but one of them slipped off because his pants were so wet. 'What happened to the rain barrel?' he asked me real slow and loud like he didn't think I could hear him. 'How'd it get broken?'

I looked away from him down toward the creek where it ran through the woods, and I thought about how fast it was probably moving with all this rain. My chest felt like I had somebody standing on it. Daddy reached out and grabbed my shirt. 'What happened to it?' he screamed.

I looked back at him, and I saw his face right up against mine and his eyes looked wild and terrifying. The smell of his breath was the only thing I could think about, and I started crying. 'Stump fell,' I finally said.

'What's that mean, 'Stump fell'?' he asked. He jerked my shirt and pulled me toward him. I put my hands on his shoulders to keep from slipping. I couldn't even look at him because I was so afraid of telling him.

'He fell,' I said. 'He was standing on top of it, and he fell.'

Daddy let go of my shirt and stepped back, and then he turned and looked at the rain barrel. I could tell that he was staring at the gutter where it was bent up and broken.

'Why was he standing up there?'

'Because we heard you,' I said. He turned and looked at me.

'What?'

'We thought we heard you and Mama inside,' I said. 'But I know we weren't supposed to be spying, especially because Mama'd sent us down to the creek and told us not to come back up to the house until we'd caught five salamanders.'

'You should've listened to her,' he said.

'But it wasn't you,' I said.

'What do you mean?'

'It wasn't you inside there with her.'

20

I was crying by the time I followed Daddy into the house because he hadn't said a word after I told him what I'd seen. I couldn't stop shaking because my clothes were sopping wet with rain. I saw an empty liquor bottle on the counter in the kitchen. Daddy opened a crinkly, wet grocery bag and pulled out another one and unscrewed the lid and took a long drink. He wiped his mouth with the back of his hand and took another. Then he picked up the empty bottle and threw it against the refrigerator. It broke, and little pieces of glass covered the floor. I hollered out for him, but he didn't even look at me. He took another drink, and then he screwed the lid back on and walked down the hall toward his and Mama's bedroom. I heard him open and close the drawers on the dresser like he was looking for something. He walked back down the hall, and I heard the glass crunching like gravel under his boots when he walked through the kitchen on the way to the front room. He picked up his truck keys off the table.

'Where are you going?' I asked.

'Go to bed,' he said. He opened the door and walked out onto the porch. I followed after him and caught the screen door before it shut in my face. He was already down the steps and heading across the driveway to his truck. He climbed in and slammed the door and started the engine.

'Don't leave!' I hollered. 'Please!' I ran down the steps and out into the rain and pulled on the truck's door, but I reckon he'd already locked it because I couldn't get it open. I beat my fists against the window.

'I'm sorry!' I hollered. 'Don't leave me here!'

It was so dark that I could just barely see him inside his truck. He looked at me through the window. I watched him pull the gearshift down, and I heard his tires on the gravel when he rolled back. I watched him turn around in the driveway, and then I watched his taillights fly down the hill toward the road. Soon I couldn't even see them through the trees, and all I could hear was the rain.

* * *

I walked up the porch steps and back inside the house. I closed the front door behind me. It was quiet in there, and I listened to the rain falling on the roof and the sound of it running into the gutters and down the spout. I knew the rain would've run right into the rain barrel if it wasn't broken. The lights were on in the kitchen, and those little pieces of glass from where my daddy had broken that bottle twinkled on the floor. It looked like somebody had come through and tossed a handful of ice into the kitchen. I walked around them as carefully as I could. I stepped on

292

a couple of pieces, and they popped under my shoes. I turned off the kitchen light and went into me and Stump's bedroom and shut the door.

I hadn't ever been at home all by myself before, especially not at night, and I kicked off my shoes and climbed up on the bed and pulled down the covers and got under them. I realized how cold I was in my wet clothes, and I couldn't hardly quit shivering. I pulled the covers over my head and thought about where Daddy could've gone, and I wondered if he would ever come back. And then I thought about how just a week before it had been me and Stump and Mama and Daddy all here together, but now everybody had gone and it was just me. I laid there under the covers and thought about how I'd bring them all back if I could, but after what I'd told Daddy I figured that even if we were all here together things wouldn't ever be the same. I thought about Stump's quiet box where it sat under our bed, and I wished Mama'd made me one too.

*   *   *

I opened my eyes when I heard a sound like Daddy's truck coming up the driveway. I turned over on my back and stared up at the ceiling and listened hard until I knew for sure that it was him. My clothes still hadn't dried all the way, but I wasn't cold anymore, and I kicked the covers off me and took off my shirt and my pants and my socks and threw them on the floor. Then I pulled the covers up over me again and turned on my side and looked out the window. It had quit raining, but there still wasn't no moon coming through the clouds and the night outside was pitch black.

My daddy parked his truck in front of the house and I heard him turn his engine off, and then I heard him open and close the truck's door and I heard his boots coming up the porch steps. It sounded like he tried to open the front door as quiet as he could, but I knew it would squeak anyway. His boots walked through the kitchen, and I heard them crunching on the glass where he'd broken that bottle. He went down the hallway to the bathroom, and I heard him open the lid on the toilet. A second later I heard him peeing. I closed my eyes and thought about how I wasn't scared anymore to be at home all by myself, and I started to get mad at Daddy for leaving me alone because I knew Mama wouldn't ever do that. I laid there and thought about where he might've gone when he left, and then I heard him coming back up the hallway. He stopped outside my door like he was trying to listen to see if I was still awake.

The knob turned real slow, and the door almost didn't make a sound when he opened it, but I saw that little bit of light from the hallway come into the bedroom and shine on the window, and I laid there on my side as still as I could with my back to the door. I could hear Daddy breathing from where he stood out in the hall.

'Jess,' he whispered.

I didn't say nothing, and I closed my eyes and pretended to be asleep.

'Jess,' he whispered again. 'You asleep?'

I still didn't say nothing, but I could hear him breathing and I knew he was still standing there looking at me. Then I heard him close the door just as quiet as he'd opened it. There wasn't any more light coming from the hallway, and my bedroom was just as dark as it was before.

My daddy walked back down the hall to the kitchen, and I heard him pick up the bottle off the counter and unscrew the lid, and then I heard him sit it back down. He opened and closed the cabinet, and then he ran water in the tap and turned it off. I heard him pick up the bottle again. I turned over on my other side, and I could see a little bit of light from the kitchen coming in under my door. I imagined Daddy in there leaning up against the counter and drinking out of that bottle and wiping his mouth with the back of his hand. I lay in my bed and listened to him in there, and then I heard something real soft and I couldn't figure out what it was. I held my breath and listened hard, and when I did I realized that what I could hear was the sound of Daddy using the broom and the dustpan to sweep up those little pieces of glass off the floor.

Adelaide Lyle

21

I drove back from that meeting with Chambliss as scared as I'd ever been in my entire life. Even though my windows were down and the air poured into my car, I couldn't hear nothing except for the rattle inside my head, the sound of it coming from deep inside that dark box where Chambliss had held my arm and echoing off the walls of the empty church. Its musty smell clung to my clothes like tobacco smoke, and the soft skin on the underside of my arm still crawled with the fear of being struck by its fangs. I prayed to God that I'd find Julie at home.

But I know what an empty house looks like, and I know you can almost feel it when you see it. I knew from the road that I wasn't going to find her inside when I got in there, but that didn't stop me from going from room to room and hollering her name. I went back out through the front door into the yard and around to the back of the house and called her and called her, and that's when I saw just how dark that sky had gotten. I stood out there in the backyard and felt that wind picking up, and I heard the thunder take to rumbling way off over the mountain. The air just changed all of a sudden, and I felt strange out there all alone with it getting so dark like that and the wind picking up and bending those tree limbs and tearing off those leaves. It felt ominous to me, like something was about to happen that I wasn't quite prepared for.

I went back inside the house hoping that she'd come in while I was outside, but I knew she hadn't. I walked into the kitchen and stood there at the counter and crossed my arms and looked out across the yard and up to the road like I thought I might see her coming down it, but she wouldn't come no matter how long I looked. I'd had me a red rotary phone put in there by the door, and I stood right there and stared at it and thought about what I should do. I thought about calling the sheriff, but I couldn't think of just what I'd tell him, and I knew better than to call over to Ben's and stir up trouble if Julie was over there.

No, Addie, I thought, *there ain't nothing for you to do but pray,* and that's just what I did. I walked into my room and dropped down on my knees right there by the bed, and I folded my hands and called on the Lord. Now, I can't say just what I prayed for and I can't say exactly how I asked the Lord to go about delivering it, but I can say that I haven't prayed for nothing else so hard in all my life.

I stayed there on my knees just like that, right there by the bed, even when I felt that dark gathering all around me and that wind picking up and those big, heavy drops of rain coming down on the roof above me.

***

When I opened my eyes, it was pitch black in my room, and I realized that I'd gotten up onto the bed somehow and pulled the quilt up over me. I laid there for just a bit and listened to that driving rain and wondered how long I'd been asleep, and then I heard just about the most awful banging on the door, and I knew then the banging was what had woken me up.

I kicked the quilt off me and put my feet on the floor and saw that I still had on my shoes. I went over to the bedroom light and turned it on and listened. Whoever was at the front door must've seen that light come on, because they took to banging even louder. I walked into the front room and pulled back the curtain on the window by the door, and that's when I saw that Ben Hall's truck had been driven right up through the yard and into the grass. He'd cut clear across the driveway and just kicked up all kinds of mud.

'Open this door, Miss Lyle!' I heard him holler out there over that storm. I turned on the floodlights and looked out the window again, but I couldn't see him. I put the chain on the door and turned the lock and opened it up. When I did, he tried to push the door open and come inside, but the chain kept the door from opening far enough to let him in.

'Where's Julie?' he asked.

'She ain't here,' I told him. 'I don't know where she's at.' He stuck his arm through the crack in the door and tried to unhook that chain, and I slapped at his hand and tried to push his arm back out.

'Stop that, Ben,' I said. 'I ain't letting you in here.' He pulled his arm out and put his face right up to mine through the crack, and when he did I could smell that liquor on his breath and I knew he was drunk for sure.

'Where's she at?' he asked.

'I've done told you,' I said. 'I don't know.' He tried to stick his arm back through to mess with the lock again, but I closed the door on his hand before he could get it in there good. He hollered and pulled it back out. I cracked the door again and looked out at him. 'I'm going to call the sheriff,' I said. 'You're drunk, Ben. You need to go on home. You can talk to Julie tomorrow if she'll see you.'

'You tell her I know,' he said. 'You tell her I know what she's been doing. I know what happened.'

'Go home, Ben,' I said. He just stood there like he was fixing to leave, and then he slammed his shoulder up against the door so hard that I thought he'd torn it off the frame.

'Stop it!' I hollered. 'I'm calling the sheriff!' He got quiet after that, and then he put his face back in the crack and looked right in at me.

'You tell her I'm going to kill him,' he said.

'You can tell her yourself tomorrow,' I told him. 'You need to go on home. I'm calling the sheriff. I mean it, now.' I closed the door and turned the lock, and then I went back to the window and looked out at the rain. I knew he hadn't moved off the porch yet, and I stood there until I saw him stumble down the steps into the yard. He was drunk as he could be, and once he got down there he slipped and fell on his backside in that wet grass. I watched him until he got inside his truck and backed it up in my yard and tore off through the grass and kicked up even more mud onto my windows. I stared out at his taillights until I couldn't see them anymore, and then I turned off the floodlights and checked the deadbolt and the chain to make sure he wasn't getting inside if he came back.

When I turned around, I saw Julie standing there just outside the door to her bedroom. She must've come in while I was sleeping. She already had her nightgown on, and her hair was down like she was fixing to go to bed. I couldn't hardly see her face where she was standing in front of that light coming from my room.

'Julie?' I said.

'I heard what he told you,' she said. 'It ain't safe to be here no more. We're going to have to leave.'

'Who?' I asked her.

'Me and Pastor,' she said. 'It ain't safe. And everybody's trying to keep us apart.'

I leaned back against the locked door and just looked at her where she stood outside the bedroom in her nightgown. *Good Lord, girl*, I thought. *What in the world are you going to do now?* It didn't take her hardly no time to show me.

★ ★ ★

Early that next morning I heard Julie whispering into the kitchen telephone. I stood there on the other side of the door trying to make out the words she was saying, but I couldn't quite tell what it was. She hung up the telephone, and when she opened the door I was standing right there on the other side. I still had on my nightgown, but she was already dressed. She looked like she was surprised to see me standing there, like she'd been caught doing something she knew better than to do. We stood there looking at each other.

'You don't think Ben meant it, do you?' I asked. 'What he said last night. He ain't capable of nothing like that.'

'I don't know,' she said. 'I ain't never seen him act this way, and I ain't never heard him say the kinds of things he's been saying.'

'A drunk man's likely to say anything,' I said. 'It doesn't mean that what he says is true.'

'You don't know him like I do,' she said. 'You don't know what he's capable of doing.' She walked past me toward her bedroom, and I turned and followed her. When I walked into her room, I saw that she'd made the bed; her closed suitcase sat on top of the quilt. I looked at that suitcase, and then I looked at her. She picked it up by its handle and stood there beside the bed.

'You're leaving?' I asked.

'Yes, ma'am,' she said. 'I have to. After what Ben did last night, after what all's happened.'

'Who were you on the phone with?' I asked her. 'Did you call Pastor to come and get you?'

'No,' she said. 'I called the sheriff's office. I

301

want somebody there with me when I go home to get my things.'

'Julie,' I said, 'I wouldn't do that. You heard him last night. Please don't go over there.' She looked at me, and then she walked toward me and brushed past my shoulder on her way out the bedroom.

'I *did* hear him last night,' she said. 'Why you think I called the sheriff?' I followed her into the front room. She stopped at the door and sat her suitcase down beside her and turned the lock and unclasped the chain. She picked up her suitcase again and opened the door. 'I appreciate everything you've done,' she said. 'And I hope to repay your kindness one day.' She pushed the screen door open and walked out onto the porch. It slammed behind her. I could hear a car running out in the driveway.

'Julie,' I said, but she was already gone. I walked to the screen door and looked out and saw Chambliss standing in the driveway. He had the back passenger's-side door of his car open, and he was setting Julie's suitcase inside. Julie climbed into the front seat and closed the door. Chambliss slammed the back door shut and looked up at me. He nodded. Then he smiled.

'Sister Adelaide,' he said.

Clem Barefield

22

I was in the bathroom on Friday morning in my underwear toweling off my hair when I heard the phone ring. I hoped that Sheila would pick it up in the kitchen. I tossed the towel onto the closed toilet lid and turned and looked at myself in the mirror. Same old thing as always: gray hair, white belly, scrawny arms. The phone in the bedroom kept ringing.

'Are you going to get that?' I hollered, but Sheila didn't say anything, and I figured she might just be waiting me out. I walked into the bedroom and sat down on the bed and picked up the phone on the nightstand.

'Hello?'

'Sheriff, it's Robby.' I sighed loud enough for him to hear me. 'I know you're about to leave the house and come into the office, but I thought you'd want to know that Julie Hall just called here looking for a police escort. She's going back out to her house to get some things, and she said it might not be safe if her husband's there. I can go if you want me to, but I thought I'd call just in case you might want to go out there yourself.'

'That's fine,' I said. 'I'll call her and let her know I'll meet her out there.'

'All right,' he said. I hung up and called Adelaide Lyle's house looking for Julie, and Miss Lyle answered immediately, almost like she'd been sitting by the phone and waiting for my call.

'Morning,' I said. 'This is Sheriff Barefield.' I hadn't hardly gotten out those words before she stopped me.

'You need to get over to Ben Hall's place,' she said. 'They done left just a minute ago.'

'Slow down,' I said. 'Who left? Who are you talking about?'

'Julie,' she said. 'Chambliss came by and got her just now. They're going to get her things. She told me they're leaving town today.'

I told her I was leaving the house right then, and I hung up and called the station.

'Yes, sir?' Robby said.

'I need you to meet me at Ben Hall's place,' I said. 'And you'd better leave right now.' I slammed the phone down on the cradle and stood up. Sheila was standing in the doorway. She had a cup of coffee in each hand.

'What's happened?' she asked.

'Nothing yet,' I told her. 'But I can't speak for later.'

Jess Hall

23

'Wake up, Jess,' somebody said. They had their hand on my shoulder, and they shook me a little bit and tried to get me to open my eyes. I rolled away from them over to my other side and pulled the covers over my head and closed my eyes even tighter to keep out the light that came in the window.

'Wake up,' I heard Daddy's voice saying. 'You're already late for school. Wake up.' He put his hand on my back and pushed on me and I bounced a little on the bed, and then he pulled the covers down and the sun came in the window and hit me right in the eyes.

'I'm awake,' I said, but I knew he didn't believe me because I still had my eyes closed.

'You ain't going to have time to eat nothing,' he said. 'We've got to leave right now.'

'All right,' I told him, but I still had my eyes closed. I heard him go back down the hall to his bedroom. I kept my eyes shut just as tight as I could. Before I knew it I was falling asleep again.

'Get up, Jess!' he hollered from his room, but I'd pulled the covers up over my head again and I was just about asleep by the time I even heard what he was saying in there. It didn't seem right having Daddy come in there to wake me up, and it made me wish that Mama was there to do it. It made me wish that Stump was there too so he could get up before me and go to the bathroom first so I could keep my eyes closed just a little while longer. I laid there and thought about that, and before I knew it I was falling off to sleep again.

I heard a car coming down the driveway from way up on the road, and I could hear the sound of the gravel crunching under the tires and kicking up and bouncing off the fenders.

I heard my daddy's bare feet walking down the hall to the front room, and I was afraid he was going to come in there and yank me up out of the bed, but I heard him open the screen door instead. It slammed shut behind him, and the sound woke me up and I opened my eyes and looked around at all that darkness under the covers. I listened for my daddy to come back inside and wake me up, and when he opened the screen door I heard his voice inside the house, but it sounded like he was far away from where I was laying in bed with those covers pulled up over my head. 'Goddamn,' he said as he ran past my bedroom on his way back to his and Mama's room. 'Stay in the bed, Jess!' he hollered. 'Goddamn,' he said again.

I laid there under the covers and listened for him to say something else, but he didn't say nothing. I could hear him in the back bedroom. He was in there opening and slamming the drawers on his dresser like he was tearing them apart looking for something.

'Who's here?' I hollered from under my sheets. 'Stay right there,' he said.

I heard him pass by in the hallway again, and it sounded like he was dropping things and they were rolling down the hallway toward the kitchen. I lifted the covers off my head and laid there and looked up at the ceiling and listened, and then I heard him push open the screen door and run down the steps into the yard. The door slammed shut behind him. I could hear him yelling something out there, and I could hear somebody yelling back. Then I heard a gunshot.

I tore the covers off me and sat up in the bed, but I didn't hear nothing else, and I wondered if I'd heard all those things in a dream.

'Daddy!' I screamed. I waited for him to say something.

It was quiet outside, and I sat there wide awake and listened. My heart thumped against my chest, and I could hear it beating in my ears too. Then I heard another shot.

I jumped up out of the bed in my jockeys and ran out to the hall, but I stepped on something and it rolled under my foot and I fell and landed on my back and hit my head on the floor. I looked over and saw the shells for my daddy's shotgun rolling all over the hallway.

I got up and ran to the screen door and pushed it open, and when I did I heard another gunshot, and I saw my daddy fall on the ground in front of somebody's old car. The sheriff stood by his police car with his gun out in front of him, and my daddy just laid there in the gravel. Blood squirted up out of his neck and sprayed all over the hood of the car and turned it red. The sheriff saw me and hollered something, but I was screaming too loud to hear what he said. He put his gun in his holster and came out from behind his door and ran up the driveway through the gravel. He stopped on the other side of that old car where somebody was sitting on the ground inside the open door. He bent down and said something to them, and then he ran up the porch steps to where I stood. He wrapped his arms around me like he was hugging me, but I didn't want him to because I knew he'd shot my daddy. I fought with him, but he held me even tighter and I couldn't get him to let me go. My jockeys were wet, and I knew I'd peed myself.

'Hold on, son,' the sheriff said. 'Just hold on, now. Let's go back inside.'

'Daddy!' I hollered.

'Hold on,' he said again.

'Why'd you shoot my dad!'

'Let's just go back inside.' I heard sirens coming toward the house from up the road, and I fought with him again, but he still wouldn't let me go. Somebody out there in the driveway was screaming, and I thought it sounded just like Mama.

Clem Barefield

24

By the time I rounded the corner on my way up to Ben's house, I saw that he'd already come down the porch steps and taken a stand at the top of the driveway in front of Chambliss's old car, the same one I'd seen him working on out in his barn the day before. Ben had on an old white T-shirt and a pair of boxer shorts, and he'd raised his double-barrel shotgun eye level and had it pointed at Chambliss's driver's-side windshield. He stood there frozen stiff, like he could stay that way forever, and I blasted my siren once to get his attention. He raised his head just enough to look over the roof of Chambliss's car, and he watched me roll slowly up the driveway toward him.

My siren must have gotten Chambliss's attention too, because his red taillights went white when he put his old car in reverse, and I heard his tires crunch on the gravel when he began to back away from Ben and down the driveway toward me. He put his arm across Julie's seat and turned around and looked at me through his back window. It struck me as strange then, and it's even more troubling to think about now, but he smiled at me. It was almost like he was proud to be playing the good guy all of a sudden — somebody who I'd come out to protect now that Ben Hall had finally made him the victim.

And then all that blood on the windows. It seems like I saw it happen before I even heard it. Chambliss's face was there on the other side of the window, his eyes narrowed like he was concentrating on staying in the gravel and not veering into the wet grass. And then I couldn't see his face at all, and I realized I couldn't see through that glass window either. By the time my ears had registered the shot I knew I was looking at bits of Chambliss's brain and skull where they'd been blown up on the back window from the force of the blast. His car kept on rolling back toward me though, faster and faster, until I put mine in park and braced myself for the impact. His car slammed into mine and rolled up over my bumper and into my grille, and when it did Chambliss's trunk flew open and I saw where he'd packed a half-dozen of those little wooden crates I'd seen inside his barn. A couple of them tumbled out onto my hood, and I looked at them through the smoke that poured out of my radiator. Then I heard another shot blow out what was left of Chambliss's front windshield, but with his trunk open and the steam gushing from under my hood I couldn't see a thing.

I opened my door and used it for cover, and I stepped out onto the gravel and drew my sidearm and pointed it at Ben. He'd walked down the driveway following Chambliss's car as it rolled backward, and now he was standing right in front of its bumper. When he saw me draw and take a position behind my door, he pointed his gun at me. I wondered if he'd had time to reload, but I knew better than to assume that he hadn't.

'You need to drop that gun, Ben,' I said. He looked at me like he didn't know who I was for a minute, and then his eyes registered some kind of recognition and he held them on me. 'This thing's over,' I told him. 'Put it down and let's go inside and talk about this. Ain't nothing else for us to do. You know that.'

It was quiet, and the two of us just stood there staring at each other. Suddenly the passenger-side door of Chambliss's car creaked open and I heard Julie tumble out into the driveway. I couldn't see her, but I could hear her breathing heavy in short, quick breaths, and I listened as she crawled slowly through the gravel like she was trying to get away. Ben waited until she'd gotten out from behind the open door, and then he took that shotgun off me and pointed it at her.

'Don't do that, Ben!' I hollered. 'Look at me! Turn that back on me!' I could hear Julie sobbing over there on the far side of the car, and I could hear her struggling to get away from him. 'It ain't going to be worth it,' I said. 'I know it won't. You know it too.'

'No, I don't,' Ben said, and when he said that he turned his head and looked at me with a face I'd never seen on him before, and I can say that it was the only time in that boy's life that I'd ever seen his daddy in him. He kept his eyes on me, but he called out to Julie.

'What about you, baby?' he said. 'Was it worth it for you? What you did in our bed, what you did in that church; was it worth it?' He turned and looked down at her. 'You're always telling me that I need to get back into the Bible, and so I got it out and looked all through the New Testament, Julie, and I found a verse for you. In the book of Matthew, Jesus said not to kill, not to commit adultery. He also said, 'You shall not steal.' But my favorite is 'You shall not bear false witness.'' His body braced like he was thinking about firing on her. 'I reckon that part of Matthew probably wasn't ever read out loud in your church. If it was, maybe y'all chose not to hear it. But I wanted you to hear it. I wanted to tell it to you.'

A noise came from inside the house, and out of the corner of my eye I saw the screen door fly open and Jess run out onto the porch. Before I could yell at him to get back inside, the screen door banged shut and Ben spun around toward Jess with his gun still raised. I reacted without even thinking about it and fired once and caught Ben in the right side of his throat. He dropped the gun and fell backward onto the gravel. I heard Jess screaming from up there on the porch, and I knew that he'd seen it.

'Hold on now, Jess,' I hollered at him. 'You stay up there. You wait for me. Just hold on.' He kept on screaming out words I couldn't understand, and then he folded his arms around his belly and hunkered down on the porch.

I kept my gun drawn and pointed it at the front of Chambliss's car, and I crept around the driver's side until I saw Ben laying there. His eyes were wide open, and his chest was heaving. He breathed heavily through his mouth, and I could hear a gurgling sound coming from his throat where he'd been shot. Blood had begun to soak the gravel around his right shoulder. I holstered my pistol and picked up the shotgun and broke it open. Both barrels were empty. I looked down at Ben. 'Goddamn it,' I said. 'Goddamn it, Ben.' He looked up into the sky and blinked like the sun was in his eyes. I sat the shotgun on the hood of the car and stepped around to the passengers side.

Julie was lying on her belly halfway into the grass like she'd crawled as far as she could, and when she saw me she screamed and backpedaled to the gravel and threw her back up against the side of Chambliss's car. When she raised her left hand to protect herself from me, I saw that it had almost been blown clean off from where she must've tried to cover her face and duck when Ben shot at her through the windshield. Her cheeks and forehead were peppered with shot. I holstered my gun and bent down to her. When I tried to touch her shoulder, she drew away from me. I heard a siren coming down the road from the highway, and I remembered that I'd called Robby for backup before I left the house.

'It's okay,' I told her. 'It's all over now. You're going to be all right.' Her eyes were wild and terrified, and she wouldn't look directly at me. I reached out slowly and took hold of her left forearm. Some of her fingers were missing. 'You just keep this raised,' I said. I propped her elbow on her bent knee. 'Keep that up, just like it is. I'm going to go inside the house and call the ambulance.' Robby pulled into the driveway and stopped his car behind mine. I stood up to make sure he'd see me. He got out and left his door open and ran up through the grass, but he stopped dead in his tracks when he saw Julie sitting against the car. He looked inside where Chambliss's body was laid out across the front seat.

'What the hell happened?' he asked. He drew his pistol.

'Put that away,' I told him. I pointed down to Julie. 'You need to stay right here with her,' I said. 'Make sure she keeps that arm up just like it is. I'm going in to call the ambulance. You stay with her.' He knelt down beside Julie. Her chest heaved, and she started crying.

I looked over the hood of Chambliss's car where Ben lay in front of the bumper. I couldn't hear him choking anymore. He'd rolled his head back and to the right like he was trying to get a look at the house behind him where Jess was still hunkered down on the porch. His eyes were open wide and fixed on whatever it was he'd been trying to see.

'The ambulance is going to be here soon, Ben,' I said, but as soon as I said it I knew it wasn't going to make any difference for him.

I looked toward the house when I heard Jess's feet coming down the porch steps. I didn't want him finding his mother all shot up too, so I ran

314

up the driveway and caught him before he got all the way out into the yard. I picked him up and carried him back up the steps, and he kicked his legs and threw his arms around like he was trying to fight me. Something warm came through the front of my shirt, and I knew that he'd wet himself and it had soaked through his underwear.

'You shot my dad!' he hollered. 'Daddy!' He called out for his mother too, but she was crying and didn't answer, and I wondered if she could even hear him.

'Come on, now,' I said. 'Let's go on back inside the house. The doctors will be here soon and they're going to fix everybody up. It's going to be all right.'

'You shot my daddy!' he said. 'I saw you!' I could feel his whole body shaking like each sob was the last and hardest he might have inside him. I held him and tried to keep his head against my chest so he wouldn't be able to look over my shoulder and see out into the yard. Once we got inside the house, I sat him down on the sofa and pulled the curtains closed behind him and shut the front door.

'Just sit right here,' I told him. He was still crying, and his whole body shivered. He pulled his feet up to his chest and wrapped his arms around his legs. 'Sit right here and wait one second,' I said. 'I'm going to make a phone call and have the doctors here real soon. It's going to be all right.' I stepped back away from him and looked around the front room for a phone, but I didn't see one. I looked back at Jess. 'Where's your telephone?' He just stared up at me without saying anything, so I kept my eyes on him and kept backing away toward the kitchen. I peered in the doorway and saw a telephone hanging on the wall right inside.

I took the phone off the cradle and held it to my ear, and when I went to slip my finger into the rotary I realized how bad my hands were shaking. I dialed 911 and stretched out the telephone cord and walked as far back into the front room as it would let me. Jess was still sitting on the sofa. He had his chin resting on his knees, and his eyes were closed. When the operator came on, I identified myself and told her that we needed a couple of ambulances immediately, and, just before I was about to hang up, I looked at Jess and thought about how his mama was sitting right out there in the driveway near the husband who'd just tried to murder her, and I made a decision that surprised me more than just about anything that had happened that morning.

'Wait,' I said to the operator. 'While I got you on the line, can you put me through to James Hall, over in Shelton?' I listened while the number was dialed, and then I heard a soft click before it began to ring. It must've rung six or seven times before he picked up. I looked down at my boots and held the phone to my ear and listened as he fumbled with the phone on his end. The clock on the table by the front door said it was 8:33 in the morning.

'Yeah?' he said. I could hear him breathing heavy into the phone, and I imagined him on the

316

other end, his eyes closed, hoping that I'd dialed the wrong number and wouldn't be bothering him again once I'd figured it out. 'Hello,' he said. He sounded like he'd either just woken up or maybe hadn't even been to sleep yet, and I couldn't help but wonder if he was hung over.

'Jimmy,' I said, whispering, keeping my voice as low as I could so Jess wouldn't hear me. 'It's Clem Barefield.'

'Who?' I left the front room and walked all the way into the kitchen. I leaned against the counter and closed my eyes.

'It's Clem Barefield,' I said again.

'What do you want?' he asked. I opened my eyes and looked around the kitchen and tried to think of what to tell him about what had happened.

'I'm over at Ben's,' I said. 'And Jess is here with me.' I paused because I figured he'd want to ask me some kind of question, but he didn't say anything, even though I imagined that his eyes were open and he was wide awake now. 'We had a little trouble over here this morning, and I just thought you should come down here and be with Jess. He needs somebody to be here with him right now, and I just didn't know who else to call.'

'What's happened?' he asked. His voice was clear and sharp, and I sensed something in it that hadn't been there before — panic maybe, or fear, or both. 'Why are you out there?'

'There was just some trouble,' I said. 'We can talk about all that when you get here.'

'Let me talk to Ben,' he said.

317

'I can't let you do that right now, Jimmy,' I said. 'Just get here as soon as you can. Jess needs you here.' I could hear him moving on the other end of the line, and I thought I heard him stumble. Then the sound of something falling to the floor. He whispered something to himself under his breath.

'Jimmy,' I whispered. 'Are you okay to drive? I mean, you haven't been drinking?' The line grew quiet, and I could tell that he'd stopped moving and was standing still. I could just barely hear him breathing.

'I'm going to pretend you didn't ask me that,' he said. He hung up. I held the receiver to my ear until I heard the dial tone kick in, and then I turned and sat the phone back in its cradle. I understood that I'd just made the kind of phone call to Jimmy Hall that he'd never considered making to me, but that didn't make me feel one bit better about making it, and for a minute I thought he might've had the right idea about trying his hardest to disappear all those years ago. I walked back into the front room and saw that Jess had his eyes open and was staring at me.

'Did you call my grandpa?'

'I did,' I said. 'He'll be here real soon.' I looked around the room and considered whether I should stand and wait or if I should sit with Jess or maybe even go back outside and get one of the paramedics to come into the house and sit with him once they arrived. Jess lay back against the sofa and folded his arms across his chest. He closed his eyes, and then he opened them slowly.

They were full of tears.

'Did you call my grandpa because my daddy's going to die?' I shook my head no and walked across the room toward him.

I thought about how I'd stared into that shotgun's empty barrels just a few minutes before, and even though my hands were empty too I felt the heft of my pistol and the kick it gave when I fired. In my head, I heard myself say, *I wish I could've done it all different, Jeff,* but by the time I kneeled on the floor in front of him I'd caught myself. 'Jess,' I said aloud. 'Jess.'

★   ★   ★

The ambulances had killed their sirens once they'd pulled up into the yard, and if somebody hadn't known everything that had taken place out in the driveway that morning they would've thought me and Jess were just two strangers sitting together on the sofa and waiting for something to happen. I'd covered him with a blanket and gotten him a glass of water from the kitchen and some toilet paper from the bathroom, and I'd sat both on the coffee table in front of him, but he hadn't touched either one. We'd hardly spoken since I sat down.

It was so quiet that you could almost make out the voices of the paramedics outside, and occasionally I'd hear Robby say something, but I couldn't quite understand it. But I could just barely hear the sound of another car coming up the driveway from the road, and I listened close as it stopped and somebody opened and closed its door. I knew it was Jimmy Hall, and I stood up from the couch and walked to one of the windows that looked out onto the driveway.

Chambliss's car sat facing the house. The doors on both sides were open, and I figured the paramedics had covered Chambliss's body by now. I could see that they'd covered Ben too where he was laying out in the gravel by the front left bumper. They'd lined up two ambulances on the passenger's side of Chambliss's car, and I watched a couple of paramedics strap Julie onto a gurney and lift her into the open doors of the ambulance closest to the house. Robby stood by her, and I could tell that he was talking to her, but I wondered just how much she was able to hear.

Jimmy Hall must've parked his truck in front of the ambulances at the bottom of the driveway. I watched him as he made his way up through the yard past them. He wasn't wearing a hat, and his gray hair was matted down with sleep. He stopped for a minute and watched them lift Julie up into the back of the ambulance, and then he turned and stared at Chambliss's car: the busted windshield, the blood-covered seats, the back window red with the same. When Hall walked past him, Robby turned like he was about to stop him from going any farther, but his eyes caught mine where I stood in the window. I raised my hand and motioned for him to hold off. Robby looked away from me and watched Jimmy as he walked along the side of Chambliss's car toward the front bumper. He came around the bumper and stopped when he saw the blue sheet that covered Ben. Robby looked up at me again, and then he looked back at Jimmy Hall. He hadn't moved yet, and Robby just turned and walked toward the cab of the ambulance that would carry Julie to the hospital.

I watched Jimmy Hall as he walked toward that blue sheet, and I watched as he kneeled down beside it. I wanted to open the front door and holler at him, let him know that he shouldn't do it, not because I was afraid that he'd damage the crime scene or contaminate the evidence but because I knew that he might not be ready, might not ever be ready, for what he'd see under there. But I also knew that fathers want to see what's become of their sons, and sometimes they can't forgive themselves if they don't. He reached out his hand and touched the sheet, but I turned away before I saw him lift it. I figured I at least owed them both the respect of that one last private moment.

Jess had opened his eyes again and was sitting on the edge of the sofa. 'What's going on outside?' he asked.

'Your grandpa's here,' I said. I stepped away from the front door and stood in the center of the room and waited. Jess looked over at me, and then he turned and looked at the door too. We could hear Jimmy Hall coming up the porch steps and then the sound of the screen door creaking as he pulled it toward him. He opened the front door and stepped inside the house. We stood staring at each other for a second, and then he looked over at Jess.

'Hey, buddy,' he said. I heard Jess shift his

weight on the sofa, and then he sniffed like he was about to cry. He stood up, and Jimmy walked across the room toward him.

'Wait,' I said. I stepped in between him and Jess, and I looked down at the fingers on Jimmy's right hand. They looked like somebody had taken his prints by dipping his fingertips in blood. He looked down at them too, and he turned his hand over and looked into his palm like he expected to be holding something that wasn't there. I leaned toward him and tried to whisper, even though I couldn't say it quiet enough to keep Jess from hearing me. 'You need to wash that off your hands, Jimmy,' I said. 'You can't let him see that.' I looked at him and nodded my head toward the kitchen. He looked down at Jess, and he tried to smile.

'I'll be right back, buddy,' he said. I heard his footsteps follow me out of the front room. I walked into the kitchen and ran the water in the sink. Jimmy came up beside me and put his hands under the tap. He still hadn't said a word to me yet; he'd hardly even looked at me.

'Jimmy,' I said, 'I can't begin to tell you about what all happened out there this morning; I don't know how to make sense of it myself. But I know that boy is going to need you right now. He ain't going to have nobody else for a long time. It looks to me like his mama's going to be all right, but right now it's just you.' Jimmy picked up a yellow bar of soap from where it sat on the lip of the metal sink. He spoke without looking at me.

'Did you shoot him?' he asked. I sighed loud enough for him to hear me, and I looked away

322

from him and through the window where I could see out into the fields that ran alongside the house. Ben's burley had been cut and staked, and it sat out there in the fields waiting for somebody to haul it in. I knew it'd be ruined if it sat out there for too much longer. I looked back at Jimmy. He'd turned the water off and was drying his hands on a dish towel. 'Did you?' he asked. He folded the dish towel neatly and dropped it by the sink.

'I did,' I said. 'But I can promise you I tried not to, Jimmy. I would've moved heaven and earth to keep from doing it. I wish it wouldn't have ended this way.' He raised his head and stood there staring out the window toward Ben's fields.

'Me too,' he said. He turned and walked back into the front room. I followed him, but we both stopped when we saw that Jess had left his seat on the sofa in the corner of the room and opened the front door without us hearing him. He stood in front of it now with his back to us looking through the screen door. We could all see that the paramedics had strapped Ben's body onto a gurney that was being loaded into the last ambulance. Although the blue sheet still covered Ben's body, his bare white feet stuck out from under it.

Jimmy put his hand on Jess's shoulder and turned him away from the door, and then he closed it softly, its hinges barely making a sound as it shut. He put his arms around Jess and pulled him toward him. Jess's shoulders heaved, and although I couldn't see his face, I figured he was crying. I heard the ambulance's engine crank outside in the driveway, and then I listened as it rolled down through the gravel toward the road.

I thought about how I'd meant what I'd said to Jimmy, that I wished it all could've been different. I stood there and watched the two of them hold on to each other, and I found myself praying that maybe this time it would be.

Adelaide Lyle

25

It was just a sad day when they had that funeral for Ben at the cemetery outside of Marshall. A whole big crowd of people were there, some of them from the church he'd never stepped a foot into, some of them folks he'd known from town and from growing up and living in this county for so long. I hadn't seen Jess since the Sunday night they'd brought Christopher's body out to my house, but I saw him there standing with his grandfather by his daddy's graveside. His little button-down collared shirt and his tie made him look even younger than nine years old, especially with all those adults standing around him in their black funeral clothes. He had his hair combed over to one side and his hands in his pockets. I could tell that he'd been crying.

Jess's grandfather had brought him. His mama wasn't there, which didn't really surprise me too much. I reckon Julie's heart had already left Ben behind while he was still alive, and his dying wasn't about to make that leaving no different. As for Jess, she'd already tried to leave him once, and I reckon she just decided to stay gone for good.

Jimmy Hall had on him a nice clean shirt and

a tie just like his grandson's, and I could tell that he'd gone and bought new clothes for him and Jess both. He had his hair combed down too and a whole mess of Brylcreem keeping it in place. He'd shaved, and even though his face was just as red as a beet it looked like he hadn't been drinking. I watched his hands during the service, especially when he raised them and let them drop onto Jess's shoulders, his fingers closing around them gently and pulling that boy back against his body, holding him there, letting Jess lean against him while he bowed his head during the prayer. Jimmy Hall kept those hands steady, even as he lifted one of them to his eyes, even as he shook the hands of the other men who'd come to pay their respects to his boy.

One of those men was the sheriff, but you wouldn't have known who he was just by looking at him. He wore a tie just like most of the other men did, but still, it seemed strange not seeing him in his uniform. I think he might've been ready to give it up by then, and he would give it up altogether not long after. I reckon he lost his will for the job after what all had happened, after what he'd had to do. But it was something to see him standing there by Jimmy Hall, both of them just a few feet away from Ben's graveside, and even then only twenty or thirty yards away from where Jeff had been buried twenty years before. These two men who'd hated each other for so long stood there side by side with nothing but their dead sons in common between them, both of them having believed, at least at one time or another, that the other man was to blame.

They'd hated each other until they were both broken, and I reckon that's when they decided it was time to leave all that behind and get on with their healing.

It's a good thing to see that people can heal after they've been broken, that they can change and become something different from what they were before. Churches are like that. The living church is made of people, and it can grow sick and break just like people can, and sometimes churches can die just like people die. My church died, but it didn't die with Carson Chambliss; it was dead long before that. But I can tell you that it came back to life once he was gone. A church can be healed, and it can be saved like people can be saved. And that's what happened to us. At one time we were like a frostbitten hand that's just begun to thaw. First the tips of the fingers come alive, and suddenly they can open and close. And then the palm begins to feel again. Upturned. Waiting. Witnessing. We began to feel again too.

It started on the Sunday somebody got to the church early and tore that old newspaper off the windows. I never found out who'd done it; I didn't ask, and nobody ever volunteered to say it was them. But I could see through the windows of my church for the first time in more than ten years, and from inside the church I could turn and see the world that had been kept out for just as long. The river across the road still ran under the bridge toward downtown Marshall, and I knew from there that it still ran clear on to Tennessee. It was the same world that we'd left behind, and it was a good thing to see it again.

That next Sunday I brought the children into the church for Sunday school for the first time in years. We held it in the back of the church while the adults held theirs down toward the front. I took the children outside during the service, but some of them wanted to stay in the church with their parents, and that was just fine with me.

A good many folks left the church after what happened to Carson Chambliss, and I reckon just as many stayed away after hearing about it. But others came, slowly: young folks mostly, people who'd moved in from outside of Madison County and hadn't had time to hear a word, good or bad, about the little church out by the river. Jess came back to us too.

Jimmy Hall brings him down for church just about every Sunday now, but he never comes with him. He's more like his son than his grandson in that respect, and while Jess is inside the church or out by the river Jimmy sits out in his truck and smokes cigarettes and reads the newspaper. But that's all right with me. He don't ever have to step a foot inside this church if he doesn't want to. It's enough for me to know that he's out there if Jess needs him. I think it's enough for Jess too.

This is a good place now, without no snake boxes, no musty smells of shed skin, no noisy rattles kicking up from places you can't see. At times I thought we'd been cast out into the wilderness, led there by a false prophet who was blind to any will except his own. Although a couple of folks take turns preaching and leading the service, we still don't have a full-time pastor. The Israelites had a Moses to lead them out of the wilderness. We're still waiting on ours.

But in the Old Testament, when God's chosen people called out, 'Save us, Lord!' He heard them, and they were saved. He was there for them because they believed. We still believe.

I think the good Lord has it in His plan to save us too.

A note from Wiley Cash

I began writing *A Land More Kind Than Home* while working on my Ph.D. at the University of Louisiana-Lafayette, where I spent five long years sweating, suffering attacks by fire ants, and missing the mountains of North Carolina. In the fall of 2003, while I was taking a course in African American literature, my professor Reggie Young brought in a recent news story about a young African American boy with autism who was smothered during a healing service in a storefront church in Chicago. I was raised in an evangelical church in the South, and stories of people who took their faith literally, especially to the point of harm or danger, have always piqued my interest. I thought about this story for a few months, and I felt compelled to fictionalize it in some way in an attempt to represent my own experiences with the church. The problem was that as a white man from North Carolina who'd never visited the Midwest, I didn't know anything about the African American community in Chicago, certainly not enough to tell the story of the young boy who'd died.

At the same time as I was taking the course in African American literature, I was also taking a fiction workshop with Ernest J. Gaines, a man who spent his literary career writing about southwestern Louisiana. Gaines taught me that

330

by writing about *home* I could recreate that place no matter where I lived. He made this clear to me one afternoon while we were visiting an old cemetery near the plantation where he was born. He pointed to a grave marker and said, 'You remember Snookum from *A Gathering of Old Men?* He's buried right there.' I soon realized that I could take that little storefront church in Chicago and put it in the mountains of North Carolina and people it with characters who I knew and understood. While none of the characters in *A Land More Kind Than Home* are based on people who actually existed, they're all amalgams of the types of people I knew growing up. In creating these people and the place they live I got to watch the sun split the mist on the ridges above the French Broad River. From my desk in Louisiana I pondered the silence of snow covered fields. While living in a place that experiences only summer and fall, I watched the green buds sprout on the red maples, and I was there when their leaves began to shrivel before giving way to the wind. I lived in two places at once, and it was wonderful.

A Land More Kind Than Home didn't simply allow me to 'return' to North Carolina, it also allowed me to revisit my own experiences with religious faith. While the novel revolves around a young autistic boy who is smothered during a church healing service, the book's three narrators all represent my experience of being raised in an evangelical church. Like Jess

Hall, the younger brother who secretly witnesses the death, I often found myself sitting in church and waiting for something to happen. As a boy I was promised that I would recognize my salvation when I felt Jesus move inside my heart; however, just as Jess does after his brother's death, I attempted to rationalize the mysteries of Christianity, and I soon realized that we often use faith to fill the empty spaces in our lives. Like Adelaide Lyle, the church matriarch who straddles the divide between religious faith and old-time folk belief, my own religious beliefs are rounded-out with a healthy dose of skepticism. While I'm always suspicious of those who pray the loudest, I can't help but have an emotional reaction when I witness a riverside baptism, and I can't account for the inexplicable peace that comes from humming an old-time gospel. But I most identify with the character Clem Barefield, the local sheriff who must sift through his own tragic past to solve the mystery of the boy's death, because, like the sheriff, I'm guided only by what I can perceive of this world, and I'm hesitant to get lost in following those who claim to be led by a spirit from the next.

I became a Southern writer because I wanted to recreate the South that I knew, and I learned to write about the South from the writers I loved. Ernest J. Gaines often recalls William Faulkner's invocation of Oxford, Mississippi as a little postage stamp of earth that he continually mined throughout his career. Gaines did the same thing in his Louisiana fiction. That's what I tried to do in *A Land More Kind Than Home*. My next novel is set in the same region of North Carolina. Fortunately, this part of the country is much larger than Oxford, and I can't imagine ever running out of stories to tell about it.

Wiley Cash, October 2011

We do hope that you have enjoyed reading this large print book.

Did you know that all of our titles are available for purchase?

We publish a wide range of high quality large print books including:
Romances, Mysteries, Classics
General Fiction
Non Fiction and Westerns

Special interest titles available in large print are:
The Little Oxford Dictionary
Music Book
Song Book
Hymn Book
Service Book

Also available from us courtesy of Oxford University Press:
Young Readers' Dictionary
(large print edition)
Young Readers' Thesaurus
(large print edition)

For further information or a free brochure, please contact us at:
Ulverscroft Large Print Books Ltd.,
The Green, Bradgate Road, Anstey,
Leicester, LE7 7FU, England.
Tel: (00 44) **0116 236 4325**
Fax: (00 44) **0116 234 0205**